The Legend of the
Sphinx

B.G. White

The Legend of the

Sphinx

Volume 2

FINAL JOURNEY

TATE PUBLISHING
AND ENTERPRISES, LLC

The Legend of the Sphinx, Volume 2
Copyright © 2015 by B.G. White. All rights reserved.

Published by Tate Publishing & Enterprises, LLC
127 E. Trade Center Terrace | Mustang, Oklahoma 73064 USA
1.888.361.9473 | www.tatepublishing.com

Tate Publishing is committed to excellence in the publishing industry. The company reflects the philosophy established by the founders, based on Psalm 68:11,
"The Lord gave the word and great was the company of those who published it."

Book design copyright © 2015 by Tate Publishing, LLC. All rights reserved.
Cover design by Rtor Maghuyop
Interior design by Mary Jean Archival

Published in the United States of America

ISBN: 978-1-63367-609-1
Fiction / Fairy Tales, Folk Tales, Legends & Mythology
14.11.26

To all the children and adults in this beautiful world who have experienced a time when all left to cling to was that last bit of hope, and you wanted to give up, but did not. You pressed forward even when all odds seemed against you. You found strength and courage in your weakest moments beyond what you ever thought possible to acquire. Your endurance is incredible and sustaining.

Contents

The Miracle

SIMON AWAKENED TO a faint voice within his ear. "Everything is going to be all right," it seemed to whisper. It took him a few minutes to realize that it was only a dream. Nothing had changed. It was real, not a nightmare! Neopoleana and Winglet's lifeless bodies still lay in this awful dark silence. In order to survive, Simon knew he must make his way to the Gruhs. He could live on mushrooms, bark, and dirty stump water. He glimpsed down at the Mother Rhue and Winglet one last time before preparing to leave.

Suddenly, a glimpse of light appeared among the shadows on the ground. Quickly, Simon looked up to see a huge ball of soft, glowing light heading in his direction. He ran to hide behind a large boulder and watched in bewilderment, feeling no fear for some reason. "What could that be?" he asked himself.

As it neared the ground, the light ball became very bright and crystal clear. Simon found himself squinting to see. "Oh my goodness, the light is traveling to where Neopoleana is lying!" he shouted then quickly became very quiet and watched in complete awe as the massive glow hovered just above the Mother Rhue a short while. Then it began to stretch upward, downward, and to the sides, becoming wide and elongated. Simon could not believe his eyes when a form began to appear and take shape. Within a couple of minutes, the light had transformed into the form of a Rhue! He knew at that moment who it was and whispered with excitement, "It is Krystallina! She looks just like the figure I saw chiseled on the monument in Neopoleana's yellow rose garden!" He then spoke with haunting mystery, "What is her spirit doing here? I guess she came to help Neopoleana turn loose of her spirit. It was she who whispered in my ear."

Soon the light form of Krystallina slowly cascaded down and covered Neopoleana's body. Simon could not move as he watched the breathtaking event. The next thing he was expecting to see was the Mother Rhue's bright, shining spirit leaving her body. "Something like this probably takes a very long time," he figured as he continued to observe.

After several minutes of staring in complete awe, Simon glanced down to check on Winglet. When he looked back up, he gasped, for he thought to have seen a flicker of light in the *golden wings*! Immediately, he closed his eyes tightly and then slowly opened them. Again, the wings flickered. Right then, Simon's heart began to pound. He moved a little closer. For several minutes, the wings remained dark. *My eyes must have been playing tricks on me*, he thought while looking down at Winglet. After a minute or so, he slowly looked up and almost had a heart attack when he saw the bottom half of Neopoleana's right wing glowing! He held his breath as he witnessed the light slowly crawl through the Mother Rhue's entire wing, glowing with a low intensity. Then the left wing started to glow from the bottom up. "Man, this is awesome!" he shouted out loud.

Suddenly, the *golden wings* lit up to their full, splendid brightness! Simon screamed and covered his eyes tightly with one hand. He quickly felt around on the ground for Winglet and pulled her farther away from the blinding, bright light. He then peeped out and spotted a nearby rock. He latched on to the baby Rhue with one hand and crawled quickly behind the boulder.

All this commotion and excitement had caused Simon to become a bit short-winded. "I don't know what is going on, Winglet! I can't look because of the bright light! It will damage my eyesight again!" he spoke in breathless words. For a while, he sat patiently, hoping Neopoleana's spirit would find its way out and join Krystallina. Every once in a while, he would peer out from behind the rock only to see bright, golden light beams. Finally, he quit looking, for he had grown very tired.

Soon Simon had drifted into a restless sleep. Like each time before, his dream carried him inside the wishing well where he was trying to climb out. Again, he saw his Mom's reflection in the water. Bronzella's ferocious roars terrorized him as she trailed behind. Furiously, Simon fought against the deep water to reach his Mom's extended hand. Just when he was about to make it, the sphinx gripped his legs, wrapping them inside her massive paws.

Simon awakened from the nightmare, panting for air and sweating profusely, and then opened his foggy eyes to see a face very close to his. He screamed and buried his own face in his hands. "Simon, it's me," a soft, sweet voice called out. He quickly realized only one person could ever have such an angelic voice such as this. Slowly, he turned on his back and peeped between his fingers. Sure enough, it was Neopoleana, and she was alive and well! The Mother Rhue was standing over Simon in all her splendor! He had a tough time even trying to speak.

"Don't be afraid," Neopoleana assured him.

"Uh…uh…Are you real or is it your spirit I see?"

Neopoleana chuckled. "Of course, I am real. Why wouldn't I be?" she asked, causing him to feel bewildered.

"Uh…don't you remember the fight with Bronzella? The sphinx killed you!"

"Well, evidently she just knocked me out," the Mother Rhue analyzed.

"No! No! Bronzella killed you! I saw your pale skin and felt your cold face. Your *golden wings* were darkened!" Simon explained with anxiousness.

"Calm down now. I was not dead, or I would not be standing here. Right now, I must know about Winglet. Did the Sphinx… ugh…kill my baby?" she asked with apprehensive compassion.

Simon gave the loving Mother Rhue a half-smile and slid over to expose the baby Rhue. Neopoleana gasped and then quickly picked her up, rocking and cradling the lifeless body in her arms as gleaming, golden tears streamed down her face. Simon could feel her grief and cried with her.

"Come with me, Simon," the Mother Rhue instructed as she walked fast to the open area right beyond the tunnel. She then handed Winglet to him and sat down upon the ground. "Lay my baby in my arms," she commanded. Simon gently placed Winglet in her open arms without asking questions. He watched in awe as the Mother Rhue folded the *golden wings* around the baby, completely encasing her. He realized that Neopoleana was going to try to save Winglet with the power from the golden light beams.

"Neopoleana, I must let you know something."

"I must have peace and quiet right now. Can it not wait?" she asked with a bit of frustration.

"I'm sorry, Neopoleana, but I believe this is news you should here now," Simon replied.

"Okay, go ahead and tell me this urgent information."

"First of all, you have been so overtaken with Winglet that you haven't noticed the huge mountain of coins over there," Simon remarked while pointing. "Someone must have found the sphinx eye and did as the legend instructed. Bronzella has been destroyed! She is that heap of gold coins!"

"This is truly wonderful news, Simon! We will never have to worry about that selfish creature again!" Neopoleana rejoiced. "I wonder who could have found it."

"I believe with all my heart that it was my mother," Simon answered with pride.

Neopoleana stroked his cheek with one finger. "Of course, it was your mother. Only she would have the kind of love filled with enough hope and faith to not give up. She searched and found answers to clues you didn't even realize were left behind."

Simon smiled and then began telling Neopoleana about the miracle. "A huge ball of light traveled downward from the dusky sky. It hovered over your body and then took the form of your sister, Krystallina."

The Mother Rhue listened intently as Simon continued. "Her spirit totally covered you. I thought she had come to help your spirit escape."

Neopoleana smiled. "Oh, Simon, you must have been very frightened to think I was dead," she responded with concern.

"I was. I just knew the Rhues were going to die, and Rhueland would dry up to nothing!"

"Simon, I was in a deep coma, yet I could feel your sadness. I could also feel the strength and energy from Krystallina's good spirit. These things were very healing to me. I fought hard to live because all of Rhueland depended on me, especially the Rhues," Neopoleana explained.

"And I was depending on you to get me back home," Simon interrupted. "Now you can!" he shouted as he clapped and jumped up and down.

Neopoleana chuckled at his jesters. "Yes, Simon! I can certainly help you with that, but first, I must see if my baby is going to pull through," she stated then added, "I want to thank you for taking care of Winglet while I was passed out."

Simon smiled in a blushing manner. "Aw, I didn't give it a second thought. I love her, and I love you and all the creatures and Rhues," he shyly spoke.

Neopoleana stroked her hand gently down Simon's face. "We have grown to love you too. Thank you for coming to our world and showing us what a little boy is all about!" she commented with love from the heart.

Simon giggled then immediately calmed down as he sat by Neopoleana's side. "I sure hope Winglet makes it," he cried.

"She has been without food and light a very long time. I know a chance exists that Winglet will not regain consciousness, but I will give her all the power from the *golden wings*. She will feel my love as never before. If anything can pull her through, this will," Neopoleana explained with all the hope and faith a loving mother could possess.

Simon was overwhelmed with the Mother Rhue's compassionate words, for he knew his mom had the same caring heart. He snuggled close and waited quietly and patiently. With renewed faith and hope of the heart, Simon knew in this wonderful land in The Third Dimension a miracle could happen. He smiled to himself as he thought of how miracles could also take place right back at Hillcrest!

Back at the Well

THE WATER IN the wishing well had calmed, and the tornado winds had slowed to gentle breezes. Beams of sunlight were beginning to trickle through the trees as darkness gave way for a new day. A few early morning birds perched on a nearby low tree branch, were chirping happy tunes. Jim and Karen were seated upon the bottom railing of the well, tired and exhausted. Jim was ready for some good sleep. "Karen, it's over now. You did what you needed to. We must get home and rest before we both collapse," he advised in a nice manner.

Karen took a slow, deep breath. "You're right. There is nothing more left to do except wait," she remarked. "You saw what happened here tonight—the strange wind, the shaking well, and thick smoke spewing from it, and the water bubbling and rushing. Do you believe now the legend is true?" she asked.

Jim sighed. "What difference does it make how or what I feel? No matter what I say, you'll just read more into it!" he exclaimed.

"You still don't believe it—even after all that you saw with your own eyes," Karen fussed in frustration.

"I just look at it differently, that is all."

"How do you look at it, Jim? You saw the exact same events that I did. Did you not *really* feel, nor see the tornado winds? Did you not acknowledge the *real* sight of the violently shaking well?" Karen anxiously questioned.

Jim snapped. "You're poking fun! Of course I saw all that, but you know we do get wind around here!"

Karen yelled, "Oh come on, Jim! It was just in the area around the well!"

Jim became firm with his words. "See how you get? That's why I need to keep my opinion to myself!"

Karen took another deep breath. "I'm sorry, Jim. You have the right to your own opinion. Go ahead. Finish explaining your realistic views of what you saw. I will not get upset," she promised.

"Are you sure this time?"

"Yes, I am sure."

"Now, just listen carefully, then maybe you will understand that what I analyze of the situation makes sense," Jim demanded. He then spoke in a professional manner as Karen tried to keep a straight face. "We don't know what Simon's lucky rock could have been composed of. There is a possibility the crystal contained a combination of compounds that created a chemical reaction when mixed with the high mineral contents of the well water," he explained with the mannerisms of a professor of science.

"Mr. Professor Sphinx, I thank you for that most logical and realistic explanation. You know it is totally absurd!" Karen criticized.

Jim rebuked, "And all this mumbo jumbo of legends and sphinx eyes isn't crazy?"

At that point, Karen walked away, heading for the car. Jim shouted, but she kept going, picking up pace until she was running. By the time she reached the car, she was bawling. As usual, Jim wrapped his arms around her. "You really think I'm crazy, don't you?" Karen sobbed.

"I don't think that at all, Karen. I just believe you love Simon so much you're willing to see any tiny tidbit of hope, no matter how far-fetched it may be."

He then lifted her chin with two fingers, so he could look into her eyes to speak words of sympathy. "Karen, I love you and Simon more than life itself. As I have said before, I miss our son every minute of every day. I do try to understand your strange feelings and the things you see, but they are not real. You are grasping at straws, seeing and hearing what you want in them."

"They seem so real! I can't believe all I have felt deep inside my heart has been my imagination!" Karen cried.

"Come on. Let's go home. We'll get some rest and talk later," Jim advised while opening the car door for her.

Karen got in, and before Jim closed the door, she remarked, "Now that the sphinx eye has been destroyed, my heart and mind do feel more settled. Simon will be coming home. You will see!"

"Of course he will, Karen. I really have no doubt of that," Jim remarked in a weak manner then ran around to his side of the car, got in, and cranked up. He looked at Karen and smiled. She returned the smile.

She's made up her mind to believe this nonsense. Oh well! I'll be here for her when she decides to come back down to reality, Jim thought as he drove away from the park, leaving well enough alone.

New Friendships Are Formed

A Time to Grieve

SIMON WAS SITTING quietly next to Neopoleana while she held the sick baby Rhue. He was almost hypnotized from watching the golden light beams flicker from beneath her folded wings. As he gazed in a trance-like manner, the sound of fluttering wings from above broke the spell. He looked up to see Flutta circling in the coral sky. "Flutta!" he shouted while watching the beautiful creature make her descent.

She lit next to him, her eyes going directly to Neopoleana then to the pile of gold coins.

"What happened here?" she asked noticing Simon's grimaced face.

He scolded her. "You flew away! I can't believe you didn't even try to help save Neopoleana!" Flutta downed her head in shame.

"Do not make Flutta feel guilty. She did as I had asked her," Neopoleana firmly stated. "However, she did take you down to Winglet as you requested now, didn't she?"

This question caught Simon by surprise but, of course, Neopoleana was right. "I'm sorry, Flutta. You did the best thing by not becoming involved. Bronzella would have ripped you to pieces for sure," he spoke in an apologetic manner.

With tears swelling in her eyes, Flutta asked about Winglet. "Is the baby Rhue still alive?"

Neopoleana answered, "She is barely hanging on, but I'm doing all I can to save her. She is under my wings, receiving full strength and power from the golden rays."

Simon interrupted, rattling about the miracle. "Bronzella hurt Neopoleana bad! She was on the brink of death, but Krystallina's spirit found her. She covered the Mother Rhue's body with powerful light! Neopoleana could feel all the good, and she felt my pain and grief! This gave her the will to fight hard to live!"

Flutta's eyes had grown big from listening to this incredible happening. She then asked about the sphinx, "What about Bronzella? Where is she?"

"You see that mountain of coins over there?" Simon replied as Flutta's eyes followed his pointing finger to the pile of metal. "That was once Bronzella!" he exclaimed.

Flutta gasped. "My goodness, the old girl just fell apart," she spoke with spirited excitement, causing Simon to chuckle.

"Sh...sh!" the Mother Rhue hushed. "I must have silence now!"

Just when the two quieted down, bubbles began to trickle out from the nearby tunnel's entrance. Simon remained calm as he watched in bewilderment. Soon marching right in behind the bubbles, Blubbles exited, followed by Gurggles. Pinka, Truffles, and Tooty made their way out. Then Blinko, Slurple, and Razzle came on through. Malo and Jetta soon appeared, with Squiggly trailing behind.

Simon was completely taken as they marched quietly and formed a circle around Neopoleana. The tiny Rhues kneeled down and began to cry, stirring emotions within his heart. *They know what the Mother Rhue is doing*, he thought to himself.

Within minutes, the tears from the Rhues' eyes developed color. Beautiful droplets of red, pink, green, blue, white, brown, purple, gray, yellow, black, and orange trickled off their tiny faces. Simon had never seen anything so amazing in his entire life! He had never noticed the beauty in tears of grief before, but the wonderful colors shining through showed him. He kneeled down and let loose of his own emotions as never before. All the bottled-up hurt, pain, and grief he had carried for so long now flowed out with his tears. It was truly precious and beautiful!

Simon felt much better after the good cry. He got up from his kneeling position just in time to hear a rustling sound in the distance behind him. He turned and looked but saw nothing. Suddenly, Razzle let out a scream of sheer terror. "Look behind that tree down there!" he exclaimed while glowing like an ember of coal.

Simon glanced at the tall, dead tree Razzle had pointed out. At first, he thought he saw an old dead treebranch protruding from behind the base of the trunk. That is until it moved! "Hey! I believe that is La'Zar's tail sticking out there!" he squealed with excitement as he ran toward the tree. Blinko cried as his snout lit up like a neon torch. "That could be a monster. It will snatch him up and eat him alive!" he exclaimed as the other Rhues cringed and huddled together.

"Oh, I'm sure Simon would not mistake his friend's tail for that of a monster," Neopoleana calmly replied.

All the Rhues watched with caution as Simon neared the edge of The Forest of Dead Trees. Soon he spotted a trail of fresh slime leading behind a nearby huge gray boulder. He smiled and knew for sure his friends were hiding. He climbed upon the giant rock and looked down to see Icky staring up at him as La'Zar peered from behind the dead tree.

"Okay, you guys! Come out right this minute!" Simon shouted with excitement and then scurried down the boulder to meet them. "I didn't think I'd ever see you again!" he exclaimed while giving them hugs. He noticed La'Zar still had his scar from the cut Bronzella had given him but didn't mention it.

"I guess you know that the sphinx turned back to coins. She won't be threatening any of you ever again!" Simon proclaimed as he wiped slime off his hands from Icky's hug.

Suddenly, Grundel stepped out from behind another large boulder. "Good gracious, how many more of you are here?" Simon asked. He could hardly believe his eyes when Frieda the spider, Rattles the snake, the two worms Crawly and Cutter, and Brat the rat all showed their faces.

"What a wonderful and nice surprise!" he shouted to all of them.

"Simon, we heard the commotion and have been hiding back here for a long time," Grundel spoke up.

"Yeah, we thought Neopoleana was a goner for sure!" La'Zar remarked.

"How's the baby Rhue?" Frieda asked.

"The Mother Rhue is still giving her light and power from the *golden wings*. Only time will tell," Simon explained.

"May we go up there and kneel beside Neopoleana the way you and the Rhues did?" Brat asked.

Simon contemplated. "Oh, that is so nice of you to want to do that, but…uh…well, I just don't know."

"Look, Simon, Bronzella is gone. We no longer have to live in fear. We are very aware that we may look scary, but we want to be friends with Neopoleana and the Rhues and creatures of Rhueland," La'Zar announced with a smile.

"Oh, I want that too! It would be wonderful for all of you to make friends, but the Rhues do not know you. They would be very afraid," Simon pointed out.

Brat agreed to his point of view then threw in a spooky comment. "The creatures and Rhues have heard many horror stories about the 'bad monsters' from Gruhland." Everyone snickered at his pun.

Frieda looked toward the tunnel. "Where are the Rhues anyway?"

Simon glanced and then realized they must be hiding inside the tunnel. "Come on, but walk slow and be very quiet," he commanded. "With Winglet sick, it is a sad time for everyone, especially Neopoleana."

"Are you sure we should go up there? We don't want to upset the Rhues," Grundel asked in a concerned manner.

Before Simon could answer, Cutter asked very boldly, "What about Neopoleana? She may not want us around her baby."

"Well, we shall be very cautious. I believe when Neopoleana and the tiny Rhues see you kneel in a show of compassion for Winglet, they will then trust you," Simon determined.

"That is such a good point. They will truly see that we are not mean," Frieda spoke with hope.

Simon led the way as the Gruhs marched in single file toward the tunnel. Each one was very quiet and obedient, not even whispering. Strange, but Neopoleana seemed completely undisturbed by the approaching creatures from Gruhland. They gathered around her in a half-circle and then proceeded to kneel down together. Soon the creatures were crying for Winglet just as they had seen Simon and the Rhues do. The Mother Rhue smiled with pleasure at the amazing sight.

Simon peered toward the tunnel's entrance to see several Rhue heads peeping out. He smiled before walking serenely in their direction, hoping they would not run farther back. When he reached the entrance and peered inside, he found the gang all huddled together. "Come on out, you guys. The Gruhs are my friends, and they will be yours too."

"We are scared of them!" Blubbles firmly replied as bubbles filled the area.

"Why?"

"We have always been afraid!" Blinko spoke out loudly.

"You weren't afraid to come over to Gruhland," Simon stressed.

"Well, Flutta told us Winglet was sick. We were so concerned over her that we never thought of the creatures," Pinka commented.

Simon smiled and pointed toward Neopoleana. "The Gruhs are also concerned for Winglet. Look at them. Their hearts are full of compassion."

The Rhues slowly broke away from their huddle to take another peek. As they watched the Gruhs pouring their hearts out, they knew these creatures were not the 'bad monsters' they had always heard about. Now they saw them differently and in a whole new light. Unlike Bronzella, these Gruhs were loving and compassionate.

"Simon, I guess I'd like to meet the Gruhs, but only if you promise to stay close by," Squiggly spoke with reluctance.

"I'm willing to meet them also," Slurple slurped out.

"Me too!" Gurggles gurgled.

Simon listened with anticipation as all the Rhues took turns indicating their desire to meet these new creatures. "Well, come on! They're getting up from kneeling right now!" he exclaimed as the Rhues watched cautiously.

One by one, each huddled close to Simon, becoming so tightly packed (like sardines) that it was hard to take even one step. Very slowly, the entire group began to inch toward Neopoleana and the Gruhs. The Rhues were so nervous Simon could hear slurps, bubbling, and gurgling. Razzle was glowing, and Blinko's snout was flashing nonstop. Believe it or not, prissy Pinka was actually trying to fluff her curls! Jetta was jumping as they slinked along while Squiggly rolled his snout up and down. Malo was so puffed up he appeared to float above the others. Tooty's horn snout was pumping out off-key notes, and Truffle's scent was strong with the smell of chocolate. Simon's mouth watered uncontrollably as he thought of sinking his teeth into a thick chocolate bar.

Finally, the group stopped very close to La'Zar, but the Rhues remained tightly huddled. "La'Zar, these are my friends, the Rhues," Simon grunted then exclaimed, "Oh, come on, you guys, loosen up! I can't even breathe!"

"It's nice to finally meet you," La'Zar politely spoke.

Blubbles poked his head out and managed to acknowledge. "We are glad to meet you too. My name is Blubbles."

Another voice shouted from within the bundle. "My name is Razzle!"

Simon finally talked the Rhues into pulling away from him. However, they stayed close while he chatted with his Gruh friends. In a short while, the Rhues began to relax and talk a little to La'Zar. Simon then decided to break the ice by introducing them to Frieda, Cutter, Crawly, Grundel, Icky, and Brat.

However, after all the nice-to-meet-yous, everyone became quiet, not knowing exactly what else to say. The Rhues began to group together once again, and the Gruhs all came together with a few giggles and whispers going on within both separate groups.

The Gruhs noticed how Pinka was snickering and pointing. Suddenly, she yelled out, "Hey, Brat! What happened to your tail! It looks like part of it was chewed off!"

That's all it took. One by one the Rhues began to chuckle. Then Simon got tickled just hearing their laughter. Of course, the Gruhs even chimed in (that is, all but Brat).

"It is not funny to get two-thirds of your tail bitten off by a dragon!" the rat cried out in humiliation.

This just added fire to the furnace. The crowd laughed louder than ever. However, Neopoleana quickly called them down.

Simon winded down enough to try to pacify Brat. "Oh, come on!" he shouted, swatting at the huge rat's shoulder. "Where is your sense of humor? It was just funny how Pinka blurted that out. We weren't really making fun of you. Don't get so personal, okay?"

Brat sighed. "Well, maybe I did take it too serious. At least my tail gets me attention." He chuckled lightly. Soon he was laughing along with the group, although on the inside, he still felt confused with his feelings.

Simon realized how loud they had gotten. "Sh, sh! Be quiet, everyone!" he scolded. "Here we are laughing and joking around while Neopoleana is trying to nurse Winglet back to good health. We should be ashamed of ourselves."

Neopoleana spoke up. "No, you shouldn't. It makes me happy to hear your laughter. I only needed silence in order to collect my thoughts. I'm sure Winglet can hear and loves it! What better medicine could a baby Rhue be given?" she elated.

Simon ran to her side with the Rhues and Gruhs following. "How is Winglet? Do you think she is responding to the golden light beams?" he questioned with concern.

"Well, take a look for yourselves," Neopoleana answered with a big smile. Simon and the creatures watched in awe as she lifted her *golden wings* slightly. Their mouths dropped open and their eyes grew big at what they saw! Winglet peered from beneath the magical wings and actually giggled! Her cheeks were becoming rosy, and her *silver wings* had returned almost to full color. The best sight was that the baby Rhue was squirming around.

The group jumped for joy then joined hands and skipped around in a circle. Tooty played a special tune as they danced and sang. They even remembered the song Simon had made up about them and sang it in harmony. Neopoleana watched in pleasure as the Rhues and Gruhs played together, rejoicing for the revival of Winglet!

Simon was still celebrating along with the group when something at the tunnel caught his eye. Was he seeing things, or was that the stone figures exiting the entrance? He looked hard to make sure his eyes were not deceiving him. "It is them!" he screamed with excitement while pointing toward the tunnel. Everyone turned to watch Tealo, Jado, Ember, and Roza march side by side in twos heading directly to the mountain of coins.

"What are they up to?" Simon asked in a puzzled manner while watching the tiny figures with their stone buckets swinging on their mitten hands. "Come on! Let's follow them!" he commanded.

The gang kept their distance behind as the stone figures made their way to the huge pile. They watched in awe as each scooped up a bucketful of coins from the mountain of metal. Then Simon was surprised to see them marching their way!

"I wonder why they're headed up here." Pinka asked.

"I don't know, but let's be really still. We don't want to frighten them off," Simon suggested.

After Tealo, Jado, Ember, and Roza neared the group, they sat their tiny buckets down on the ground. Simon noticed their pails were so tiny, each contained only two or three coins. He stood very still, consumed with wonderment, as the figures took their place forming a circle around him! They began to march around, looking him up and down, leaving Simon totally bewildered. The figures then picked up their buckets and marched in single file in the direction of the tunnel.

"Now what in the world was that all about?" Simon pondered while the creatures watched the stone figures move onward, paying no attention to anyone. They marched like tiny, toy soldiers through the tunnel's entrance and were soon out of sight.

"I can't figure out why those little rascals were giving me the once over, but I guess they're going to clean up all those coins," Simon commented.

"They love to build beautiful works of art, you know. I'm positive that is what they will do with the coins," Pinka determined.

"Well, a project like that should keep them busy for a very long time!" Malo exclaimed.

Just then, Neopoleana interrupted the conversation. "Simon, will you and the Rhues and Gruhs please come here?" she called.

"Sure, Neopoleana," Simon obliged as he and the creatures walked in her direction.

Winglet was peeping out from under the *golden wings* again. Simon noticed her cute face squinted up in a shy grin. He chuckled before giving the same expression back to her. The baby

Rhue quickly covered her face with her hands and then slid back under the wings, out of sight, causing Simon to giggle. "When do you think Winglet will be well enough to come out," he asked the Mother Rhue.

"It will be quite awhile yet. She must gain strength and endurance," Neopoleana explained. She suddenly realized that Simon and the Rhues and creatures were staring at her. "Is something wrong?" she asked.

"Uh...well, what is that crusty streak across the side of your face?" Squiggly asked as he walked close and pointed to the area. Neopoleana quickly lifted her long, elegant, and slender hand to her face to feel an elongated scab.

"That is where Bronzella cut you during the fight, isn't it?" Simon asked.

"Yes. She sliced through my skin, penetrating deeply," the Mother Rhue replied, causing the entire group to cringe as if they felt the pain.

"Will you have a scar like La'Zar?" Blinko asked.

"It is possible. We'll just have to wait and see," she answered, then immediately gave orders. "Now let's get back to why I called you over here! Actually, I have an offer to make to the Gruhs, but the Rhues and you need to know the details also," she spoke while glancing toward Simon.

The group looked very curious, so Neopoleana responded with excitement, "Oh, it is something good! I believe it will make everyone happy!"

"We are listening," Frieda informed her.

"First, I wanted to let Simon and the Gruhs know that I was keeping a watchful eye on them earlier," the Mother Rhue spoke, causing the group to look at one another in amazement. "When Simon ran to you with no fear, I knew you had been good friends to him. Then when you came and kneeled down and cried for Winglet, it touched my heart deeply. I see much good in you. You are truly full of love and compassion." The creatures shyly smiled.

Neopoleana continued without interruption. "I wanted to let you know that Winglet will grow fast over the next few months. Her tiny, sparkling winglets will grow into long, flowing, magnificent *silver wings*. They will then contain the same magical power and light as mine. There will be more than enough for our existence, and I'm sure Winglet would agree that we would love to share this wonderful power with you," she proudly explained, looking at the Gruhs.

Everyone continued to listen intently as the Mother Rhue elaborated. "Gruhland would again flourish with colorful flowers, trees, plants, and shrubbery. There would be more food selections to choose from, not just mushrooms, thornbushes, and bark. The enchanting lavender sky would light your day."

The Gruhs looked at one another in total surprise of such a generous gift. "We have always heard that Gruhland was once such a place as you described. Is this true, Neopoleana?" Grundel asked.

The Mother Rhue sighed a little and then smiled. "What you heard is true. My sister, Krystallina, gave Gruhland power and light from her beautiful crystal wings. Of course, this was many eons ago. None of you creatures existed at that time," she explained.

"Bronzella killed Krystallina!" Simon suddenly yelled out, causing gasps among the creatures and little Rhues.

Neopoleana spoke up. "All of that is behind us now. My sister was kind. Her spirit can still be felt here in these lands. It would please Krystallina for Winglet and I to share our power with the Gruhs."

"Your offer is so kind and generous," Frieda acknowledged. "However, we have only known dusky darkness in Gruhland. This would certainly be a dramatic change. May we discuss it among each other first?" she asked.

Neopoleana agreed. "Oh, by all means. This should definitely be a group decision. Take your time with it."

The Gruhs walked away to a nearby boulder and huddled together behind it to hold their meeting in secret. "Well, what do you think of Neopoleana's offer?" La'Zar asked the group.

"Oh, I just think it's wonderful!" Frieda exclaimed.

"Well, I love my mushrooms and I want them to stay. For this, they need a cool, moist place," Icky firmly stated.

"I think having flowers to pick and smell would be totally awesome!" Frieda spoke out.

"I believe having light and being able to see such a beautiful sky would make us feel better," Grundel evaluated.

"I agree," Crawly shouted. "Plus, we would gain strength with the light and power from Winglet's *silver wings*.

Cutter procrastinated. "I just don't know. I'm used to the way things are now in Gruhland. Why change them?"

Rattles spoke his mind. "It doesn't really matter to me whether we do or don't."

"I am totally, positively against any change whatsoever! I can hide from mean dragons and from Sqhawk in the darkness!" Brat anxiously shouted. "I'm certainly not ready to lose the rest of my tail!" he cringed.

"What about you, La'Zar? How do you feel about Neopoleana's generosity?" Frieda asked.

"I guess I'm sort of in the middle. I want the light, but not every day."

"Well, we need to make up our minds one way or the other!" Cutter declared.

"Some of us want light and some don't, while others want it part of the time. How do we solve this problem?" Crawly asked.

"I have a suggestion," Frieda spoke out.

"And what is it that you suggest?" Icky asked with a tone as if Frieda couldn't possibly have a solution.

"Well, actually it's very simple," the smart spider bragged, causing the creatures to roll their eyes.

"We're waiting to hear your fantastic idea!" Brat exclaimed.

"I believe we should accept Neopoleana's offer, but with a stipulation," Frieda suggested.

The creatures looked at each other in a puzzled manner. "Look, can't you just spit out the solution in simple terms?" Icky scolded.

"We don't have all day! We're getting hungry!" Grundel added.

"Well! You don't have to be so rude!" Frieda huffed.

"Aw, come on. We're anxious to hear what you have come up with," La'Zar prodded.

Frieda smiled and then explained. "We can let Neopoleana know we will accept her offer if she can leave a portion of Gruhland dark."

The Gruhs looked at each other with expressions of shock. Why, this was a simple yet good solution because it would solve the problem. "Frieda, I must say, you are a genius," La'Zar complimented as the Gruhs applauded. Frieda blushed shyly but felt proud on the inside.

"Come on, group! Let's go tell Neopoleana that we accept her offer," Cutter shouted while leading the way.

"That is, of course, with the stipulation," Crawly pointed out, creating snickers, giggles, and laughs among the Gruhs.

Neopoleana looked up, and Winglet peeped out when they heard the creatures approaching. "It didn't take you long to reach a decision," the Mother Rhue spoke, sounding rather surprised.

"We have decided to accept your most generous gift," Frieda announced, being the spokesperson. "However, we would like part of Gruhland to be left dusky dark at all times. Some of the Gruhs feel more secure in that atmosphere."

"That would not be a problem whatsoever. In fact, I like the idea very much!" the Mother Rhue exclaimed.

Everyone clapped and cheered, and then Simon spoke up. "While you were gone, the Rhues let me know that they would like to visit The Forest of Dead Trees!"

"We would be delighted to show them around!" Grundel elated.

"Hold on!" Neopoleana shouted. "I do not recall being in a discussion about the Rhues taking a trip to The Forest of Dead Trees. I just don't know if that is such a good idea. You know we still have Sqhawk to deal with."

This comment caused the Rhues to hunker down and look toward the coral sky. "That old buzzard would eat us alive!" Razzle cried.

"Well, I think we're plenty big enough to take care of you," La'Zar boasted.

"Look what happened to Simon! Bronzella was huge, but Sqhawk managed to get him! He's lucky to be alive!" Pinka squealed.

Frieda analyzed, "Simon was captured because he wasn't on guard at all times in the open areas, and all Bronzella had on her mind were the *golden wings*!"

Simon frowned at her remarks. "We would be more cautious than that!"

"There are eight of us to watch after the Rhues. Old Sqhawk would not dare come near!" Brat bragged, showing bravery.

"He's right. We will have the Gruhs' protection. There is nothing to fear!" Tooty agreed.

"Can we go? Please, Neopoleana?" Malo begged in a sympathetic manner as the others looked on.

"I do agree there are plenty of 'huge creatures' to look after you. I guess it will be all right, but only if you promise to stay very close to the Gruhs!" the Mother Rhue responded with a bit of reluctance.

Immediately, the group started cheering. "Hold it!" Neopoleana shouted. Silence prevailed right then. "You must stay for only a short while. Is that understood?" she ordered.

"Yes, ma'am!" the Rhues shouted together.

"When we do return, Simon will be going home, won't he?" Gurggles asked.

"Oh yes, of course! He needs to get back to his mom and dad. Also, Winglet should be well enough to travel by then,"

Neopoleana replied. "So scoot on out of here. Behave too!" She chuckled.

"We will!" Slurple shouted with excitement as they waddled to board the Gruhs. Crawly stretched out so Blubbles could hop upon his back while Gurggles chose to ride with Cutter. Slurple and Squiggly climbed upon Brat as Tooty and Malo hitched a ride with Grundel. Truffles scurried to grab a ride with Frieda, burrowing down in her soft, fuzzy back. Blinko ran and jumped upon Rattles from behind, like a cowboy pouncing on a horse. Finally, Simon helped Pinka upon La'Zar's back. Immediately, she shivered at the touch of such cold, scaly skin.

"Well, isn't anyone riding with me?" Icky protested as he glanced toward Razzle and Jetta. They were the only two left with no ride and squinted as if they had just eaten a green persimmon at the thought of getting on that slimy creature!

"Well, come on!" Icky demanded. "A little slime isn't going to hurt you."

With puckered faces, the two slowly walked up. "You go first!" Jetta suggested with her scrunched face.

"Why can't you go first?" Razzle firmly asked.

"Look, you two!" Simon yelled. "Just climb upon Icky! You're wasting time!"

Jetta gave Simon a grimaced look. "Well, we don't hear you offering to help!" she shouted.

"Look, I can't be helping you off and on Icky. It will become a habit that would wear me out. Therefore, you must figure the problem out," Simon weakly explained.

Razzle snapped, "The truth is you don't want to be coated with slime!"

"Whatever!" Simon snapped back.

After a few snarls at each other, Razzle proceeded to scale Icky's side. The drippy, thick slime was so slippery he immediately slid back down, creating laughs among everyone.

Quickly, Jetta helped Razzle up from the ground and then helped push him up Icky's side. Finally, he made it to the top of the snail's back and took a seat in the middle of the dry, cracked shell. Then Jetta tried to slink up Icky's side but couldn't get a grip on his slimy skin. "Come on, grab my hand!" Razzle shouted as he bent forward, hand extended. Jetta clasped her hand in his, and he started to pull her up. Kerplunk! Both of them went slipping and sliding down, screaming for dear life! Simon and the creatures laughed their heads off at the funny sight.

"I give up!" Jetta shouted in frustration. "I can walk fast, and that is just what I'm going to do!"

"Me too!" Razzle cried out.

La'Zar yelled out a suggestion to them. "Hold on a minute! You're jumping the gun! You can climb on my back, and then I'll stand next to Icky so you can jump on his back."

"That's a great idea!" Jetta expressed.

"I don't know why we didn't think of it ourselves," Razzle added.

"Hey! I'm sorry to tell you, but that will not work," Simon shouted.

"Why will it not work?" La'Zar belted.

"Well, the Rhues have small legs and can't take the long jump from Icky's back to yours. They would definitely fall!"

"Oomph, I suppose you're right," La'Zar muttered.

Jetta and Razzle sighed deeply. Then the other Rhues joined in with their sighs from the frustrating situation.

"I can solve the problem," Frieda bragged in a subtle manner.

La'Zar smirked. "Oh yeah, I'm sure you can."

"I'm only trying to help! You should appreciate it!" Frieda exclaimed.

"Oh, but we do!" Jetta shouted. "Tell us what you have in mind."

Frieda rolled her eyes at La'Zar. "I will be happy to share my idea with you. You can help push Razzle up Icky's side like before. In the meantime, I will be spinning a silk rope. I will then toss it to Razzle, who can hold one end tightly, letting the other end dangle. Jetta can grasp the rope and climb up!" she explained with pride.

The group (except for La'Zar) cheered at this most brilliant solution. "I know this idea will work. We'll be waiting, Frieda! Go ahead and spin the rope!" Simon exclaimed.

Jetta pushed Razzle up Icky's side, while Frieda got busy secreting thick, clear silk from her "silk purse."

"Hey, that stuff looks like nectar. Can we eat some?" Malo asked with drools of excitement.

"Certainly not. It will glue your insides together!" Frieda scolded, causing Malo to feel totally humiliated for having even asked. Giggles from Simon and the others didn't help him to feel any better either.

Frieda took the glob of silk and began her spinning technique. Everyone watched in awe as the glob stretched out, becoming an elongated strand. Soon this long piece of silk was spinning around so fast that it made the group feel dizzy just watching. After the spinning ceased, a strong yet narrow rope had been made to fit perfectly in Razzle's tiny hand. Quickly, Frieda tossed it up to him. He grinned from ear to ear as he held tightly to one end and let the other end dangle. "Come on! I've got a good grip!" he yelled.

The gang watched in anticipation as Jetta grasped the rope tightly then pressed her feet firmly into Icky's slimy body, using it for an anchor to begin her strenuous climb. As everyone held their breath, she moved upward, hand over hand. As she neared the top of Icky's back, Simon covered his mouth to stifle his gasp. Finally, she reached the very top and swung in behind Razzle. Everyone sighed with relief and then shouted with joy, "Yeah, Yeah!" Jetta pulled in the rope and draped it around her neck, saving it for later.

The trip to Gruhland could now begin. With cheering and clapping, the Gruhs began to move onward. "Good-bye, Neopoleana and Winglet. We'll be back soon!" Simon shouted.

The Rhues laughed at Winglet as she peeped out from underneath the *golden wings* to wave.

"Have fun! I love you!" the Mother Rhue shouted.

Flutta, whom everyone had forgotten about, woke up from hearing the commotion and crawled out from beneath a huge red-and-gold bush. "What's going on?" she sleepily asked.

"Hey, Flutta. We forgot you were even around!" Simon yelled. "You sort of sneaked off to sleep, didn't you?"

She was stretching her wings and legs. "Boy! I was really tired! However, I feel much better now."

"Winglet is getting better!" Simon announced.

Flutta was elated. "What wonderful news to wake up to! It just makes my day!" She then questioned in wonder, "Why in the world are you guys boarded on the backs of the Gruhs? Are you going somewhere?"

Simon enlightened her. "Yeah, I will be going home soon, so we're taking a short vacation trip to The Forest of Dead Trees."

Blinko chimed in, "Would you like to come with us?"

"No, I need to fly back to Rhueland and check on the other creatures. I'm sure they are worried over Neopoleana," Flutta answered.

With a glowing face, the Mother Rhue responded, "Oh, thank you so much for being so considerate."

"We need to head on out," Simon exclaimed as the Gruhs lined up in single form. La'Zar was at the front of the line and slowly moved on with the others following. The Rhues glanced back when they heard Flutta cranking up her wings then watched her take off in the direction of Rhueland. While waving at Neopoleana one last time, they chuckled at Winglet's tiny face peering out from under the *golden wings*.

Soon the Gruhs were traveling over big rocks and huge boulders. The Rhues giggled as they bounced up and down, loving every minute of the ride. Simon thought back to when he was traveling down through the well on Bronzella's back. That ride was fast and smooth compared to this bumpy one! He then looked up toward dusky darkness and wished Neopoleana could spread out her wings to light up the lavender color of Gruhland's sky. His thoughts then went inward to his mom and dad, his friend Doug, his dog Bingo, and Hillcrest. He sure missed them, but he smiled, knowing it wouldn't be long before he would be back home! He glanced toward Pinka. *I even miss Angel Marie Wilson*, he thought.

Suddenly, Truffles shouted, interrupting Simon's thoughts. "Hey, is that The Forest of Dead Trees over there?"

Simon looked up to realize they were nearing the edge of the forest. "Yes, we're almost there!" he squealed with excitement.

The Gruhs climbed over the last few boulders as the Rhues shouted together, "We're almost in Gruhland!" Blubbles was making bubbles and watching them float across The Rivers of Strength while Tooty played a catchy tune on her horn snout. The group sang joyfully while moving on, getting closer to their "vacation spot."

Soon they were past the last boulder. The Gruhs halted for a moment, and the Rhues didn't waste any time in jumping off their backs, heading fast toward the dead trees. Simon hurried down La'Zar's side and ran to catch up with them. "Hey, you guys, slow down. You don't know this area. You could get lost, then Sqhawk could find you and…ugh…well…eat you alive! You know very well what the Mother Rhue said!" he scolded.

The Rhues froze momentarily with fear. "We're sorry, Simon. We promise to stay close to you and the Gruhs like Neopoleana told us to do," Truffles spoke with shaky words. They waited until the Gruhs caught up with them and then proceeded to enter the forest.

The Gruhs were glad to be back home so they could fill their hungry stomachs. The Rhues observed with complete fascination as La'Zar immediately chose a tree loaded with bark, ripped off a long, crunchy piece, and chomped down.

Crawly and Cutter were busy plowing up the woods dirt, while Icky searched for a cove of mushrooms. Rattles found an empty nearby hole and crawled in to investigate. Grundel made the ground shake like an earthquake as he stomped off toward the thornbushes.

Simon was thinking of how Sqhawk had her nest in a thicket of thornbushes on the far side of Gruhland when suddenly a noise close by in a very tall tree caught his and the Rhues attention. They looked up to see Frieda climbing high, searching for a nice, remote hiding place. She would also be surrounded by plenty of dead leaves on which to munch.

Brat yelled out just before disappearing into a thicket of weeds, "I'll be out after dinner!"

The Rhues then followed Simon to the thickest bunch of mushrooms they had ever seen. Icky was already enjoying the delicacy when they walked up. "Are these mushrooms good?" Simon asked. Icky's mouth was full of the tasty treats, but he tried to answer. "Th…a…goo!" he muttered with pieces of mushroom spewing from his mouth.

"That is so gross!" Simon exclaimed as he picked bits of mushrooms off his shirt that Icky had spit on him. "I couldn't understand a word you said. Your mouth was full."

Icky finished chewing and then swallowed. "I said these mushrooms are excellent. In fact, they are the best I have ever tasted."

"That's better," Simon remarked while brushing away the last few tidbits of half-chewed mushrooms.

Suddenly, a loud noise caught their attention. *Bam! Bam! Bam!* It was Slurple slamming his snout up and down, over and over, beating it hard against the ground. Simon ran fast to him. "What is wrong, Slurple?" he asked excitedly.

"He slurped a big piece of mushroom up his snout!" Squiggly quickly spoke up.

Simon screamed, "What? I can't believe this!"

Bam! Bam! Slurple was getting desperate. He was choking, and time was running out! "Hold on, Slurple! I'm going to help you!" Simon shouted as he looked around on the ground.

"Hurry, Simon! Slurple is turning a funny color!" Blinko yelled with anticipation.

Simon found a dead tree branch lying nearby and quickly picked it up and ran to the choking Rhue. "Don't move, Slurple!" he screamed while drawing back the limb. Fast, he came down with a hard whack across Slurple's snout, hitting right where it bulged. The strike broke the mushroom in several smaller pieces. "Now blow your snout hard!" Simon ordered as he and the Rhues moved back.

Slurple puffed up, then blew his snout straight out. A spray of mushroom pieces flew from his nostrils, going in every direction. "Ouch! Ouch!" he screamed in agony as the last few pieces sailed out. "That hurt! I believe you broke my snout!" he cried.

Simon exclaimed, "I'm sorry, but I had to do something. You were choking to death!"

Soon Slurple's snout began swelling right in the center. It began throbbing, looking almost like a beating heart. The swollen area was now a burgundy color from turning red on the purple snout. Simon felt bad for the tiny Rhue, but at least the mushroom was out, and Slurple was alive!

"Your snout may be hurt, but Simon saved your life!" Pinka spoke out.

"You wouldn't be here right now if it weren't for him," Truffles added.

"They're right, Simon. You are my hero, and I thank you!" Slurple obliged while giving his friend a warm, "slurped" hug.

"Oh, I was glad to help." Simon blushed. He then gave some good advice. "Now listen, guys. You can't suck any type of food in Gruhland up your snouts. You must use your hands to put it in your mouth and then chew it. I suppose it will be all right for you to taste the food here, but you can't overdo it. You were meant to eat nectar only. Anything else could make you sick."

Of course, the Rhues were hungry and insisted on tasting the mushrooms, so Simon broke off a tiny piece for each one. They put the mushroom bits in their mouths and chomped down. In a matter of seconds, the Rhues were puckering up and spitting out the bitter food.

"We don't like it!" Pinka shouted with a squelched face.

"Well, I didn't think you would. I can't stand them myself." Simon chuckled. "You want to try some bark?" he smirked.

"No, I don't think so," Squiggly bluntly answered. Each Rhue joined in to say they wanted no part of Gruhland's food.

"I'm hungry," Pinka whined.

"I am starving!" Malo shouted.

Simon was very understanding. "I'm sure all of your little bellies could use some nectar. I just don't believe you're quite ready for Gruhland. Let's just head back to Neopoleana and Winglet. We can go to the nectar field and eat well!" he exclaimed.

"That is the best idea yet!" Pinka agreed. She then sassily fussed. "This place is so boring! The Gruhs only think of themselves! They are supposed to be looking after us, yet they are just feeding their faces!"

Simon responded, "Calm down now, Pinka. The Gruhs mean well, I'm sure. At least we have this time together."

"It won't be long before you will be going home, right, Simon?" Blinko asked with a tone of sadness.

"The time is drawing near," he replied in a poetic manner.

"We will never see you again. You shall be gone from us forever and ever," Gurggles cried.

"Well, this is your world in The Third Dimension. My world is in Hillcrest," Simon explained. "But let me tell you guys one thing!"

"What, Simon? What do you want to tell us that will ease our grief?" Jetta questioned.

"I want you to know that each one of you Rhues and each Gruh will live in my heart forever," he spoke as a tear rolled from his cheek.

"You will be in our hearts forever and ever too," Pinka responded with a warm pink blush. She then ran for a hug as the other Rhues followed.

"Let's find all the Gruhs so we can head back," Simon elated while hugging the last tiny Rhue.

"Yes, let's hurry. I'm ready for the orchid fields!" Malo shouted.

"I'm ready too!" Squiggly echoed. "We shall eat and then take a long nap."

Immediately, Simon walked to the cove of mushrooms with the Rhues following close by. "Are you full yet?" he asked Icky who was still chomping.

This time, the big snail finished chewing and swallowing before speaking, "Let me get one more bite!"

"All right, we'll be calling in the other Gruhs," Simon responded. "Frieda! We are ready to go back to Rhueland!" he yelled up the tall, dead tree. "Frieda, Frieda!" he called again and again.

Finally, Simon's screams awakened the giant spider, which had fallen asleep while munching on leaves. "Uh, what?" she sleepily asked.

"Wake up, sleepyhead! We're ready to leave!"

Frieda felt as though she needed a longer nap. "But we just got here, didn't we?" she asked.

"We've been here long enough. The Rhues are hungry for nectar already!" Simon shouted.

"Let me get woke up, and I'll be down," Frieda confirmed as she began stretching all of her eight legs out tight like rubber bands. After they bounced back to normal size, she grabbed one last mouthful of dead leaves to nibble on during her trip back down the tree.

Simon was searching for La'Zar around the stand of giant trees of bark. He finally spotted the scaly lizard almost a half mile from where he had started and was amazed to see that all the trees in La'Zar's path had been stripped of their bark! *They now look naked as jaybirds*, Simon thought. *My goodness! He sure can eat fast!* As he approached the full lizard, he shouted, "La'Zar! You're eating up all the bark! Aren't all the trees going to be ruined?"

"These trees grow more bark in no time. There is always an endless supply," La'Zar informed him.

Simon was bewildered. "I have never in my life heard of such a thing!" he exclaimed.

La'Zar snickered. "Simon, remember you are in The Third Dimension. These lands and our world are completely different than what you are used to. Even we are different," he pointed out.

"That is true," Simon agreed. "However, you guys are very much human in the ways that count the most."

La'Zar looked somewhat puzzled. "How is that, Simon?"

Simon pondered a minute or so. "I'll try to explain it. Back home, our creatures do not talk, nor feel with their hearts as you do. Only humans do this. The creatures here are just awesome!"

La'Zar had a surprised look. "My goodness, I couldn't imagine not being able to speak!" he exclaimed.

Simon chuckled. "I'm glad you can, but what touches my heart the most is how deep you feel. Both the Rhues and creatures possess such deep compassion and love. It's incredible, and I have learned so much about my own feelings from just being around you," he commented with pride.

"Do humans possess feelings?" La'Zar asked.

Simon grinned. "Of course they do, but in my world, everyday life is hectic. In your world, it is different somehow. Maybe it's the simplicity. It is like you have more time to stop and feel, and it comes from your hearts. Most people I know are so busy, they don't take the time to really feel, you know, with their hearts," Simon explained.

La'Zar smiled. "I'm glad you like our world. You could stay, you know?"

"No, I couldn't do that. I love and miss my mom and dad. I must go back to where I belong," Simon replied with a hint of sadness. "However, I'm sure that everyone who knows me will definitely see a change."

"Oh, I'm sure they will," La'Zar agreed. "Now come on. We've got some hungry Rhues waiting!"

As they strolled past the last few naked trees, Brat suddenly scurried out of the nearby thicket. "Scare somebody half to death, would you?" Simon scolded.

"Well, I didn't know you were close by." The huge rat snickered, finding Simon's fright amusing. "You thought I was Sqhawk, didn't you? Caw! Caw! I'm going to eat you alive!" Brat rolled with laughter.

"Cut it out! Frightening someone out of their wits is not funny!" La'Zar fussed.

"I bet when that ole mean dragon had you by your tail, you weren't laughing," Simon reminded the frisky rat.

"Oh, okay, I get your point. I'm sorry," he apologized while turning to hide his grin.

"Come and walk with us. The Rhues are waiting in the open area beyond this thicket," Simon prodded.

Brat squealed, "Alone!"

Simon calmed him down. "Don't get so worked up! Frieda and Icky are with them."

Brat crawled up beside Simon and asked, "Why are the Rhues waiting?"

"We are heading back to the tunnel and then on to Rhueland. The Rhues aren't quite ready for this land. Besides, they are hungry. They need to eat nectar, you know."

"We should have realized there was no food in Gruhland fit for the Rhues to eat. I guess we were just too excited over bringing them here," Brat stated. "I can imagine how famished they must be, especially after seeing us jump into eating no sooner than we got here."

"Did you find good food down in the thicket?" Simon asked.

"I munched on twigs and dead, rotten leaves!" Brat exclaimed while lapping his tongue around and around his mouth.

Simon squelched. "Yuck! How gross can you get?"

"Don't knock it till you try it!" the old rat exclaimed with a snicker.

"Brat, may I ask you a question?" Simon asked, changing the subject.

"I don't see why not, but I do not understand why you have to ask if you can ask me a question. How would I know if you can ask if I don't know the question first?" Brat smirked.

Simon sighed with confusion. "Huh? I think I know what you mean."

"What is the question?" Brat asked, seeming a bit impatient.

"I would like to know—will your ever grow your tail back?"

"Nope. It is gone forever!"

"Do you miss it?" Simon asked.

"Actually, I try to forget about it. Then someone comes along and points it out!" the rat shouted with frustration. "I guess it stands out more, because now it is different from other rat tails," he analyzed.

Simon agreed. "Yes, that is exactly what it is. Your tail is just different, and others notice and wonder about it."

"I do understand and accept that, but it sure bothers me when certain creatures find it amusing then point and laugh," Brat criticized.

Simon knew Brat was talking about the time when he and the Gruhs and Rhues laughed at Pinka's remark about his tail. "I thought you were over that! You joined in and laughed along with us," he exclaimed.

"Yeah, I snickered. So what? It still upsets me on the inside," Brat admitted.

"Oh, Brat, I'm sorry. I did not realize this, and I'm sure no one else knew," Simon apologized.

"Sometimes I get confused with my feelings. They all seem to run together, and then I don't know how I really feel," Brat tried to explain.

"I understand exactly what you mean. I have felt the same way many times myself," Simon assured him.

Brat questioned in a surprised manner, "You mean these feelings are normal?"

"Oh yes!" Simon exclaimed. "There have been lots of times I have felt very different from others—like I didn't fit in."

"I would have never known this if you had not shared your true feelings with me," Brat responded.

"That's because it is hard to read the true feelings of others. I couldn't tell how you really felt either. So now, we both have learned something about each other," Simon pointed out.

"I actually feel better just knowing that someone has gone through the same thing. Talking about my feelings and hearing of yours did help me to understand," Brat proclaimed.

Simon suddenly realized that La'Zar had gone ahead of them. He could see the huge lizard and the Rhues waiting out in the open area. "Are Rattles, Crawly, and Cutter back?" he yelled as he approached the gang.

"Rattles finally came out of the hole and has gone to get them," Frieda replied.

"Which way did he go?"

"See all that loose woods dirt? Rattles just knew to follow it," Razzle remarked.

"All of you stay right here together while I go to check on them," Simon ordered.

"Please hurry. We want to leave," Pinka whined.

Simon followed the loose dirt for almost a mile it seemed. There, at the end of the road, was a mountainous mound of solidly packed black dirt with large holes all through it. "Crawly! Cutter! Rattles! Are you there?" he shouted.

Soon a giant snake head popped from one of the holes. It was, of course, Rattles. "Crawly and Cutter are on their way. They were really caught up in some serious digging in this mound," he informed Simon.

The two waited a short while by the huge, round "worm house." Finally, Crawly and Cutter wiggled on out. "That was fun. Cutter can move some dirt with those sharp-edged teeth of his!" Crawly shouted with excitement as dirt spewed from his mouth.

Cutter soon poked his head out and gave a wide grin, showing his pearly whites with dirt stuck all between them. Simon and Rattles chuckled at the sight. "We can certainly see you two have enjoyed yourselves. However, we must go now. The Rhues are getting rather cranky from being hungry," Simon informed them.

"We know. Rattles had already told us. Let's get going!" the huge worms shouted with enthusiasm.

"We'll stop by the thornbushes for Grundel," Simon suggested. "I bet he is so full, he can hardly move."

As they walked on, he realized this would be the last time he would see Gruhland. *No one will ever believe I have been to these lands in The Third Dimension. Maybe I will just keep it a secret forever. That way, these special creatures will be safe in their own incredible world*, he thought.

Simon's thoughts faded as they approached the thornbushes and saw Grundel standing near a thick tree of the sharp needles. "Grundel, we're ready to leave!" he yelled loudly. The giant dragon did not respond.

"Grundel!" Simon screamed as the group moved in. The dragon remained motionless. He crept near his ear and shouted at the top of his lungs, "Grundel!"

The huge creature slung his head upward, creating a rushing whirlwind of air. "You almost hit me with your big head!" Simon complained.

"What? What?" Grundel muttered.

"You were asleep, weren't you?"

"I must have dozed off," the sleepy dragon responded.

"Well, it's now time to go," Simon informed him.

"Okay, okay!" he cranked.

They marched onward, heading back to the rest of the group. Grundel was completely awake by the time they got there, enjoying the sound of the Rhues as they clapped and jumped for joy when they saw the gang approaching. "We finally made it back," Simon remarked. "Now, is everyone here?"

"I think so," Squiggly shouted out.

"Okay, get on your rides!"

The Rhues scurried with excitement. Jetta slid the rope off her neck and handed it to Razzle. With Simon's help this time, she pushed him up Icky's side. He took a seat and then tossed Jetta the rope. It seemed to be getting much easier for the two to get situated.

Simon helped Pinka atop La'Zar's back and then climbed in behind her as the other Rhues finished boarding their rides. "Let's get going, La'Zar!" he commanded. Soon the group was on their way out of The Forest of Dead Trees.

More Trouble Ahead

As they approached the huge rocks and boulders, Simon began to sing. This time, he had made up a song for the Gruhs. Tooty joined him with catchy notes pouring from her horn snout, filling Gruhland with wonderful music. It went like this:

> Icky the snail may seem a bit sticky
> And his slime will make you balk
> But it will hold an enemy tight
> If you don't believe me,
> Just ask old Sqhawk!
> Slime! Slime! Slime!

Crawly moves over and under
And through the dirt
It's easy for him to form a huge mound
Without ever making a single sound!
Wiggle! Wiggle! Wiggle!

Cutter has teeth to snip through
Thorns and thistles
If you need his help,
All you have to do is whistle.
Snip! Snip! Snip!

Rattles is actually a very nice snake
But if you anger him,
You will hear his rattle
And know he is ready for battle.
Rattle! Rattle! Rattle!

Do not be afraid when Frieda comes near
This huge, black spider wants to
Spin you a gift
What a friend so dear!
Spin! Spin! Spin!

Have you seen a giant gray rat?
Part of his tail was eaten by a dragon
If you happen to see him scurrying,
Just yell!
Brat! Brat! Brat!

I hope you get to meet my friend La'Zar
He's the greatest lizard by far!
You will always know when he appears
For on his face, he bears a scar
Slink! Slink! Slink!

He can bellow huge puffs of smoke without lagging
But there is no need for him to be bragging
'Cause he is Grundel, my good friend, the dragon
Puff! Puff! Puff!

No sooner had Simon finished his song than Razzle blurted out, "Sh! Sh! I heard something."

The Gruhs came to a sudden halt, and everyone got very quiet to listen. "I don't hear anything!" Malo exclaimed.

"Me either," Pinka agreed.

"Well, I know I heard something," Razzle confirmed with confidence.

Simon popped questions. "In what direction was the sound? What kind of noise was it?"

Razzle became very unsure of himself. "I think it was way off somewhere. It sounded like a faint scream, I think," he answered.

"It could have been anything," Truffles deemed.

"Maybe Neopoleana is calling us," Gurggles suggested.

"There is no point in guessing. We'll just keep our ears open," Simon determined.

"How do we open our ears?" Blubbles asked with a snicker.

"Very cute, Blubbles. You know that was just a figure of speech!" Simon snapped as the others laughed at the humorous idiom. "Oh, come on, Gruhs! Get going!" he commanded.

Soon they had reached the last stretch of boulders. One huge, flat rock extended out into The Rivers of Strength like a pier.

Blinko squealed in delight, "Let's walk out over that boulder! We can get a better view of the rivers!"

Simon was hesitant with a reply. "Well, I just don't know about that."

"Oh, please!" Tooty begged with a toot from her snout.

"Yes, Simon, the boulder is huge. We'll be safe," Jetta pleaded.

"Uh…well…the boulder is thick and wide. I'm sure it's strong enough to support us," Simon analyzed. "Okay, we'll walk out there, but don't get too close to the edge. It's dangerous!" he warned.

The Rhues clapped with excitement as Brat took the lead with Slurple and Squiggly holding on tight. Simon noticed the excited rat was moving much too fast! However, just as he shouted for him to slow down, Brat tripped over a loose rock. He lost his balance and lunged forward, sending Slurple sailing over the boulder into The Rivers of Strength! Squiggly held on to Brat's fur with all his might and was spared from being plunged into the fiery heat of the deadly molten rivers!

At that point, nothing could be heard but eerie silence. Then gasps of horror from the group began to slowly wail through the air. Pinka quickly clasped her three-fingered hands against her face and cried out in agony, "Oh gosh! Slurple has turned into Jell-O in the boiling water! He is dead!"

All the Rhues became extremely upset. Malo puffed out like a toasted marshmallow as Blubbles and Gurggles covered the area with hundreds of different-sized bubbles. Blinko's neon snout lit up to full brightness and wouldn't go out while Tooty's snout played nonstop rusty notes. Jetta paced back and forth in one spot atop Icky's back as Razzle glowed to a crimson red and cried like a baby. Squiggly lashed his long snout against Grundel's back like a whip, and Truffles's chocolate scent became so strong it was almost pungent.

Simon was just as terrified at Slurple's accidental fall, but for the Rhues' sake, he did an excellent job of keeping the bad feelings inside, though it was all he could do to keep from screaming out. He noticed how sad the Gruhs were, especially Brat, and figured they were also keeping their emotions inside. *Like me, they're doing it for the Rhues*, he thought.

Quietly, Simon wrapped his arms around Pinka. "Sh! Sh!" he softly whispered while cradling her gently. "It was just an accident. Slurple never felt a thing, I'm sure."

"I love Slurple, and I don't want him to be dead! He is gone forever!" she cried with anguish.

Simon held Pinka until she seemed to run out of tears. He then slid down La'Zar's side in anticipation of helping with the other grieving Rhues. Just as his feet touched the ground, he thought for an instant he heard sounds coming from beneath the boulder. "Hey, you guys! You must get quiet! I can't be sure, but I believe I heard cries!" he shouted.

The Rhues hushed to a dull sobbing and listened intently for more sounds. Suddenly, there it was again; a faint cry for help! Simon quickly got down on his knees and crawled toward the edge of the boulder. The Rhues and creatures held their breath as he inched his way close to the end. Soon he spotted six small fingers clutching the edge of the rock. Simon knew it was Slurple and became very excited. "Hold on, Slurple! We're going to pull you in! We will save you!" he shouted to the terrified Rhue.

"Hurry up, Simon. I can't hold on much longer," a very tired Slurple begged as the hot molten bubbled below.

"Just hang in there (no pun intended on Simon's part) a little while longer, and don't talk!" Thinking smart and fast, he commanded, "Bring me your rope, Jetta!" The tiny Rhue hurried down Icky's side and scurried fast, dragging the rope behind her.

"Can we help?" Frieda asked.

"No, just stay back. We don't need excess weight on this cliff!" Simon ordered.

As he grasped the rope from Jetta, Simon noticed Slurple's tiny fingers were slipping. "Hang on, little fellow!" he shouted while preparing to toss it down.

Right at that very moment, out of nowhere, Sqhawk swooped down, the tip of her right wing brushing the surface of the hot molten! She squawked so loud with pain it was deafening. However, the old hawk had managed to snatch Slurple up into her massive beak and fly off.

Everything had happened so fast the group was left stunned. With big eyes and gaping mouths, all they could do was watch in frozen terror as Sqhawk flew fast out of sight with Slurple dangling down, his tiny feet kicking violently.

Suddenly, Jetta cried out, "Sqhawk's going to eat Slurple alive!"

Truffles raged, "I hate Sqhawk! I hate that mean old hawk!"

"I hate her too!" Blinko agreed in angry tones.

"I hate Gruhland!" Pinka cried as she ran toward the other Rhues.

Soon they had all huddled together, crying with grief again. Simon put his arms around the group, and the Gruhs circled around to sob with pain and hurt for Slurple. Simon noticed the different colors of tears once again like he did when the Rhues cried for Winglet.

"I'm going to be sad forever and ever!" Pinka cried through her pink, teary eyes.

"We love Slurple and don't want him to be gone forever!" Squiggly wept.

"I know it seems hopeless, but there's a chance old Sqhawk will not...uh...uh...you know!" Simon wished he hadn't said this.

"Eat Slurple alive!" Tooty shouted out. "Just say it! Sqhawk is going to eat Slurple for dinner!"

"Sh! Sh! Calm down now, Tooty! We don't know that for sure. After all, Sqhawk caught me one time and I'm still here!" Simon proclaimed.

"Simon!" Icky yelled, remembering the rescue. "We are wasting time! Sqhawk has taken Slurple to her nest. We need to try to save him like we did you!"

Simon screamed with hope, "Icky's right! We have got to get going now! Come on, gang, board up!"

The Rhues scurried to their rides and boarded them quickly. In just a few short minutes, the Gruhs were heading back across the rocks and boulders. "I'll spin an extra rope when we get there!" Frieda exclaimed.

"And I'll secrete extra thick slime!" Icky volunteered.

"I'll churn plenty of smoke and have it ready to send smoke signals," Grundel proclaimed.

Razzle protested. "I doubt very seriously if we need to prepare for anything!"

The Rhues gasped. "How can you say such a thing? Where is your hope?" Gurggles questioned.

"Well, Sqhawk is going to remember how Simon was rescued by the Gruhs. Do you really think or believe she is just going to sit by and wait for that to happen again?" Razzle asked, creating fear among the group.

Blubbles yelled out in terror, "You're right! Sqhawk will not wait! She will gobble Slurple up fast!"

"That mean old hawk has probably eaten him already!" Pinka cried.

"Okay, okay, that's enough! I'm certainly glad the Gruhs didn't think like that when Sqhawk had me in her clutches. I wouldn't have stood a chance of being freed!" Simon scolded. "Now let's move onward with faith and hope in our hearts of rescuing Slurple. Is that understood?" he firmly commanded.

"Yes, sir!" the Rhues responded, showing respect.

The group moved onward, traveling at a fast-paced speed heading back to The Forest of Dead Trees. Soon the stand of dead trees was within their sight. The Gruhs pushed ahead, moving fast into the woods.

"We'll be there in no time," Simon remarked, trying to hide his anxiousness. He was actually wondering if the Rhues could read his bad thoughts of Slurple being doomed, which had crept into his mind. "We will have Slurple out of Sqhawk's nest before that old crow can blink an eye!" he boasted, hoping to cover up his negative attitude. The Rhues smiled and agreed with him.

"Hey! The open area is just ahead!" La'Zar shouted with excitement.

"Man, you Gruhs are awesome. Look how quickly you got us here," Simon bragged.

Suddenly, La'Zar came to a halt, gasping. Simon looked into the near distance and then gasped himself. "What? Am I seeing things?" he shouted.

Pinka strained around Simon to look. "I don't believe this! If you're seeing things, then I am also seeing things."

"I do not believe our eyes are deceiving all three of us," La'Zar pointed out.

"Hey! What's going on up there?" Brat shouted as he approached the area.

"All of you come and look for yourselves," Simon prodded. The Gruhs moved forward as the tiny Rhues stretched and squelched to see ahead. When they finally reached a point to where each could get a gander, the entire group gasped at one time. Just ahead of them, standing out in the open area was Slurple! Sqhawk was less than three feet from him!

"From hereon out, keep very quiet," Simon advised. "We don't know what old Sqhawk is up to, and we sure don't want to endanger Slurple's life even further. We will just observe them for a while."

The group hid behind a huge, gray boulder and peered around to watch. They stared in bewilderment as Slurple took a seat upon the ground and started playing in the woods dirt! "He doesn't seem to be afraid!" Simon commented with wonder, sounding a bit confused.

"I bet that dirty old bird told him to act as if he wasn't afraid, or she would eat him alive right now!" Squiggly analyzed.

"I bet Slurple is a decoy for Sqhawk!" Razzle added in agreement.

"You know, you guys could be right! Sqhawk is using Slurple for bait to lure us in. It is definitely a trap!" Simon shouted, almost getting too loud.

"Oh, look! Sqhawk is walking toward Slurple!" Truffles exclaimed.

All the Rhues and creatures strained to get a peep. "Get your heads back!" Simon ordered. "She's looking this way, so just let me do the spying! Sqhawk is less likely to notice only one head."

Simon slowly peered from behind the boulder to see Sqhawk pecking woods dirt! "For crying out loud, that big old bird seems to be entertaining Slurple! What a snow job she's giving him!" he exclaimed then asked in a frustrated manner, "What is going on with this insane creature?"

Every now and then, Sqhawk and Slurple would gaze toward the boulders. "They keep looking this way as if they are watching for us," Simon determined.

Sqhawk finished loosening the dirt, creating a neat sandpile for Slurple, who quickly jumped into the center of the mound and contently began sifting the dirt through his hands. Sqhawk calmly sat near, with the little purple Rhue being completely wrapped up only in play.

"Well! I just don't know what to think!" Simon told the others, sounding more confused than ever. "However, there is one thing that I'm convinced of—Sqhawk is waiting for us!"

"What should we do?" Blubbles asked.

"I really don't know, but we must do something!" Simon harked.

"We could just rush out and storm Sqhawk. This would catch her off guard, and she would probably fly away," Brat suggested.

Simon frowned. "That is not a very good idea. The old hawk would surely snatch Slurple up first. He would be doomed without a doubt!"

"Maybe we should get Neopoleana to handle this situation," Frieda suggested.

"Well, you know the Mother Rhue has used a lot of energy on Winglet. She's got to be drained. No, she couldn't possibly handle that huge bird right now," Simon determined.

"Then what are we going to do?" Pinka whimpered.

"I believe you guys should stay here and let me try to talk with Sqhawk," Simon suddenly blurted out.

"What!" Gurggles exclaimed.

Tooty cried out. "She will get you, Simon! Sqhawk will finish what she started—eating you alive!"

"We don't know that! Look, this is something I must do for Slurple's sake. Plus I have no other choice!" Simon snapped. "Now all of you stay quiet and don't be showing your heads!" he ordered.

"You mean you are going right this minute!" Razzle screamed out.

Simon whispered loudly, "Sh, sh! You must stay calm, and please be quiet! There is no use in me putting this off. I must do it now!"

"Be careful," Pinka begged as Simon slowly crept around the boulder, exposing himself in the open.

Soon he was walking toward Sqhawk and Slurple. Both looked up and spotted him. Simon froze, but before he could move again, Slurple quickly jumped up from his sitting position and squealed, "Simon! Simon!" The happy Rhue scurried in a waddling fashion toward him, screaming his name all the way.

Finally, Simon was able to move. He took off in a run toward Slurple and then jerked him up quickly after they met. Slurple hugged Simon around the neck. "I thought maybe you weren't coming for me," he cried.

"There is no way we would forget you!" Simon exclaimed as he ran fast, heading back to the boulder with Slurple in his arms.

"But...but Simon," the Rhue tried to speak.

Simon interrupted. "We'll talk after I get you out of harm's way—away from that savage old hawk!"

"Simon!" Slurple shouted.

"Not now!"

The Rhues and Gruhs jumped and squealed with excitement as they approached. Slurple seemed a bit dazed as Simon sat him down. "You just took off with me!" the Rhue fussed as Simon gasped for air trying to catch his breath.

"Of course I did, you silly Rhue! Didn't you want to be rescued?"

"Well, did it look as if I needed to be?" Slurple asked.

Malo chimed in. "What are you saying, Slurple? Was Sqhawk not making you pretend to not be afraid?"

Before Slurple could answer, Pinka scolded him for being so naive. "Sqhawk was just taunting us with you!"

"What does that mean?" Slurple asked, looking confused.

Pinka looked totally embarrassed, for she had only used the word "taunting" because she had heard Simon use it. Quickly, Simon jumped in with the answer. "It means that Sqhawk was just playing around with our emotions. She was pretending like she wasn't going to eat you, you know, just having a little fun."

"Sort of like Bronzella's tactics, right, Simon?" Truffles exclaimed.

"Exactly!" Simon agreed

Suddenly, the Rhues became horrified to see Slurple chuckling about the situation. The Gruhs shook their heads in total disbelief, and Simon was most flabbergasted! "I absolutely cannot believe this! You really think this ordeal is funny? Sqhawk really had you fooled, didn't she, Slurple?" he rattled in disgust.

"I'm sure she's had us all fooled for a very long time," Slurple remarked lightheartedly.

Everyone looked perplexed. "How is that?" La'Zar asked.

"Think about it. As huge and strong of a bird as Sqhawk is, if she had really wanted to eat me, then she would have. In fact, she would have already eaten all of us. Sqhawk really has been pretending, but not in the way you think," Slurple conveyed.

"What in the world are you talking about?" Simon asked, being more confused than ever. "What kind of garbage has this hawk filled your head with?"

"Well, I do not believe it was garbage!" Slurple replied defensively. "You never gave me a chance to explain what really happened back at the boulder! You need to know. All of you need to know right now!" he exclaimed.

"Go ahead, Slurple! We're listening!" Truffles shouted.

"Simon, do you remember when you were getting the silk rope ready to toss to me?" he asked, looking straight toward him.

"Yes, of course, I remember."

"For your information, right at that moment, I lost my grip and could no longer hold on! I was starting to fall into the raging hot molten of The Rivers of Strength!" Slurple cried as the group stared in total bewilderment with their mouths gaping! "Yes! Sqhawk saved my life! She is a hero!" he exclaimed.

"We had no idea!" Tooty gasped with her hand over her mouth.

Simon didn't know what to think or say, being speechless for the moment. After all, Sqhawk had captured him, threatening to eat him alive, causing him much pain and anguish. Slurple noticed his perplexity and asked, "Do you truly believe you outran Sqhawk awhile ago?"

Simon just stared at him with a blank look and did not reply. "Of course, you don't!" Slurple answered himself. "I'm telling you that Sqhawk is not who she has been pretending to be! She wants to talk to all of us and tell her story. Don't you think we owe her at least this?" he asked.

Finally, Simon began coming out of shock. "Well, after the way that old hawk treated me, I still don't trust her! How do I know to what extreme she will go? She probably wants to grab us all up at one time—a bigger dinner for Sqhawk. Don't you get it?" he shouted, causing the Rhues and creatures to flinch.

Slurple still defended old Sqhawk. "Look, she assured me that we did not have to fear her. She gave her word. She even apologized for having frightened the wits out of you and swears that she would have never really eaten you."

"Hahaha!" Simon laughed. "Guess what? Bronzella handed me a line too. I trusted her, and look where it got me. No, I will not go through that again!" he firmly made clear. The Rhues and creatures joined in agreement (that is, all but Slurple).

After downing his head in deep thought for a minute or so, Slurple yelled out, "Hey, Simon. You never answered my question?"

"What question was that?"

"Do you truly believe in your heart that you outran Sqhawk awhile ago?"

He stammered. "Uh…uh…well…I was so anxious to get you away from her, I never had time to think about such a thing."

"Sqhawk didn't even try to chase us," Slurple pointed out. "Aren't you the least bit curious about her motive?"

"Her motive is to eat us alive!" Simon shouted. "You cannot trust her! After taking me to her nest and scaring me half to death, no! She killed any trust I could ever have!"

Squiggly firmly agreed. "Yeah, Slurple, Simon's right. Let's just get out of here. Neopoleana is waiting for us."

Suddenly, Icky yelled very loud. "It's too late! It's too late! Sqhawk is headed this way!"

The group glanced in sequence toward the open area. Sure enough, Sqhawk was flying fast in their direction. "Hurry and huddle together, and keep your heads low!" Simon ordered as the group scrunched tightly together behind the gigantic boulder. Simon and the Rhues took positions low among the creatures.

It didn't take long for the speedy bird to reach the huge rock. The Rhues trembled with fear as they heard her thunderous landing above. It was so loud the group thought the gigantic rock was going to crumble down and bury them alive!

Soon Grundel decided to take matters into his own hands, so to speak. The brave dragon began snorting and huffing, building up fiery smoke. "Just give me the word when to make my move, Simon! I'm going to fight the old crow!" he stated with courage.

"Hold off for now. I think I will ask her some questions first just to see if I can get her trapped in her own scheme," Simon spoke, almost bragging.

"Why waste your time! Why play games with Sqhawk?" Pinka questioned.

Before he could answer, Slurple cut in. "Leave Simon alone. Let him ask Sqhawk all the questions he wants. Maybe he and the rest of you will learn something," the determined Rhue exclaimed.

After hearing Slurple's scolding, Pinka squinted her nose at him. Simon couldn't help but grin. It never ceased to amaze him how cute these little Rhues were, even in times like this. He then cautiously crawled out from beneath the boulder and immediately asked Sqhawk, "What do you want? You're scaring the Rhues out of their wits."

Sqhawk snickered. "None of you seem very frightened to me. I've been sitting here on this overhang listening to your every word."

"So what?" Simon spoke in a haughty manner.

"So I thought it was funny how you and the Rhues were going back and forth, arguing over whether you should speak to me or not," the huge bird replied with a chuckle.

"Just let me know what it is that you want!" Simon ordered.

"Well, for starters, you could thank me," Sqhawk calmly spoke.

"Thank you for what?" Simon asked with disgust.

"Oh, I believe you know for what. I'm sure Slurple told you that I saved his life," Sqhawk firmly responded.

"Oh yes, of course he did, but so what? What does that prove? Slurple is naive to you!" Simon backlashed.

After hearing Simon's last remark, Slurple became defensive and cut in, "How dare you call me naive! Just because Bronzella had you fooled doesn't mean that is what Sqhawk is doing!"

"I'm sorry, Slurple, no offense intended! I was just trying to get a point across to Sqhawk," Simon explained.

He then immediately looked up and questioned the oversized bird. "Okay, Sqhawk. Now what's really up with you? Why didn't you eat Slurple? Are you taunting us until we wear down or something?"

Before Sqhawk could respond, Frieda jumped in to give a piece of her mind. "You are a mean and arrogant old hawk! Now either let us go, or we will fight you! This game-playing is getting old!"

Sqhawk's True Self

At that point, Sqhawk downed her head. "I know how you all must feel about me, and I don't blame you. All I can say is I'm sorry. I should have never carried things as far as I did by capturing Simon and torturing him the way I did," she spoke with compassion.

"My gosh!" Simon suddenly screamed out. "I can't believe you are going even further with all this hogwash of the self-pity act! Come on, Sqhawk! Get real!" he harshly scolded.

Sqhawk raised her head, surprising Simon with tears flowing from her eyes. "Now you have turned on the tears! What a great actress you have turned out to be!" He poked fun while laughing and shouting out "bravo" as he applauded.

The entire group joined in with snickering and claps—all but Slurple. "Stop it! Can't you see that Sqhawk is hurting? She has changed and wants us to forgive her!" he cried.

Simon was firm. "Forgive her? After what she did to me! How could I ever trust such a conniving old bird? She doesn't deserve it!"

Sqhawk cut into the conversation. "He's right, Slurple. Why should any of you ever forgive or trust me? I really don't deserve it! But would you please listen to my explanation? That is all I ask."

"Why should we?" Simon asked with a smirk. Sqhawk could not answer.

Slurple preached. "You keep forgetting that she saved my life! If it had not been for Sqhawk, I would have been turned to Jell-O by The Rivers of Strength! No matter what you say or think, you owe it to Sqhawk and to yourselves to at least listen to what she has to say!"

Simon sighed. "Well, I guess it won't hurt to do that," he reluctantly agreed. "Okay, go ahead with what you need to say, Sqhawk! We're listening."

"Do you mind if I fly down there? All of you are going to have stiff necks from looking up so long."

"I just don't know about that!" Simon exclaimed.

"Oh, come on, Simon. Our necks are killing us already!" Malo begged.

"Well, all right, but keep your distance. Is that understood?"

"It is," Sqhawk replied while zooming down, staying a good distance away.

"Thank you, Simon. This means a lot to me," she praised.

"Just go ahead and make your little speech, okay?"

Sqhawk sighed, for she realized Simon had a really big grudge against her, and for good reason. "I just don't know where to begin. It's such a long story."

"Just calm down and try to relax," Slurple softly consoled the bird as Simon rolled his eyes.

Sqhawk took a deep breath. "Well, I wasn't always like this. I'm sure La'Zar remembers when I got along with all the creatures."

"That was a long time ago," La'Zar responded as he looked toward Simon. "However, what she says is true. There was a time when none of the creatures feared Sqhawk." Simon just shrugged his shoulders.

"Not even Brat was scared of him?" Pinka asked.

The rodent shouted out, "No, not even me! Sqhawk only chased the wild rats, which lived out in the far-off fields."

"Do any of you creatures remember when I changed?" Sqhawk asked.

All the creatures looked at each other, and then Frieda spoke out, "I remember well! It was shortly after Bronzella arrived in Gruhland."

Icky raged, "Yes, it sure was! You turned your back on us and became like the sphinx!"

"Well, I know this sounds very cowardly, but actually I did this for you in a way," Sqhawk explained in a confusing manner.

"For us? You doubled our fears!" Grundel shouted. We had you and Bronzella to contend with all these years! Come on now, you can do better than that!" he protested.

"But it is true. I actually helped you by *acting* like Bronzella."

"Let us hear more of this lame excuse for an explanation!" Brat shouted out.

"It is almost laughable," Frieda snickered as the other creatures joined in.

Sqhawk downed her head in shame and embarrassment. "I truly did what I thought would be best for all the creatures," she cried softly.

"Keep talking!" Icky ridiculed.

"When Bronzella arrived here, I could see that she wanted control of the land and the creatures. She approached me one day and told me what an asset I could be to her. The sphinx asked me to help with her dirty work, which went against Gruhland!"

"What is it she wanted you to do?" Frieda asked.

"Oh, it is horrible! I can barely think about it, much less speak of it!" Sqhawk cried out.

"You must tell us so that we can get some understanding to your reasoning for turning your back on us," Cutter exclaimed.

"Cutter is right. You must not waste any more time. Tell us now what Bronzella wanted you to do!" Crawly demanded while the other creatures chanted in agreement.

"Uh...uh...well, the sphinx wanted me to kill any creature who tried to stand in her way of controlling Gruhland," Sqhawk bellowed out. The entire group gasped in horror.

"Hold on. You haven't heard the worst yet!" Sqhawk cried in anguish.

"What is it? Please tell us! You can't leave anything out!" Truffles exclaimed.

"Oh, this is so painful! Uh…uh…Bronzella told me…uh… uh…she told me that she had killed Krystallina!" Sqhawk wailed in agony.

Everyone sucked in their breath with loud gasps of horror! Then, for a few moments, there was silence. Sqhawk continued. "You know, at that time, we had heard the magical stories of Neopoleana's beautiful sister but never really knew exactly how she had died. I was totally devastated! From that point on, I flew off and kept my distance. I taunted Bronzella every chance I got to prove I was just as vicious as she. I figured this would help keep her off your backs."

"Like when you captured me?" Simon asked.

"Exactly. I determined this would keep Bronzella from ever thinking of messing with me. I had to make my act appear real to everyone in order to convince Bronzella that I was just as mean, selfish, and arrogant as she," Sqhawk explained.

"Well, you certainly had us fooled," Frieda remarked in agreement.

"Don't you see I had to? However, I want to let you know that I haven't been happy with the deception I've been carrying. I have felt guilty all these years," Sqhawk cried.

"We still do not quite understand your reasoning," La'Zar spoke with confusion. "Can you explain further?" he asked.

"Well, if Bronzella thought that I was friends with the creatures of Gruhland after I had refused to do her dirty work, then she might have killed all of you anyway!" Sqhawk screamed. "It just happened that Simon wished up the sphinx at the same time all this was going on. Bronzella saw an opportunity with him. Since she couldn't use me, the sphinx decided a different approach," he explained.

"I'm beginning to see what you mean," Simon commented, giving Sqhawk hope of being understood.

"Bronzella knew the creatures would be too afraid to warn you of her, so she devised a plan where you would steal the *golden wings.* She then would have all the power ever needed to control these lands her way!" Sqhawk exclaimed.

"And you couldn't warn me, because Bronzella would have then destroyed us all!" Simon determined.

"That is exactly right, Simon. I had to continue with my tough bird act to make it look real. I did it to spare you and the creatures from being killed by that wicked sphinx!"

"Sqhawk saved all of you, and she saved me from liquidizing in The Rivers of Strength!" Slurple shouted. "We should forgive her. After all, she has been living in her own torment all these years."

"I agree with Slurple. Sqhawk has a good heart. I can see it," Pinka commented.

Simon looked unsurely at the giant bird, showing reluctance. "Well, Sqhawk! What you say makes sense, but I'm not totally convinced we can trust you."

"Don't forget, Simon! Sqhawk was our friend before Bronzella entered the picture," La'Zar reminded him.

"Sqhawk could have flown to Rhueland anytime to eat us up," Malo pointed out.

"You guys are right about all that, but I still carry much fear. It isn't easy to forget the bad feelings Sqhawk instilled in me!" Simon explained while cutting his eyes toward the old bird.

"All I can say is that I'm truly sorry. If you can't forgive me, I will understand and fly back down to my thicket, never to bother you again," Sqhawk promised.

"Well, Neopoleana is helping me to get back home soon. It is the creatures and Rhues I'm concerned about," Simon responded.

"I know you will not believe this, but I would help look after them, that is, if I could just have the chance. Maybe this would help in some way to bring some peace within my guilty heart," Sqhawk cried with compassion.

At that moment, Slurple ran to the giant bird, stretching out his tiny arms. Sqhawk lowered her head, and the tiny Rhue wrapped his arms around her neck as far as they would reach. Soon, before

Simon could call him back, Pinka ran to join Slurple, followed by Malo. In no time, all the Rhues had clamored around the sad bird. Simon and the Gruhs stared in amazement, for they knew the Rhues had made their minds up to trust Sqhawk! "I guess if the Rhues can trust and forgive you, then I can," Simon softly spoke, causing Sqhawk to be so overwhelmed with gratitude she could not speak. Several tears trickled down her face, flowing into her mouth, which was slightly gaping with a smile of happiness.

Simon joined the Rhues who were singing and dancing with excitement from having made a new friend as the Gruhs rejoiced over having an old friend back again.

Journey Back to the Tunnel

Soon the excitement had winded down. It was now time to head back to the tunnel. From there, they would travel to the nectar fields and eat to their hearts' content then sleep like babies for a while.

"I am so hungry!" Malo shouted.

"I am starving!" Jetta cried.

"We're all hungry," Simon pointed out. "So let's get going!"

The tiny Rhues began scurrying about to find rides when La'Zar suddenly screamed out, "Hold it! I have something to say!"

Everyone came to a quick halt and silence prevailed. All eyes were upon the giant lizard. "Has anyone, besides me, stopped to realize that this is the last journey we will have with Simon? As all of you know, we can't fit through the tunnel's entrance."

"Oh! We have been so excited over making friends with Sqhawk that we never thought of that. We're sorry!" Pinka apologized.

"I have thought about it," Simon chimed in.

"Why didn't you say something?" Squiggly asked.

"I guess I didn't want a bunch of sad faces on our trip back to the tunnel," he replied while viewing the already low-hung heads of the Gruhs. "Cheer up now! We'll say our sad good-byes when the time comes. Right now, let's board up and then enjoy our time together traveling back to the tunnel. Come on! Let's get going!"

Immediately, the Rhues scampered to their rides, choosing the same Gruh each had traveled to Gruhland on. That is, all but Razzle and Jetta. They had latched on to their new friend, Sqhawk. "We are tired of putting up with Icky's slime. Since Sqhawk is here and we now trust her, Razzle and I can fly back to the tunnel with her!" Jetta squealed with anticipation.

"Wait just a minute! I don't know if I like that idea!" Simon spoke with tones of hidden mistrust.

Sqhawk immediately bellowed, "You still don't trust me, do you?"

Simon hesitated. "Uh...well, it's not really that I don't trust you. It's...uh...I think we should give this some time," he lamely explained.

Sqhawk responded with wisdom. "Well, I guess I understand that. I shouldn't expect your full trust right away. The trust I had broken will be regained over a period of time."

Jetta and Razzle pitched a hissy. "We trust Sqhawk now and want to ride with her!" Jetta whined.

"I don't want slime on me again!" Razzle cried.

Both he and Jetta began stomping their feet and wailed at the top of their lungs. Simon scolded them. "Look at you two! You are throwing temper tantrums. Neopoleana would be disappointed. She wouldn't stand for such behavior! Besides, you can't just go flying in on Sqhawk. The Mother Rhue would have a heart attack!"

Jetta and Razzle downed their heads. "Now go board Icky so we can be on our way," Simon ordered. The two Rhues obeyed, immediately walking toward Icky, who was sneakily grinning. Jetta pulled the rope from around her neck, helped Razzle up, and then climbed the rope with ease. Everyone cheered at how the two had mastered this climb.

La'Zar took the lead after Simon and Pinka were seated. They had just begun their journey when Sqhawk belted out a shrill cawing. "What about me! Do I just stay her alone?" she screeched.

"Oh no. I assumed you were coming along with us. That is why we didn't tell you bye," Simon explained.

"What about Neopoleana and Winglet? I heard you tell Razzle and Jetta that I would probably frighten them if I just showed up. I certainly don't want to cause any more scares!" Sqhawk pointed out with concern.

Simon thought for a minute. "I tell you what! When we get near the tunnel, just drop back. I'll explain to the Mother Rhue how you had been just acting all this time and that you are now our friend. If everything goes well with her, one of us will let you know," he explained.

Sqhawk grinned from ear to ear. "Wow!" she exclaimed. "My stomach has butterflies from just thinking of meeting such royalty as Neopoleana!"

The Rhues chuckled, for they could not understand Sqhawk's overanxiousness of meeting their mother. However, Simon understood completely. "I know how you feel" was all he said to the anxious bird.

Finally, the group was on their way. The trip back was peaceful and quiet. Tooty played a few slow, mellow tunes as the Rhues sang. The Gruhs walked slowly, for they wanted to extend their time with Simon. He and the Rhues realized this, and even though they were hungry, no one rushed them along. Simon relaxed and added this special journey with his friends to the list of other special memories he had stored in his mind.

It still seemed like very little time had passed before the tunnel came into sight in the distance. Simon took one long, last look across The Rivers of Strength. The teal-green and fuchsia-pink rocks appeared brighter and more beautiful than ever. The Gruhs stopped so he could listen to the rushing and bubbling of the hot molten. As they marched onward, a solemn kind of sadness began to loom over the group. However, everyone remained quiet, not speaking of it.

Suddenly, Simon got a glimpse of Neopoleana in the near distance. "Okay, Sqhawk, this is as far as you go," he uttered as the curious bird strained to get a peek at the magnificent queen.

Sqhawk gasped in awe of her. "She's just like I had pictured—tall, statuesque, and splendidly beautiful." The tiny Rhues blushed and giggled out of pride for their mother.

As La'Zar moved on, Pinka suddenly cried out, "Oh, look! Winglet is out from under the *golden wings*!" Everyone looked ahead to see the baby Rhue pouncing around Neopoleana. The silver color had returned to her wings and downy coat, sparkling like tiny diamonds beneath the dusky sky. She was fluttering and flying around better than ever!

Soon the creatures were within shouting distance. The entire group seemed to yell together all at once, "Hey, Neopoleana! We're back!" Winglet immediately escaped from the Mother Rhue's arms and flittered toward them. The Rhues quickly jumped from their rides to meet the baby halfway. Simon took his time just enjoying watching their happiness.

Special Times at the Tunnel

The Rhues "captured" Winglet, causing her to giggle with delight. Tooty scooped her up in her arms and ran to Neopoleana. "There is no doubt that Winglet is well now," Simon commented as he walked up to join the group. The Gruhs slowly made their way up, stopping to watch all the Rhues take turns hugging their mother. Of course, Simon didn't miss his big hug.

After everyone had settled down, Simon announced he had something important to tell the Mother Rhue. She took a seat upon a large rock. "Go ahead, Simon. I will listen to what you say, but first I want to ask if all of you enjoyed your trip to Gruhland."

"That is part of the reason I need to talk to you," Simon began, sounding rather mysterious. "We did enjoy the actual trip, but when we were crossing the boulders, there was an accident," he blurted out. The Mother Rhue gasped but did not interrupt.

Simon continued. "Slurple fell over the edge of a boulder that stretched out and over The Rivers of Strength." Fear consumed Neopoleana's every fiber, and she flung her hand across her gaping mouth. Simon consoled her. "Please don't get so upset, Neopoleana. There's Slurple over there. You just gave him a hug a minute ago."

All the Rhues and creatures snickered, causing the Mother Rhue to blush. She quickly tried to hide her embarrassment, for it wasn't like her not to be on top of things. "Just to hear that one of my little Rhues was on the brink of disaster is upsetting!" she clarified. "Now continue with this amazing story."

"Yes, ma'am. Slurple was hanging from the boulder's edge by his hands. The Rivers of Strength were rushing, gurgling, and bubbling below, and he was beginning to lose his grip."

Everyone seemed to be hypnotized by the haunting manner and dramatic tones Simon used in relaying this true story. "However, this was about to change. We spotted Slurple, and *I* immediately yelled for Jetta to bring the rope that Frieda had made. *I* encouraged him to hang on. Just as *I* tossed him the rope, Sqhawk flew down and snatched him up, and then flew off in the direction of her thicket! *I* kept the Rhues calm, and *I* made them and the creatures realize that we needed to help Slurple. *I* reminded them to keep their faith and hope," Simon bragged. Now this caused many snarls among the group, for it was obvious that Simon was being a little conceited.

"What happened then, Simon?" Neopoleana asked.

"We went back across the boulders toward The Forest of Dead Trees in hopes of rescuing Slurple. We found him sitting in an open area. Sqhawk was pecking up dirt for him to play with. To make the long story short, Sqhawk had rescued Slurple! She explained to us how she had been putting on an act so Bronzella wouldn't use her to do her dirty work. The old bird cried and apologized. Then we forgave her and became friends," Simon finished up in a hurry.

"That is just amazing," Neopoleana commented. "Do all of you feel that Sqhawk is now trustworthy?" she asked the group.

"We certainly do!" Slurple shouted out as the other Rhues nodded in agreement.

"We also believe Sqhawk can be trusted," Frieda remarked. "She was our friend before Bronzella came, so her story is credible to us."

"What is your opinion of Sqhawk's motive to put on an act for such a long time, Simon?" the Mother Rhue asked.

"I want to trust Sqhawk, but she scared me so bad it is difficult to do so," he responded.

Neopoleana gave an evaluation. "I'm sure Sqhawk realizes it will take time to build complete trust. However, since she saved my baby from the fiery Rivers of Strength, I believe we should give her a chance. After all, the creatures knew a different Sqhawk before Bronzella entered the picture. This makes her act seem believable."

As the creatures and Rhues shouted and clapped in agreement, Simon looked at the Mother Rhue and smiled. "Sqhawk is waiting right beyond that open area," he informed her.

Neopoleana squealed, "Oh, she is!"

"Would you mind if she joins us?" Simon humbly asked.

The Mother Rhue chuckled. "I think it is time for me to meet this special bird," she replied.

Simon beamed. "She is rather anxious to meet you also!"

"I'll go get her!" La'Zar volunteered and then took off in a fast run.

Neopoleana scooped Winglet up in her arms, for she knew an unfamiliar creature would surely frighten the baby Rhue. Everyone watched in anticipation for La'Zar and Sqhawk to come into sight. Soon they got a glimpse of him just over the hill. Sqhawk was flying low, right above the giant lizard's head. Even though it had been only a couple of minutes, all the tiny Rhues ran to the edge of the open area to greet them.

Winglet clung tightly as the Mother Rhue held her close to her breast, gently patting her back. She peeped at the huge, strange, and mysterious bird coming her way. "It's okay. Sqhawk won't hurt you," Neopoleana consoled.

As they approached, the Mother Rhue could see that Sqhawk was nervous. She spoke with gratitude. "Everyone tells me that you saved Slurple's life."

Sqhawk hesitated then blurted, "Uh…it was the least I could do. For years, I acted like a big bully!"

Neopoleana looked into her eyes. "Simon told me the story. He also said you apologized and asked for forgiveness."

"Uh…yes, I'm truly sorry for having deceived the other creatures for so long, and I'm sorry for terrorizing Simon. Can you forgive me, Neopoleana?" the humble bird begged.

The Mother Rhue showed wisdom in her words. "I believe that you have earned forgiveness. In time, you shall earn more trust."

Sqhawk was elated. "Oh, thank you! That is all I ask for. I'm grateful for another chance."

Everyone cheered, and the Rhues ran to hug Neopoleana in a show of appreciation. She handed Winglet to Simon as the group formed a line. One by one, each got a big, warm hug. Blubbles was last in line. As she reached her loving arms out to him, he asked, "Neopoleana, will you ever run out of hugs for us?"

The Mother Rhue smiled with delight. "No, my child. I will always have plenty. They come from an endless supply of love within my heart." She then squeezed Blubbles so tight a couple of giant bubbles oozed from his snout and floated upward to the dusky sky.

Simon was busy letting Winglet get acquainted with Sqhawk. "Look, Neopoleana! The baby Rhue is petting Sqhawk's head," he shouted with excitement as Winglet chanted "Sqawt! Sqawt!" in her usual baby talk. Everyone laughed and laughed.

Just then, Jetta walked up and tugged at Neopoleana's fury leg. "Mama, Mama!" she yelled, causing the Mother Rhue to look down at her in awe.

"What did you call me?" she asked.

"I accidently called you Mama," Jetta replied with apprehension.

"Oh no, Jetta, do not apologize for that. I really like it. It makes me feel very special."

"I guess she heard me talk about my mom so much, she picked up the term," Simon explained.

Neopoleana was feeling a mother's true devotion. "You know what? That is exactly what I am. I am the Rhues' Mama, and they are my children. I love them with all my heart," she expressed.

Simon choked back his emotions as the other Rhues came running to her shouting, "Mama! Mama."

Jetta chimed in, "I want to show you what I can do, Mama!"

"You do?"

"Yes. It's a surprise!" the tiny Rhue elated as she stood with her hands behind her back.

Neopoleana got Winglet and sat upon a nearby rock as the others gathered around to watch. Jetta quickly pulled the silk rope out from behind her. "You still have the rope I made!" Frieda shouted.

"Yes, I love it! Now, watch what I can do!" Jetta boasted.

She then began to jump rope like a school kid. Neopoleana watched with excitement and pride. Soon the Gruhs joined in the fun, stomping their feet to the beat of each jump. Tooty began to play some upbeat notes of fun music, which flowed from her horn snout. The Rhues clapped to the beat as Jetta shuffled her feet with each jump. Simon cracked up with laughter at the sight, not even realizing Winglet was loose from Neopoleana's arms. She was fluttering all around Sqhawk, having lost all fear of this giant creature.

In a short time, each Rhue had learned to jump rope. Simon joined them in their play as the Mother Rhue watched with pleasure. The Gruhs danced to the sound of Tooty's music, and Winglet continued to play with her new giant bird friend, Sqhawk.

Sad Good-Byes

As the fun and games came to a close, Neopoleana looked at Simon. She didn't have to say a word. He knew, just as the creatures knew, that it was now time to leave. Slowly, the Gruhs walked toward their friend and formed a circle around him. "It's time for me to travel on to the far tunnel," he spoke rather sadly.

"We know, Simon. As much as we wish you could stay, we realize this is something you must do," La'Zar spoke with compassion.

"Your mom and dad need you," Icky commented.

"Yes, and I need them," Simon responded as he walked up to face Crawly. The huge worm lowered his head so Simon could wrap his arms around his neck. "Crawly, you know I will always carry your love in my heart. I will never forget watching you build your huge mound houses." Tears streamed down the worm's face like a leaky faucet. Simon gave him a kiss on the forehead and moved on to Cutter.

"Cutter, you snipped through that thicket to reach me when I was trapped in Sqhawk's nest. I will treasure your friendship always," he cried as he hugged the worm's neck.

He then slid over to Rattles and stroked the snake's smooth, cold body. "You know I'll always love you. I will remember the music you played with your rattles as we sang." With giant tears streaming from his eyes, Rattles leaned his head over for a hug, getting Simon's arms soaked. However, they weren't cold like his skin. These beautiful droplets were warm and filled with love.

Brat was waiting next to Rattles. Simon looked into his sad eyes. "I enjoyed the talks we had. I learned so much from them," he cried.

Brat smiled. "I learned a lot about my own feelings from you. I love you, and I'm going to miss you."

"I'll miss you too," Simon choked out as he hugged him and then kissed him on the cheek.

He then walked over to his giant spider friend. "Frieda, you are wonderful!" Simon squealed as he rubbed her fuzzy body. "You're always there to help and never hesitate to spin a rope when there is a need."

"Please don't forget me, Simon," Frieda sadly spoke.

"You know I won't."

Simon wiped a lonely tear from under his eye as he moved toward Grundel. "I will think of you often and forever remember your smoke signals," he cried while giving the sad dragon a warm hug. He then kissed Grundel's cheek gently and patted him on the head.

Simon turned to Icky, who was sobbing. "Please don't cry. We have made some wonderful memories," he begged his slimy friend.

"I know, but I wish you could stay longer so that we could make more!" Icky wept.

"I love you and will think of you every day," Simon consoled the sad snail as he hugged his slimy neck. "You know I never really minded your slime," he whispered, prodding a smile from him.

Simon then walked up to La'Zar, who already had his head down for a hug. He wrapped his arms around his cold, scaly neck but felt warmth from the reptile's heart. He then gently brushed his index finger across the scar. "I'll always remember how you stood up to Bronzella for me, and the rides upon your back were awesome!" he whispered.

Tears were pouring from the ebony lizard's eyes. "How will my heart ever stop aching?" he asked.

Simon felt so much compassion. "In time, I believe our hearts will heal. We shall have precious memories forever to make us smile," he spoke with passion and new wisdom. He then kissed the bridge of La'Zar's nose. "Now don't be getting in fights with the wild dragons! You don't need any more scars," he quipped.

Sqhawk had been watching the sad good-byes from atop a small boulder. She figured as much trouble as she had caused, Simon wouldn't have a hug for her. So when he shouted, "Come down here, Sqhawk!" the old bird was completely taken off guard, being literally startled.

She approached him with a downed head. To her amazement, Simon began stroking his hand across her massive wing. "I'm glad we were able to settle our differences. I'm sure you are a much happier bird now that you no longer pretend. Look at all the new friends you have made and the old ones who came back," he calmly stated.

Sqhawk showed genuine humbleness. "Thank you for your forgiveness. I will forever be grateful. I hope in your heart you can believe me when I say I will always love you."

"Of course, I believe you!" Simon exclaimed as he hugged the bird tight. "Guess what? I feel the same about you. I love you, Sqhawk!" he added while patting her head.

Simon then turned, facing Neopoleana. "Are you ready, Simon?" she softly asked.

"Yes, ma'am, I'm ready," he answered respectfully.

All the Rhues scampered, running between the Gruhs' legs toward Simon. Together, they began their walk to the entrance of the nearby tunnel. The Gruhs followed along, whispering of a surprise they had for Simon. Neopoleana trailed a short distance behind, carrying Winglet in her arms.

Soon everyone paused at the entrance and, for a few moments, there was complete silence. Then Frieda spoke out loudly, "Simon, we have a nice surprise for you!"

A smile seemed to cover half his face as he beamed, "Oh man! What is it?"

"We have made up a song just for you!" Frieda pronounced with pride.

"How sweet you Gruhs are! I can't wait to hear it!"

"We would like to confer with Tooty first. Maybe she would like to put some music to our song," La'Zar spoke while looking in the orange Rhue's direction. Of course she was thrilled and immediately joined them to discuss the appropriate tune for their masterpiece.

Simon waited upon a teal-green and fuchsia-pink rock, playing with Winglet, as Neopoleana spoke of their journey to the far tunnel. He was in great anticipation of seeing his mom and dad and his best friend, Doug. Thinking of wrestling with his dog, Bingo, made him chuckle. Even Angel Marie Wilson crossed his mind as he glanced toward Pinka.

Soon La'Zar interrupted Simon's thoughts. "We're ready now!" he exclaimed as the other Gruhs and Tooty took their positions, forming a half-circle around Simon. The Rhues quickly gathered around. Soon the Gruhs were singing in harmony as Tooty played her "saxophone" snout. Simon reflected back on the times he had spent with the creatures in Gruhland as he listened. The song went like this:

In Our Hearts

> We have only known you for a short while,
> But the love you brought to our world will
> Last a lifetime
> For it is locked inside our hearts
>   Forever and forever
>
> Thank you for all the kindness you gave
> For you helped to make our world a better place
> And you will be in our hearts

Forever and forever

You must leave and return to your world
But a part of you will always be near
Our memories will hold you so dear
And you will stay in our hearts
        Forever and forever

After the Gruhs had finished this slow heartfelt melody, everyone clapped and cheered. Simon brushed away the tears and then choked out words, "That was wonderful! I shall carry it in my heart forever. Thank you so much for all the joy you brought my way while I was here in Gruhland. I will cherish every memory." He smiled, then immediately informed Neopoleana that he was ready to move onward.

"Okay, Simon. I'll take Winglet with me and fly on ahead to Rhueland," she replied while picking her up. She then turned to speak to the Gruhs, "Don't forget, Winglet will grow fast over the next few months. I will be training her in how to use the power from her *silver wings*. We will be back when she is ready to help brighten part of Gruhland."

"That will be so wonderful!" Grundel exclaimed as the other Rhues smiled.

Winglet was giggling and squirming almost beyond control. "Why is she so restless?" Frieda asked.

"I believe she is trying to get out of your arms," La'Zar assumed.

"She must want to tell us all good-bye," Crawly determined.

Neopoleana agreed. "I believe you are right. Do you want to say bye-bye to the Gruhs?" she asked the baby Rhue in high-pitched tones.

"Yah...Ma-Ma, I do," Winglet replied in baby talk.

"Oh my, Winglet just called me Mama! I am ecstatic!" the Mother Rhue elated as everyone cheered. The baby Rhue buried her face in Neopoleana's soft downy fur and giggled.

"You go right ahead and say your good-byes," Neopoleana encouraged as she loosened the baby's grip. Winglet immediately flew to the Gruhs, fanning her tiny winglets in delight. She flew to each one saying "bye-bye" followed by a tiny giggle. Everyone chuckled at her cute show of expression. Without anyone realizing, this helped to ease the pain and sadness everyone was feeling.

"Come to me, Winglet!" Neopoleana suddenly called out. The tiny Rhue quickly flew to her mother's arms.

"Bye, everybody. I'll be back!" the Mother Rhue shouted as she prepared to spread her wings. All the creatures immediately closed their eyes, and Simon shielded his with his hands.

"I'll meet you in Rhueland!" she yelled to Simon. "Take good care of the little Rhues!"

"Oh, I will!" he promised while peeking through his extended fingers to see the splendid Mother Rhue soar across The Rivers of Strength. He and the creatures got a glimpse of Gruhland's enchanting lavender sky and then watched in awe as Neopoleana crossed the point where it met with Rhueland's crisp, coral sky. Within seconds, the lavender color faded as darkness once again consumed Gruhland. With this, the Gruhs' spirits were dampened, but they kept their smiles for Simon. Of course, he was doing the same thing for them.

"Well, you guys, the Rhues and I better move on now. Neopoleana will be waiting for us," Simon spoke, trying hard not to use any tones of sadness.

"Remember, I love each of you with all my heart," he choked out while again fighting back tears. "I will never forget you!" he cried then turned to scoot the Rhues through the entrance to the tunnel. He did not look back.

"Good-bye, Simon! We love you!" he heard the Gruhs shout. "You will be in our hearts forever and ever!" He could tell by their shaky voices the creatures were crying with sadness, just as he was. He wanted so badly to turn around and run back to his friends, but he knew this would only delay what must be done.

Besides, the Rhues were very hungry and needed nourishment, so Simon pushed forward for as long as he could. However, when the sounds of the Gruhs' good-byes completely diminished, a sad, lonely feeling consumed him. He could go no further. He came to a halt and sat down to sob.

"Please don't cry, Simon," Pinka said with compassion as all the Rhues gathered close to give comfort with hugs and kind words.

"We know your sadness must be hard to carry, but the Gruhs understood that you had to leave," Jetta remarked.

"They will miss you but will have good memories to recall," Squiggly commented.

"Right now, your mom and dad are sad from missing you. You must finish this journey and hurry back to them," Tooty pointed out.

Simon smiled. "Thank you, guys, for trying to cheer me up. I do feel better now."

The Rhues smiled as Simon got up from his sitting position. Soon the group was moving onward through the darkened tunnel. The Rhues stayed close by his side as Simon wondered over and over how he would ever be able to say good-bye to them.

Another Reflection

Back at the Well

IT HAD BEEN two days since Jim and Karen's experience at the wishing well. Today, Jim had returned to work at the clothing store, but Karen was still on a leave of absence from the law firm. She knew she needed to return to work soon, but she just wasn't quite ready. Her spirits were low, but by no means had she given up hope on Simon returning home. Even though the eerie, strange feelings had left her body, Karen knew in her heart that her son had still not left the mysterious land. She clung to the faith and hope of seeing him one day soon, for this is what kept her going.

Jim had brought Bingo back home. The hyper dog had calmed down some, and Karen was glad to have his company. Simon's bedroom door was kept closed so he wouldn't be tempted to stay in that room.

This morning, Karen was cleaning the house for the first time in days when the phone rang. It was Patricia Shatterly, who called on a regular basis to check on her. "Hi, Patricia!" Karen greeted.

"How are you doing? When are you planning on returning to work?" Patricia questioned.

Karen rolled her eyes at her friend's nosiness. "I'm doing somewhat better. I'll probably go back within the next two weeks," she answered.

"That's good. How is Jim?" Patricia asked.

"He went back to work today but still constantly worries over me," Karen informed her then immediately asked, "What about Doug?"

"Of course you know he misses Simon, but he's still managing to keep up his schoolwork," Patricia replied.

"That's good," Karen acknowledged.

"Have the police turned up anything?" Patricia asked with concern.

Karen sighed. "No, I haven't heard from them in days. I'm sure they will call me if they find or hear anything of significance."

Patricia suddenly changed to another subject. "I'm coming to town to take care of some business. Would you like to join me? We could do some shopping!"

Karen sighed again more deeply this time. She knew she needed to get out of the house, but her energy level was almost completely gone. "I'm not really up for shopping, but why don't you stop by here after you finish your errands? Bingo and I need some fresh air and exercise. I'm up to par maybe for a short walk," she stated.

"That sounds perfect. I could use a nice, relaxing walk myself!" Patricia exclaimed. "I'll be at your house in about two hours, right at lunchtime."

"Great! I'll whip us up a cool, light brunch," Karen volunteered. "We don't need a heavy meal to *weigh* our walk down," she chuckled.

Patricia agreed by returning a chuckle. "That sounds good. I'm leaving right now."

After she hung up the telephone receiver, Karen noticed her spirits have been slightly lifted. She finished dusting and vacuuming the living room before scampering off to the kitchen to see what she could put together for lunch. After opening the fridge door, she frisked through the overly crowded shelves. "Wonderful!" she elated. "Everything I need for salads is here. Thank goodness Jim kept up the grocery shopping." She got the head of lettuce, a tomato, and other items out and then placed them on the countertop.

Before Karen could get started with her lunch preparation, Bingo scurried into the kitchen, wagging his tail and yelping. "You hungry, aren't you boy?" The frisky dog barked once, as if answering her with a yes.

"We're going for a brisk walk in a couple of hours," Karen told the dog while opening a can of his favorite flavor of dog food—beef and gravy. "How does that sound, boy?" she asked before placing the bowl in front of him. Again, Bingo barked but twice this time, causing Karen to laugh. The old mutt quickly gulped the moist, tasty treat down then went to his nearby water bowl and lapped up all the cool liquid in no time!

"My goodness, you ate as if you were half-starved to death!" Karen exclaimed.

Bingo yelped a couple more times before heading off to the living room sofa for a nap. Karen snickered at the funny dog and then began preparing the salads after putting on her usual favorite blue apron. She was humming as she worked; something she had not done in weeks. However, she didn't dare question her good mood. Instead, she actually relaxed and enjoyed it.

After finishing up the food preparation, Karen put the two salads in the refrigerator and headed upstairs to spruce up. She put on a tad of makeup, brushed her hair, and tied it back into a ponytail, then changed into something comfortable to walk in. After hunting down her well-worn jogging shoes, she was ready to go and darted out of the bedroom.

However, Karen halted in front of Simon's closed bedroom door feeling a strong urge to go in. This time, there were no strange feelings gripping her body; just a strong, uncontrollable desire. Slowly, she opened the door and stepped inside. For some unexplained reason, she wasn't upset for the first time in weeks, feeling instead, her son's presence within the room. She smiled and then spoke out loud, "Simon, I know you're on your way home. I feel it in my heart."

Just then, Bingo pounced up the stairs and ran into the room yelping with excitement. "You feel it too, don't you, boy?" Karen asked him. Of course, as usual, Bingo responded with a quick bark.

"We will be waiting for you, Simon," she pronounced while pulling Bingo back, scooting him out the door and quickly shutting it. The two then scurried down the stairs to wait for Patricia.

Karen flopped down on the sofa with Bingo jumping up to join her. He laid his head gently in her lap while she stroked his forehead and scratched behind his ears. The mutt was literally in dog heaven and drooled several round circles of saliva onto Karen's knit jogging pants. She really didn't mind for she was now strangely calm being in her own heaven with good thoughts of her son.

Just then the door bell rang, startling Karen and causing Bingo to quickly leap down and run to the front door. Karen followed and stopped to take a fast peek between the mini-blinds as Bingo barked and growled like a ferocious guard dog. As everyone knows, Bingo's bark is certainly bigger than his bite, for this old mutt wouldn't hurt a fly.

"Be quiet, Bingo. It's just Patricia!" Karen scolded while opening the door.

Patricia was amazed at how refreshed Karen looked. "You look more relaxed than I've seen you in a long time!" she exclaimed as Bingo whined and lapped at her ankles. He had finally recognized Patricia's scent and was begging to be petted. She patted his head but avoided squatting down for the usual face washing.

"You look good too, Patricia. The beach trip was wonderful, wasn't it?" Karen asked.

Patricia smiled. "It was. It really helped both Doug and me to get away for a while."

Patricia continued the conversation as she and Karen walked into the living room. "You know, it's been tough raising Doug alone, but he's doing well." She then took a seat upon the sofa. Karen joined her, for she knew where this conversation was headed. "Doug misses Simon and wonders what happened to him. They are best friends!" Patricia exclaimed. "It's times like this that I wish Doug's father was still here."

"You've done excellent with Doug!" Karen proclaimed. "Don't ever think you haven't been anything less than a good mother!"

"I just wish Frank could have lived to see his son grow up," Patricia spoke with tones of sadness and frustration. "Why did he have to be killed by that drunk driver? It was never fair!" she cried, remembering back with anguish. "Doug was only a year old. He missed out on so much."

Karen wrapped her arms around Patricia to comfort her. She never realized how the pain of Frank's sudden, tragic death still haunted her friend. "Come on, Patricia. Let's have lunch and then take our walk."

"I'm sorry for bringing that up," Patricia apologized. "I don't know why it all came back at this particular time."

"Don't you dare feel guilty or apologize for being human!" Karen scolded. "I'm glad you could confide in me. You know that you can talk to me anytime about anything. After all, isn't that what friends are for?"

The two then got up and headed for the kitchen. Before they reached the doorway, Patricia grabbed Karen's arm and looked her in the eyes. "Hey, don't forget. You can also talk to me about anything," she reminded her, causing Karen to wonder if Patricia sensed something. A few guilty pangs ran over her, for Karen knew she wasn't practicing what she was preaching by concealing her own feelings about Simon.

After lunch, Karen brought a tray of steaming, hot coffee into the living room. Bingo stretched out on the floor beside them to nap while the two reminisced of old times. Karen had the opportunity but never mentioned the strange feelings she had been experiencing. After all, her belief in the connection of a legend to the disappearance of her son would be hard to explain. It was difficult enough trying to convince Jim of the validity of her beliefs. There was certainly no way Patricia would buy into such a far-out theory!

Soon Bingo interrupted the two with a loud yawn as he stretched his legs, ready to pounce up. "Well, since Bingo is raring to go, I believe this is a good time for our walk," Karen suggested.

⌾〰〰〰⌾

Soon the three left for their overdue excursion. It was a nice, rather crisp afternoon, just right for a quiet stroll. Bingo kept a few steps ahead of them, sniffing the dirt and cool grass in the patches beside the sidewalk. Karen breathed the outdoors air deep into her lungs. She had not been outside in two days, and it felt wonderful!

Suddenly, Karen remembered they would be walking past the wishing well. She wondered if Bingo would become excited again and sure hoped that he wouldn't. Patricia would then get suspicious for sure. "We can cross the street and go another way if you'd like," she suggested.

Patricia immediately replied, "No, I would like to see the wishing well. That is, if you don't mind. It won't upset you, will it, Karen?" she asked.

A half-smile curled one side of Karen's mouth. "Oh, of course not!" she exclaimed, trying to look confident.

Patricia smiled. "You have really come a long way with your emotions. I am so proud of you, and I know that Jim is."

"Actually, this is the first day since Simon has been gone that I've felt this good. Jim doesn't even know that I'm feeling better," Karen responded, not wanting Patricia reading too much into her improved mood.

"It's nice to have the old Karen back. Jim will be ecstatic," Patricia elated as they came in sight of the wishing well.

Karen immediately noticed something that shocked her. Jim's car was in the side lot of the park. Bingo took off running toward the well, barking and wagging his tail. Karen called for him to come back, but the mutt paid her no mind.

Patricia caught her attention when she asked, "Isn't that Jim's car?"

They paused to observe. Karen responded, "Yes, that is Jim's car all right. I wonder what he's doing here."

As they walked toward the wishing well, both noticed a man sitting on the bottom railing of the well. "That is Jim, isn't it?" Patricia asked.

"Yes, it is him," Karen replied as she picked up a fast pace, Patricia following behind.

Bingo ran directly to Jim, yelping with excitement. "Hey, boy. What are you doing here?" he asked while looking up to see Karen and Patricia headed his way. He frisked Bingo's smooth black coat then quickly stood up to be greeted by his wife.

"What are you doing here?"

Jim chuckled rather nervously. "I took a long lunch break and just decided to come here for some quiet time. You know how the first day back at work can be," he replied.

Karen just stood staring at him with a manner of suspicion. Patricia quickly commented, "Yeah, it can be hectic, but it's nice running into you here."

Karen wanted so badly to question Jim on why, of all places, he chose to come here. It had been only two days since all the mysterious events had occurred right at this place. It was hard for her to keep quiet, but she had to hold off because of Patricia.

"I guess knowing how Simon always came here is what drew me," Jim remarked.

"I understand completely," Patricia responded. "Karen and I were walking. I also wanted to stop to be near a place Simon enjoyed with Doug."

Karen was quiet, wrapped up in thoughts. *Jim must believe the legend and is expecting to see more. That's why he is here! He's waiting for another event to take place right here at this wishing well.*

"I've got to get back to work now. I'm already over an hour late," Jim spoke, interrupting her thoughts.

"Uh...oh sure, Jim. I'll walk back to the car with you," she spoke while reaching for his hand.

"I'll be right back, Patricia!" she shouted.

"I'll just stay here and watch Bingo's fascination with that squirrel in the tree," Patricia remarked.

When they were out of hearing distance of Patricia, Karen asked, "Why are you really here, Jim?"

"I told you why!"

Karen showed desperation. "Why is it so hard for you to admit that you know and saw something strange happening at the well? You feel Simon's presence the same as I do, don't you?" she questioned. "You know as well as I he is in a strange land! You know our son is trying to get home!"

Jim snapped, "Karen, please, just leave it alone. You did what you had to do, and no miracle has happened!"

Karen cried out, "No, it hasn't—not yet! But two days ago, something happened here to change things for Simon. He will be coming back!" Her emotions then took over, causing her to rehash events. "Jim, you saw with your own eyes how the well water bubbled and rushed around, causing the well to shake. You felt the tornado winds! You saw smoke bellow from the well!"

She then sobbed with anxiety. "The strange feelings left me the night I crushed that 'evil eye.' Why can't you just admit there is a connection with *The Legend of the Sphinx* and Simon?"

Jim became very anxious. "Look, as I have stated at least a hundred times before, we were under very severe stress. This can cause our bodies to feel and our minds to see completely differently from the norm. I really don't know what was and what wasn't real that night!" he preached.

"All I can say is that you are here at this well, and I don't believe you have given up hope!" Karen exclaimed. She then lowered her tone. "I don't know what you're afraid of, Jim. You must be patient. Simon will be home." This comment caused Jim to roll his eyes. After all, Karen had been the impatient one from the start.

"What's up with you, Karen?" he asked with curiosity. "Your mood is so upbeat today."

"I can't explain it," she replied. "It's just something that I feel deep inside. Even though I can't see Simon, I can feel him. I know that since we did our part to destroy the sphinx, it somehow made things easier for our son. He is happy now, and he is on his way home!" Karen elated.

All Jim could do was reach and pull his wife close, hugging her tight. "You're something, you know that?" he asked with a slight chuckle.

Karen squirmed from his embrace. "Bye, Jim," she sweetly remarked, giving him a quick peck on his cheek. "You've got to get back to work!"

Jim reached for the handle on the car door and then turned around. "By the way, you look cute today," he smiled, giving a wink.

"I'm glad you noticed," Karen teased as Jim got inside and cranked up the car. She grinned while waving in a cutesy manner as he drove away with a big smile across his face. She stood in place a few moments and then took off, heading back to the well.

Patricia was still watching Bingo taunt the squirrel when Karen walked up. "That dog is obsessed with that squirrel. He's been aggravating the poor critter for the past fifteen minutes," Patricia fussed, feeling a bit of compassion for the rodent.

Karen snickered and then called Bingo over to her. "You ready to go, boy?" she asked while kneeling. He yelped a couple of times before giving her a few wet tongue laps.

"How gross!" Patricia shouted with a snarled face.

"Well, I don't have a problem with it whatsoever!" Karen snapped. Both of them then busted out in laughter.

"We need to get together more often," Patricia suggested as the two sat down on the railing of the well.

"Yeah, I know," Karen agreed. "It's been fun today, hasn't it?"

"Yes, and I think we've been good for each other," Patricia remarked. "It's always nice to have someone to talk to, isn't it?"

Karen quickly jumped up. She was having a hard time keeping a straight face, wondering again if she was doing the right thing in not sharing more of her feelings about Simon with her friend. "Come on, Bingo. We've got to go!" she shouted.

Of course, the dog had already scampered back to taunt the poor squirrel. Looking up through the leafy tree limbs, Bingo barked a couple more times before darting back to the well.

"I guess I do need to get home before Doug arrives from school," Patricia remarked as they began their walk toward the street.

Karen couldn't help but glance back at the wishing well. The strong urge that had hit her so many times before flooded through her body. She wanted to run and peer down inside but tried fighting the desire. However, it soon became overwhelming. "Hold on to Bingo. I'll be right back!" she ordered before bolting away.

"Where are you going?" Patricia asked as she grabbed hold of the yelping dog, which squirmed to be loosed.

"Please, just wait right there for me. I'll only be a minute!" Karen shouted as she approached the well.

Why must I do this?" she asked herself while stepping up on the railing. She glimpsed back to make sure Patricia wasn't following and then slowly leaned her head over the water.

Why can't I leave it alone? Karen asked while staring down through the water as if trying to see beyond the bottom of the well. This and her thoughts of Simon soon became hypnotizing, and she remained motionless, being in a fixed stare.

Suddenly, a reflection appeared right beneath the water. It was Simon's face again, but this time it was different. He had a big smile! Karen gasped. "Simon, I see you! When are you coming home?" she cried, only to see his image fade away almost as fast as it had appeared. "Simon, come back! Let me know something!" she shouted in desperation.

Bingo heard Karen's cries and quickly jerked loose from Patricia's grip. The dog jetted toward the well, barking with excitement. Patricia ran in behind him shouting, "Karen, are you all right?" When she reached the area, Karen was sitting on the bottom railing, pale and a bit shaky but trying to maintain her composure.

"I heard you shouting. Were you calling for Simon?" Patricia asked in breathless tones above Bingo's high-pitched barks.

"Be quiet, Bingo!" Karen ordered. Her tone was harsh and hurt his feelings so bad he yelped and whined like a child being scolded, but he did get quiet. "Now what did you say?" she asked Patricia, pretending not to hear the first time.

"I heard your shouts. It sounded as though you were calling to Simon. Were you?"

"Oh, I just got a little carried away," Karen chuckled, concealing her true emotions.

Patricia pressured her. "Well, you sounded pretty desperate to me! What is it, Karen? Out with the truth! You look as if you've seen a ghost."

Karen quickly stood up. "You worry too much! As I said, I got carried away with my thoughts of Simon. Just because I've been in a better mood doesn't mean I never think of my son and become upset! He's on my mind a hundred times a day!" she firmly snapped.

"Why are you getting so defensive?" Patricia questioned.

"It's because you're giving me the third degree!" Karen exclaimed. "You act as if I'm falling apart or something!"

"Well, excuse me for being concerned." Patricia smirked.

"Let's just get out of here!" Karen yelled. "Come on Bingo (who was already headed back to torment the squirrel)! We're going home!" she proclaimed.

The two marched out of the park in a huff without speaking. Bingo whined as he ran ahead of them. When they reached the small grassy hill that led down onto the street, Karen spoke in an apology, "I'm sorry for having snapped at you, Patricia. I know you're just trying to help."

"Oh, that's all right. I should have realized you are still under severe stress."

"Yeah, but I did overreact," Karen admitted.

"Aw, we both did." Patricia chuckled.

Soon both were laughing as if nothing had ever happened. They walked back to Karen's house to have a snack before Patricia would have to leave. Bingo chewed on his rawhide bone while the two friends enjoyed hot tea and cookies in the kitchen with light conversation.

"That was delicious, but I must be on my way," Patricia said as she got up from the small table.

They walked quietly to the front door. "Keep in touch with me now," Patricia whispered as she hugged Karen. "Remember, if at any time you need a friend to talk to, don't hesitate to call me," she added.

Guilt feelings grabbed at Karen, but she smiled. "You know I will."

She stood in the doorway until Patricia drove away then walked into the living room and plopped down on the sofa with Bingo joining her in his usual cozy spot. As she stroked his fur, Karen's thoughts immediately returned to the wishing well and Simon's reflection. She had a clear image in her mind of his smiling face, and though her initial reaction to this reflection was shock, it was now actually calming. The illusion of her son's happy expression told Karen that he was safe and no longer afraid. How thankful she was for this clue, for it would make her wait less of a burden!

"Should I tell Jim about this?" she asked Bingo as if he understood her words. The old, limp mutt never even lifted an ear. Hard chewing on his rawhide bone had worn him out, and the touch of Karen's hand stroking his fur had put him into a restful sleep. She just laughed while fluffing the pillow.

"Jim will probably just think I'm seeing things again, but I'm going to tell him anyway!" she muttered then buried her head deep into the overly soft, feather-stuffed cushion. Soon she was in a very relaxed state and drifted off to sleep.

A Fun Surprise

Karen napped peacefully all afternoon until Jim's blusterous voice shook her senses. "Wake up, Karen!" he prodded while shaking her upper arm near her shoulder.

"Oh, hi, Jim. I can't believe I slept so long," she answered.

After rising up, Karen noticed that Bingo was gone from his spot and asked, "I wonder where Bingo is? He was sound asleep on the floor when I dozed off."

"Oh, he's probably up in our bedroom," Jim replied.

"Gosh. I need to get up and start making dinner! I bet you are starving!" Karen exclaimed.

"I tell you what," Jim remarked, smiling and sounding rather mysterious. "Why don't you get dressed and let me take you out. It's been awhile, and it will do us both good."

Karen's face lit up like a Christmas tree. "I would like that!" she bubbled with enthusiasm. "But do you think we could go to a nice, quiet place?"

"Nothing else would do!" Jim blurted.

Karen smiled from ear to ear. "I'll get up from here now and get dressed," she exclaimed while bolting up from the sofa. "Thank you, Jim. I love you," she whispered softly before taking off upstairs. As she reached the last step, she whirled around and yelled out, "I think I'll take a long, hot bath first!"

"Take your time. It's still early," Jim assured her. "While you're doing that, I'll call and make reservations. Does 7:00 p.m. sound good to you?" he asked, shouting up the stairs.

"Uh...well, yes," Karen muttered, having been caught off guard with the word "reservations." She went running back down the staircase, stopping on the last step and facing Jim. "Where in the world are you planning on taking me?"

Jim looked into her eyes, grinning very slyly. "Why, to The Steak Palace, my dear," he answered in a tone as if he was king and Karen was queen.

Karen decided to play along in his game. "Oh darling, that sounds superb!" She smirked while strutting around the living room then extending her hand for Jim to kiss. After he touched her hand gently and kissed it softly, they busted out laughing. She gave him a quick hug and then ran back upstairs to get dressed, giggling all the way.

Karen turned on the bedroom light to see Bingo sprawled right in the middle of the bed. Hoping he wouldn't wake up, she tiptoed to her closet. "I hope I can find something special to wear," she spoke with apprehension while opening the door to a packed rack of dresses, pantsuits, skirts, and blouses. "Oomph!" she grunted while frisking through each piece of clothing. Soon Karen came to her rather short, sassy red dress. A pleasant smile immediately emerged upon her face. "This ought to do it," she perkily remarked while snatching the dress from its hanger. This cute little red dress would almost certainly compliment Karen's good mood!

By the time she got her hot, lavender-scented bubble bath ready, Bingo was awake. He heard Jim and quickly ran downstairs, leaving Karen glad to enjoy the soothing soak without interruptions. She rested with a smile of happiness upon her face in the tub of hot bubbles up to her neck. "Jim's in a wonderful mood," she said to herself. *This evening at dinner, I will tell him what I saw at the wishing well. He was looking for clues there today, and this will reinforce his hope*, Karen thought as she closed her eyes, totally emerged in pleasant feelings.

After twenty minutes in the relaxing, hot tub of bubbles, Karen got out to get dressed. She went a little heavier on the makeup and even put her hair up. It had been so long since she wore high heels, so she practiced walking in them before going downstairs.

Jim was watching television with Bingo curled up beside him. When Karen walked inside the doorway and spoke, he looked up. His eyes almost popped from their sockets and his mouth dropped open as he gazed at the beauty before him! Bingo even yelped with excitement.

"How do I look?" Karen asked really cutesy as if Jim's expression didn't say it all.

"Karen, you look absolutely gorgeous!" he exclaimed in awe.

"Well, I'm glad you like it," she replied with a smile as the two hugged.

"It's almost 7:00 now. We better get a move on," Karen suddenly blurted while pulling loose from Jim's embrace.

"May I do the honor of escorting you to the car?" Jim asked as he extended his arm to her. Karen smiled then cupped her small hand around his muscular biceps.

Bingo whined as the two went out the front door. "Don't worry, boy. We'll be back," Jim consoled the dog as he closed the door and led Karen to the car, opening the door for her like a gentleman.

Reminiscing

At The Steak Palace, Jim and Karen danced and joked around, just like they did fifteen years ago when they were dating. "Karen, it's good to see you like this—happy and relaxed." Jim smiled as they swayed to the music out on the dim-lit dance floor.

"Well, I'm hanging in there," she replied.

"I'm proud of you," Jim commented while suddenly whirling her around.

"Show off!" She giggled.

"Why not?" Jim boasted.

The two laughed all the way back to their cozy corner table for two. "Whew, that was so much fun!" Karen gleamed. "I'm glad you brought me here."

"Me too," Jim agreed. "Now, what would you like to order?"

"You sound like the waiter!" Karen laughed.

After they finally calmed down, the *real* waiter took their orders of medium-rare T-bone steaks, salads, baked potatoes, and tea to drink.

In the midst of casual conversation, while waiting for their food, the live band began to play a memorable tune; a love song entitled "My Lady Loves Red." Jim and Karen looked into each other's eyes as they held hands. "Isn't it odd that you just happen to be wearing a little red dress tonight, and the band plays that song?" Jim asked.

Karen gave a warm smile. "It is magical and enchanting. I was wearing a red dress in this same restaurant fifteen years ago when that same song was played," she exclaimed in wonder of it all.

"I remember," Jim whispered. "Care to dance, my love?" he asked then stood up and reached for her hand. The two were the life of the dance floor, waltzing until the very last note faded away.

"Oh, Jim, thank you for this enchanting night," Karen remarked as they sat down just as their food arrived.

"I should be thanking you, Karen," Jim responded. They exchanged smiles and then wasted no time cutting into the thick, cooked-to-perfection steaks.

"This food is delicious!" Karen raved.

"For what it's going to cost me, it should be!" Jim commented, sounding as if he were complaining.

Karen grimaced. "Now don't gripe! You wanted to put on the ritz. This place was your idea," she pointed out. "Haven't you enjoyed yourself?"

Jim immediately apologized. "Oh, Karen, I'm sorry. That was a weak joke, wasn't it? I don't regret even one minute of this precious time with you. I cherish it!"

Karen smiled and realized how lucky she was to have a husband like Jim. She also realized they were almost finished with dinner.

A Turn for the Worst

"Jim, I have something to tell you!" Karen blurted out of midair.

"What is it, honey?"

"It's something that happened today," she answered, provoking Jim to question further.

"What happened?"

"Something happened at the wishing well," she spoke in riddles again.

Jim sighed deeply. "Karen, can't this wait? Our night has been so good."

"I'd like to tell you now," she answered with a half-smile trying to cover up building anxiety. Karen knew that if she didn't tell her story now, she might not ever let Jim know.

"All right, Karen, if you insist. Now what happened that can't wait?" he asked in an already agitated manner.

"It concerns Simon."

Jim snapped. "For gosh's sakes, I figured that! Now stop beating around the bush, just tell me what happened!"

"Well, you don't have to be so pushy!" Karen popped back.

"I didn't know that I was," Jim moaned. He then tried to change the mood. "Look, we've been having some fun. Let's don't get all worked up over something *stupid*," he spoke, using the absolute wrong word, causing Karen to frown and roll her eyes. Jim quickly explained. "You know what I mean. I meant we were *acting* stupid. In fact, we've been going on about this whole thing way too long. Just spit it out, Karen," he stressed.

Karen took a long, deep breath as Jim waited impatiently. "I saw a reflection of Simon today in the water at the wishing well," she began.

"That is nothing new. You've seen our son's reflection several times—"

"Just let me finish!" Karen cut in. Jim sighed but got quiet.

Karen recalled the happening. "This time, it was different. Simon had this huge smile across his face." Jim did not respond. "Did you hear what I said?" she asked firmly.

"I heard."

"Isn't that good news? Doesn't it tell you that Simon is happy and safe? What do you think, Jim?" Karen rattled with questions.

"What am I supposed to think?"

"You were at the wishing well earlier today looking for clues, weren't you?" Karen asked, her tone becoming very frustrated.

Jim blasted, "That is absurd! I told you why I was there. It was nothing more and nothing less!"

"I don't believe this! You really think I'm just seeing things again, don't you, Jim?" Karen screamed, causing other patrons at the restaurant to glance their way. At that instant, she demanded for him to take her home.

Here we go again! Jim thought as he got up from the table, quickly getting some cash out of his wallet for the tip. Karen marched on ahead in a huff and bolted out the door while Jim was left feeling embarrassed from the stares he was getting. He stood in line for what seemed to be at least thirty minutes trying to keep a straight face.

After paying the check, Jim walked outside to see Karen standing by the car. He shook his head in disgust. "You didn't have to prance off mad! People were staring at us, you know? You could have least waited for me!" he fussed.

"I didn't feel like it!" Karen smarted. "You know, Jim, you worry too much over what everyone else thinks. That's the problem with you!"

Jim became defensive. "I don't like creating a scene and having people staring, pointing, and whispering my way! What's wrong with that?" he exclaimed while walking around to Karen's side of the car.

"Oh, just never mind! You wouldn't understand anyway!" she screeched in Jim's ear as he fumbled to get the car door unlocked. He then quickly ran back to his side of the car.

"You're a gentleman, all right," Karen mumbled under her breath as she opened the door to get in. Jim quickly cranked up and backed out of the parking space, heading home.

Neither one spoke until he pulled into the driveway. "I thought you would be excited about me seeing Simon's smiling reflection in the wishing well," Karen expressed.

Jim turned off the engine and then looked directly at his wife. "It was supposed to be the end of this nonsense! You crushed the rock and sprinkled it into the well water and nothing has happened! Simon is still gone! You need to leave it alone, like you promised me!" he harshly scolded.

Karen's eyes welled with tears. "But something is happening. It's just taking more time than I anticipated. What am I supposed to do, keep all my emotions bottled up?" she sobbed.

Jim downed his head then reached out his arms, pulling Karen close. She chanted with mixed emotions of tears and laughter, "I just want so much for you to believe in miracles, because I know one took place at the well, and I know another will happen in the near future. I feel it deep inside me. Our son is coming home!"

"Karen! Karen! Please!"Jim begged. "I do believe Simon is alive. I haven't given up hope on him returning home," he confessed.

"I know you have hope, but you don't believe our son is in a strange land. You don't believe there was a sphinx. Even after all the weird happenings at the wishing well, you still do not believe!" she shouted.

Jim sighed. "I just don't think it's wise for us to get caught up in wishing wells and legends. They prey upon the deepest parts of our imaginations, bringing about unrealistic feelings," he explained.

Karen became firm with her words. "The feelings are real to me! I cannot turn loose of this gripping connection I have with Simon! I refuse to give up on what my inner being tells me!"

"You're his mother, of course you have a strong connection to our son," Jim pointed out. "However, that is all it is. Anything beyond that is a figment of your imagination. All I ask is that you try to see this ordeal in a realistic manner."

"I have, Jim, and what I feel goes deep. It is real!" Karen proclaimed.

Jim was totally frustrated. He took a deep breath. "Come on, let's go inside. You need a good night's rest," he encouraged. "We'll talk some more tomorrow, okay?"

Karen gave him a quick smile. "Okay."

Jim's Secret

While Jim fixed some hot, bedtime green tea, Karen got ready for bed and then slid underneath the soft, cozy covers. Bingo startled her when he suddenly pounced up, stretching out in his usual comfortable spot at the foot of the bed. Karen sat up and talked to the mutt while scratching behind his ears as he drooled in delight. "Bingo, you know I'm right, don't you, boy?" she asked.

Of course, he barked one time, and she took his answer to be yes. "Simon is in an unusual place, isn't he?" Bingo let out a big yelp. "Yes, you know it, and you feel it just as I do."

Why doesn't Jim just accept his feelings? she asked herself.

Just then, Bingo jumped off the bed. Jim could be heard coming up the stairs. Karen smiled at him when he entered the bedroom with the tray as Bingo whined and begged for a pat on the head. "The tea smells wonderful! Oh, thank you," she remarked while propping the pillow behind her back.

"You are welcome. I made enough for both of us so I can join you," Jim elated.

As they sipped the green tea and talked, Bingo fell asleep on the well-worn, oval rug on Karen's side of the bed. Jim tried to make Karen understand how he felt. "I don't think you're crazy or anything," he assured her. "I just believe that you are letting the love you have for Simon blind you to reality." Karen sighed but did not interrupt. "Please try to understand where I'm coming from. I'm concerned that you have become obsessed with this legend thing."

Karen snapped, "I'm not obsessed! You have your point of view and I have mine. Do you not want me to share my true feelings with you?"

Jim remained calm. "Of course, I do. I just wish you would think more down-to-earth."

"Oh, I understand. You want me to think like you! I have discovered a different way of thinking, so that makes it unreal!" Karen blurted, catching Jim completely off guard.

"Uh…well, it is far-out," he mumbled.

"Why do you believe your way of looking at this is realistic and mine is not? That is only your opinion," Karen quickly came back with the punches.

"Well, you do have to admit this whole thing with this legend idea seems really far-fetched," Jim exclaimed.

"Believe it or not, I do see how far-out it sounds, but I also know what I feel, and it is real," Karen argued. "Do you not feel the deepest part of you telling you what happened at the wishing well is real? Can you really sit there and tell me that you do not feel anything at all?" she asked Jim.

He had a very haunting chill come over him from Karen's questioning but kept it to himself. "As I said earlier, I do believe Simon is alive and will be home again. I have a connection to our son also. I am his dad!" he stressed. "I'm just not letting my imagination take over and run wild!"

"I truly believe you are denying your real feelings. You're scared of them, and you're afraid of what others will think!" Karen firmly stated as if reading Jim's mind.

He shook his head while getting up from the bed, jerking the tray off Karen's lap. "I do understand how you want this legend to be true and real. You are hoping for a miracle! There is nothing wrong with hope, but we must separate fact from fiction," he remarked before leaving the room.

It is a fact that I saw the reflection of that sphinx, it's a fact that the water rushed and bubbled from the crystal powder, and it's a fact that I saw Simon's reflection several times, Karen thought to herself. She then turned over, facing the wall, and closed her eyes. With a weak smile, she whispered, "I have separated fact from fiction. You need to do the same, Jim."

Karen drifted off into a rather restless sleep while Jim clamored around in the kitchen, washing up the teacups and sweeping crumbs off the floor. He then walked softly upstairs and peeped inside the bedroom. *Thank goodness Karen is finally getting some much-needed sleep,* he thought while pulling the covers up around her. He kissed her cheek gently then tiptoed out of the bedroom, yawning wide. Jim realized at that time he too could use some rest.

He took a quick hot shower and frisked off with a fluffy, soft bath towel, stopping to inhale the fresh scent the dryer sheet left behind. "I guess I'd better brush my teeth," he mumbled, dreading the chore. As he stood in front of the mirror polishing his pearly whites to a glisten, Jim's thoughts went to Karen's questions about feeling something deep inside. He suddenly stopped and stared at his own reflection. "I do feel something telling me Simon is in a strange place. Part of me does say this legend is real," he whispered with haunting chills to the image in the mirror.

Quickly, Jim rinsed his toothbrush, trying to dismiss all thoughts of strange places and legends. "Why can't I just tell Karen I feel these things too?" he asked himself with anguish. "If I do, she will just read too much into them. It will make the whole situation worse," he justified his reasoning.

I know most of this is coming from our imaginations, Jim thought while crawling under the covers. He then glanced over at Karen and smiled. She had finally quit tossing and turning and seemed to be sleeping peacefully. Bingo had moved up to the foot of the bed and was stretched out over her feet.

Jim reached up and clicked off the table lamp. "Sweet dreams, Karen," he whispered before rolling over. "I love you, Simon. Wherever you are, please stay safe and come home soon. We miss you, son, and our hearts ache for your return," he cried with inward grief.

He then brushed the tears away and closed his eyes. With a wide yawn, he stretched out, getting into a comfortable position. Before drifting off to sleep, his last thought went to Simon's big smile; the one he had seen earlier that day. Do you not see? Jim had seen the reflection of his son's face in the wishing well!

Another Journey Begins

To the Nectar Fields

SIMON KNEW THE journey through the tunnel was drawing to an end for him and the Rhues, for the darkness was beginning to fade. Neopoleana's *golden wings* had brightened Rhueland once again, and flickers of the gleaming rays reached partially into the mouth of the passageway.

Suddenly, Blubbles screamed out, "There's a giant monster! He's going to eat me alive!"

The other Rhues became so frightened that they huddled together and screamed so loud you could hear their echoes deep inside the tunnel. "Calm down!" Simon demanded. "Okay, Blubbles! Where is this big monster?" he asked the shaking Rhue.

"Over there in front of the wall," Blubbles replied, pointing to the lighted portion behind him.

Simon almost laughed his head off. "That is your shadow!" he exclaimed. "It's just bigger than you."

Blubbles and the other Rhues peered out from their huddle cautiously to see this strange shadow. Simon explained about it. "The darkness behind us and the light coming in caused you to cast a huge silhouette of yourself." He then stepped into the light and turned to face the wall to show the Rhues his own shadow. They flinched when a gigantic boy appeared on the wall. Simon laughed and pretty soon was putting on a big show for his skeptical audience. He twisted his arms, fingers, and hands into different shapes to create huge images of different creatures for them to watch. The wall reminded Simon of a huge flatscreen television, and he was really proud of his showmanship, noticing how the Rhues were completely captivated with his performance.

Soon Blubbles joined in to put on his own show. Everyone chuckled with delight when he cast a mean-looking image and told the others it was Bronzella. Each one then took a turn to cast shadows and to create "monsters."

Simon let the Rhues enjoy their play for a while before calling out to them. "Come on, you guys! Neopoleana will be waiting for us. You are hungry, aren't you?"

The Rhues squealed with excitement, immediately taking off in waddling runs. "Yummy, yummy! We want nectar!" they shouted together.

"Slow down! You will be too tired to eat," Simon scolded.

"Okay, we'll just walk fast," Pinka sassily replied as she sashayed on ahead of the others.

That's the way Angel Marie Wilson walks. I guess I'll be seeing her soon back at Hillcrest. I have this feeling my mom and dad haven't given up on me. I wonder what was going on with them when Bronzella was falling apart at the seams, Simon thought. His friend came to mind. *Man, I can't wait to see Doug! I bet he thinks I'm gone for good! Maybe I'll give him one of my stones.* He slid his hand down into his pocket to make sure they were still there.

Simon's thoughts ended with the interruption of cheering Rhues. "We're at the end of the tunnel!"

"I see Neopoleana—I mean Mama!" Truffles squealed with anticipation.

The group picked up speed, running as fast as they could toward the tunnel's entrance. "Mama, Mama!" the Rhues were shouting as they ran out to her open arms.

Simon ran out behind them and was completely surprised at what he found. All the creatures, except for the stone figures and Chuckatoo, were waiting for their return! "Flutta, Turckle, Fuzzle, Bunnita!" he called out with excitement and then stopped to hug each one. "Bunnita, I'm so happy that you came to greet us," he expressed with delight.

"What about me?" a baritone voice drummed out from behind him.

Simon quickly turned around. "Oh, Trog! I never thought I'd see you again!" he shouted while immediately hopping upon the giant frog's back.

"Would you like a ride to the nectar fields?" Trog asked him.

"Yeah, that would be fun."

"I want to ride with you," Pinka whined.

"Will it be okay for her to join us?" Simon politely asked.

"Well, come on. Hop up on my back," Trog bellowed.

"Everyone needs to get a ride to the nectar fields!" Simon commanded the others.

Squiggly agreed. "Yes, we are starving!"

He then asked Fuzzle if he and Tooty could ride with him. "I would be happy to give you a lift," the soft, fuzzy caterpillar answered. Squiggly and Tooty grasped her silky coat with their small hands and pulled themselves up, giggling all the way to the top.

"What is so funny?" Fuzzle asked out of curiosity.

"Your fuzz is tickling us," Tooty chuckled, letting out a couple of toots from her snout.

Gurggles, Blubbles, and Truffles hurried to board Flutta. "We get to fly to the nectar fields," each one boasted.

"Gosh, you guys seem heavy. I believe you have grown," Flutta commented.

"I don't see how we could be very heavy, since we're completely empty of nectar," Blubbles spoke, shooting out bubbles.

"Are you losing your strength or something?" Gurggles asked as hundreds of tiny bubbles gurgled from his snout. Truffles snickered at the remark, causing the others to join in with laughs. Flutta did not find this remark amusing and gave a glaring look. Quickly, the Rhues apologized for their bad behavior.

Blinko and Slurple had already boarded Turckle. "I'm not too fast, but I'll get you there," the aged turtle promised.

Slurple immediately complained. "Gosh, this is a rough seat! Try to get us to the nectar fields as fast as you can!"

Turckle turned and gave a grimaced stare. "Oh, stop your whining! Just be happy you have a ride!" he advised.

Blinko agreed. "That's right! We'll get there soon enough. A little discomfort is not going to kill you," he shouted. Slurple slurped his snout at Blinko in an arrogant manner, and then Blinko blinked his snout on and off rapidly back at him.

Attention was called toward Bunnita's shrill cries. "Halt right there! Don't come any closer!" she demanded.

Jetta, Malo, and Razzle stopped dead in their tracks. "We just wanted to get a ride with you," Razzle spoke nervously.

Bunnita then informed the three tiny Rhues that only one could ride upon her back. "I can carry only a light load. I do not want my back getting out of shape," she professed. Her display of such pride brought frowns from everyone, especially Neopoleana. However, no one dared to interfere with the "perfect rabbit's" wish. After all, she had come a long way with her attitude.

Suddenly, Jetta bolted toward Bunnita and scurried up the side of her soft, furry body. Razzle and Malo were left in shock at first and then screamed out. "It's not fair! Jetta is fast! Of course she got the ride!" Malo cried. Neopoleana wanted so much to get involved but knew it would be best to let the Rhues solve the problem their own way. Of course, she observed and listened, being ready to step in at anytime.

"There are no rides left!" Razzle shouted. "We certainly cannot walk all alone by ourselves."

"Maybe Flutta can make room for at least one of you," Simon suggested. Flutta quickly responded. "Forget that idea! I'm overloaded as it is. I wouldn't be able to get off the ground."

"What about you, Trog?" Can you handle one smaller Rhue?" Simon asked.

"Sorry, but you and Pinka are my limit. It will already be hard enough for the two of you to hold on since I leap so high," Trog explained, puffing up his massive throat.

"We were left out! All the rides were grabbed up before we even had a chance to get one!" Malo cried out in frustration.

"Calm down," Simon softly spoke. "The rides weren't intentionally hogged up."

The Rhues looked puzzled, for they had never heard such a word as *hogged*. "What does that mean?" Malo asked with curiosity.

"What does what mean?"

Malo shouted, *"Hogged!* What does *hogged* mean?"

Simon cackled with laughter. "Oh, that word originated from the name of an animal we have back in my world. A hog eats just about anything anytime you feed him. In other words, he hogs his food down," he explained through his snickering.

"Yeah, like you, Malo!" Razzle smarted off, causing all the Rhues and creatures to laugh at the nasty remark.

"I do not hog down nectar!" Malo shouted in defense.

At this point, Neopoleana knew it was time to intervene. "Hold it—hold it right this minute!" she commanded. There was complete and utter silence. "Razzle, that was not a nice thing to say to Malo," she scolded.

"I was just having some fun."

The Mother Rhue preached her wisdom. "Yes, but you were having your fun at Malo's expense. Now his feelings are hurt from your words. Pointing, snickering, and making fun of others only shows a weakness within oneself. This is what I see to stand out."

Razzle realized Neopoleana was right and felt ashamed for having made such a rude comment. With his head hung low, he apologized. "I'm sorry, Malo. I love you and didn't mean to hurt your feelings. Will you forgive me?" he asked with compassion.

Malo gave a half-smile. "That's okay, Razzle. I know you didn't mean to poke fun at me," he replied. The other Rhues and creatures gave their apologies for having laughed as Simon watched in complete fascination. He realized how much the Rhues and creatures in The Third Dimension were so much like human beings in his world.

Just then, a familiar voice from atop a nearby boulder echoed loudly across the group. Smiles abounded on everyone's face when they looked up to see Chuckatoo! They had been so engrossed in the present situation that no one had seen the huge bird descend from the coral sky. "Hi, Chuckatoo!" Simon shouted as he ran toward the giant gray boulder. The Rhues and creatures followed, shouting their greetings.

Simon listened in awe as Chuckatoo's gigantic orange upper beak clacked loudly against his lower beak when he spoke, "What's going on? What's going on?"

"We're heading out to the nectar fields," Simon answered.

"When are you going home? When are you going home?"

"We're going to the far tunnel after we eat. Neopoleana will open it with the power from her *golden wings* so I can journey home," Simon explained.

"Can I go to the tunnel with you? Can I go to the tunnel with you?" Chuckatoo begged, pacing back and forth.

"We would love for you to travel with us, wouldn't we, guys?" Simon asked the group.

All the creatures answered with a firm yes, and the Rhues clapped and shouted with excitement, dancing around in circles.

Razzle and Malo wasted no time hitting on Chuckatoo for transportation. "Can you give us a ride?" Razzle asked in anticipation. "The other Rhues *hogged* the creatures up for rides, leaving Malo and me standing alone to walk!" Simon snickered at this remark and then glanced toward Neopoleana, who was shaking her head in dismay.

"Yes, I can do that! Yes, I can do that!" Chuckatoo gladly obliged.

"Oh boy!" Razzle and Malo shouted together while dancing and jumping up and down. The creatures and other Rhues chanted their joys.

Simon hastened the big bird. "Fly on down here so Razzle and Malo can climb upon your back. We really need to be on our way."

"Stand back! Stand back!" Chuckatoo ordered as he prepared to take flight from the boulder. His huge, flapping wings created so much air current that it blew Razzle and Malo three feet backward! As Simon felt the wind beat against his face, it reminded him of hurricane season back home.

After the somewhat awkward landing was finished, Razzle and Malo quickly regained their composure and hurried to grab their ride as if it also would be taken from them. Chuckatoo had stretched his long, colorful wing down and out like steps cascading from an airplane. He even sounded like a pilot of sorts as he commanded, "Get on board! Get on board!"

The two Rhues marched proudly up to the strong, tapered wing, waving and singing, "We have a ride! We have a ride!"

Chuckatoo's headdress flowed down his back, giving Razzle an anchor to hold for the flight. Malo took a seat behind Razzle, latching his tiny arms around his waist. "We're ready to go!" they shouted together.

"Wait a minute!" Neopoleana ordered. "Let me go ahead of you. I need to feed Winglet first so that I can hurry to the tallest tree for a while. The baby Rhue will be staying with me while all of you eat and nap," she announced.

"Bye-bye!" Winglet shouted as the Mother Rhue took to the coral sky faster than a jet.

"Bye!" the group yelled while watching her disappear from sight.

Soon Chuckatoo was reeling his wing back in, preparing for takeoff. "We'll meet you at the orchid fields! We'll meet you at the orchid fields!" he shouted as he took off with Razzle and Malo squealing with excitement.

Flutta cranked up her wings and took to the sky with great speed, trailing in behind Chuckatoo. In just a few short seconds, she zoomed past him with Gurggles, Blubbles, and Truffles screaming like kids on a sonic ride at the fair.

The other creatures began the journey with Trog leading the way. After being bounced around a few times, Simon was wishing he had rode with Flutta. Pinka was already concerned over her pink curls getting mussed but kept the silly worry to herself this time.

Bunnita hopped behind Trog with Jetta sitting atop her back very prim and proper. Simon looked back and thought, *Jetta is acting perfect to impress Bunnita.* He seemed to think this was cute anyway.

Tooty began playing a catchy tune on her horn snout. Soon Truffles joined in to sing solo to a song he made up that went well with the notes. It went like this:

> We're slinking along
> We're slinking along
>
> Up and down
> Up and down
>
> High and low
> Near and far
>
> Here we go
> There we go
>
> Ha! Ha! Ha!
>
> (*Truffles would clap after each Ha!*)

Simon was surprised at Truffles's beautiful voice and smiled with pleasure at the happy little song.

Turckle was falling farther and farther behind, but Blinko and Slurple took it in much better stride than they had anticipated. I guess they were enjoying his "tales of wisdom" too much to notice the rough seat. Before they hardly knew it, the luscious orchard blooms were in sight!

Blubbles, Gurggles, Truffles, Razzle, and Malo were already lapping up nectar when the others arrived. Simon quickly slid down Trog's side and looked around for Squiggly, spotting him latched to a nearby gray orchid. He took off quickly in the Rhue's direction. "Squiggly! Squiggly! Don't forget, you must bring me some of that delicious juice!" he shouted. Squiggly was too engulfed in the pleasure of eating to even notice another's presence. Simon then shouted at the top of his lungs, "Squiggly, I'm hungry too!"

His hunger cries were finally heard. "Let me eat just one more snoutful, then I'll get some for you," Squiggly responded while plunging his extra-long snout down into the center of the orchid to retrieve more of the sweet confection.

Simon's mouth began to water just watching Squiggly gobble the delightful syrupy nectar down with gulps of pleasure. *The next snoutful will be mine*, he thought with anticipation while wiping drools of saliva from his mouth and chin. He then proceeded to make his "hand cup" and beckoned for Squiggly to hurry and fill it. Quickly, the little Rhue filled his snout to the brim and ran to Simon, squirting the luscious nectar into the "cup" until it overflowed. Simon would slurp the treat down almost as fast as Squiggly could dish it out.

He was devouring the second "cupful" of sweet liquid when screams from the Rhues startled him. "Simon! Simon! Malo is in trouble! Help! Help!"

"Where are you?"

"We're over here in the open area," Blinko shouted with distress. "Hurry! Malo is floating away!'

"What?" Simon shouted, feeling perplexed as he ran fast to them with Squiggly following.

'Where is Malo?'

"Up there!" Razzle exclaimed, pointing toward the coral sky. Sure enough, the puffy Rhue was floating like a hot-air balloon. He had eaten so much nectar, it swelled him up to the size of a blimp.

Fear gripped Simon. "Oh no! Malo is headed in the direction of The Rivers of Strength, just like Winglet had done!" he screamed.

"Well, at least Bronzella can't eat him alive!" Tooty commented.

Simon rolled his eyes back and sighed. "For goodness' sakes, don't you realize when Malo deflates, he will then plunge downward, falling into the hot molten?" he exclaimed, causing Tooty's eyes to grow big.

He gave a quick look to Flutta. "Can you get Malo down?'

Flutta became anxious. "Gosh, he is so blown up there is no way he could stay on my back," she exclaimed.

"What about you, Chuckatoo? Couldn't you latch on to Malo with your beak?" Simon asked in desperation.

"My sharp, curved beak would cut Malo! My sharp, curved beak would cut Malo!" the anxious bird squawked out in shrill tones.

"We have got to do something soon!" Simon cried. "Malo is floating farther and farther away! Please help me come up ideas!" he ordered the others.

It was quiet for a short time as everyone tried to think of ways of rescuing the poor Rhue. Suddenly, Jetta spoke out, "Maybe my rope will help!"

Simon squealed with surprise. "Oh, Jetta! You still have that silk rope?"

"Why, yes! It's around Bunnita's ear. She wanted to wear it for a necklace, but since it would not fit, I put it over her ear."

Simon wasted no time. "Hurry over here, Bunnita! We need that rope now!" he commanded. Bunnita quickly hopped up and tilted her head back, and then she lunged forward, flinging the rope from her ear.

Simon hurriedly picked it up off the ground and ran to Flutta. "Take this rope to Malo and place it in his hand. Tell him to hold on to it tightly. You can then grab the other end of the rope with your mouth and pull him in," he ordered. "Hurry now! If Malo goes up any higher, the high altitude could cause him to explode," he spoke with terror, causing anxious sighs from within the group.

Flutta latched on to the silk rope and zoomed up into the coral sky then turned and raced toward Malo. "Hold on to this rope. I'm going to get the other end of it and pull you in," the excited butterfly explained.

"I'm scared! I want Mama!" Malo cried.

"I know you do, but right now, we must think only of getting you down from here," Flutta spoke with compassion. "Just hold on to the rope really tight. And don't be scared! I'll have you down in no time," she explained, trying to sound calm. Flutta then placed the sturdy rope in Malo's hand. He wrapped his three tiny fingers around it tightly as Flutta zoomed downward and grabbed the other end with precision.

Everyone was watching the coral sky with anticipation. Soon they got a glimpse of Flutta reeling in Malo. Cheers of joy broke out! When the heroic butterfly reached the open area, she released the rope. Simon chased the dangling twine like a kid chasing the tail of a kite. More cheers rang out when he jumped up and grabbed hold of the rope. "I have him! I have him!" he screamed with relief.

The Rhues took off in a waddling run as Simon brought Malo in. Soon he had the distressed Rhue close to the ground. "Don't turn loose of the rope! I'll just float away again!" Malo cried.

"Don't worry! I'm holding the rope tightly. You're safe now!" Simon assured the shaking Rhue.

Malo looked a mess with his mouth and snout covered in dried white nectar, but he was clearly relieved to be out of the sky, away from the dangers of The Rivers of Strength. "I'm going to be afraid forever to do anything!" he suddenly blurted out.

"Why are you going to be afraid forever, Malo?" Simon asked. "This was just an accident. You ate too much, and it blew you up. That is why you floated away."

"Well, so many other bad things have happened to frighten me. Now, this incident has made me more scared than ever!" he tried to explain his feelings.

"Oh, Malo. That doesn't mean bad things will keep happening," Simon responded.

"It doesn't?"

"No, it doesn't! But don't get me wrong! Accidents will happen. However, you should never let fear rule your life. Your world has so much for you to see, touch, and learn about. Don't shut yourself away from this beauty. Enjoy the mystery of it all!" Simon lectured.

"How do I not be afraid?" Malo asked in a pleading tone.

"Hmm…that is a tough question to answer, to tell someone how not to be afraid," Simon replied then contemplated a few minutes. With a bright smile, he answered, "You must learn not to be afraid. If you do not, then you will live in fear forever. Why should you be frightened of bad things happening before they occur?" he asked with wit, surprising himself with having retained so much his mom and dad had taught him.

Simon continued his lecture with not only Malo but with all the Rhues and creatures listening attentively. "If you are cautious and think before acting, and you obey all the rules, then your chances of accidents are less. However, if you do have one, you deal with it then. Do you understand what I'm saying?"

Malo replied with pride, "Yes, I think I do. It was like with the accident I just had. I *hogged* nectar down and got overfilled. I should have stopped when I knew it was enough." Right then, out of the blue, anxiousness set in. "Razzle was right! I am a *hog*!" he screamed and cried, almost letting go of the silk rope.

"Be careful! You can't turn loose of the rope until after you shrink back down to normal size," Simon shouted. He then began stroking Malo's forehead with a soothing touch. "You are not a hog. You were just hungry and ate too much," he explained. Haven't you learned from what happened?"

"Uh…yes! You are right! I have learned."

Simon was delighted. "Good! That is what counts the most," he elated while patting Malo on his head. The Rhue shyly smiled.

"Look!" Gurggles suddenly yelled out, pointing to Malo's belly, which was deflating like a tire on a car going flat. The Rhues and creatures shouted with joy as they watched the pouch return to normal size. Finally, everyone could relax. This is when they realized how tired they were.

"Time for a nap! Time for a nap!" Chuckatoo screeched before flying high into a nearby tree. Trog hopped off to doze alone while Flutta found a cozy spot behind a huge, green bush. Bunnita had fallen asleep right where she sat.

The Rhues stretched and yawned then huddled together against Fuzzle's soft, squishy body. Simon collapsed next to them, quickly drifting into a fretful sleep, returning to the usual dream of the wishing well, his mom's reflection, and Bronzella!

Homeward Bound
(Journey to the Far Tunnel)

Neopoleana Shares a Word of Wisdom

SIMON WAS AWAKENED by the sound of Neopoleana's soft, majestic voice. "Wake up, wake up. We must be on our way to the far tunnel." Slowly he opened his sleepy eyes to find himself still snuggled against Fuzzle's body with the Rhues huddled close by.

"I've been watching you sleep. You were talking," Fuzzle whispered.

"I was talking in my sleep?"

"Yes. You were saying something about a wishing well and Bronzella. You were screaming with terror and calling out for your mom!" Fuzzle replied.

Simon remembered his dream. "Oh, yeah. I saw my mom and dad at the wishing well with their heads lowered over the water. They were calling for me."

"Soon you will be back home, then the dreams shall cease," the Mother Rhue assured him while gently nudging the Rhues awake.

"May I ask you a question, Neopoleana?" Simon asked.

"Simon, remember what I told you?"

He thought for a minute and then smiled for remembering what it was. "Yes, ma'am! I should not ask if I can ask a question, because you will not know if I can ask the question until after I have asked it." He then gasped. "Whew! That didn't sound quite the way you told me. Did I say it correctly?"

Neopoleana couldn't help but laugh. "I understood what you said, Simon. Now what is it you wanted to ask?" At this point, Winglet had snuggled up on the Mother Rhue's lap. The Rhues and creatures were awake and had quietly gathered around, listening to the two of them talk.

Simon had to think a minute on how to ask his question. "It is hard for me to explain this, but I'll try," he began. "For some reason, I have this strong feeling that sometimes my mom and dad know I'm here. I even dream over and over that Bronzella is chasing me up through the wishing well. I see my Mom's face each time, but I cannot reach her!"

He stopped talking, glancing toward Neopoleana. "Go ahead. Continue, Simon," she beckoned.

Simon continued with wonder. "I can feel my mom and dad so strongly that it is like seeing them. Does this make sense? Is it real or just my imagination?" he questioned.

Neopoleana put her arm around him as she smiled down into his eyes. "It is part of the deep love and devotion your family shares. It is a real yet unseen bond that can never be broken. Even though you are worlds apart, you are still connected through this bond, for your feelings can travel great distances to reach the ones you love," she explained with great wisdom.

Simon was spellbound with Neopoleana's insight, and he now understood his feelings. "So, my mom and dad's love for me is reaching all the way to Rhueland. That is like them being here with me. Is that correct?" he asked.

The Mother Rhue gave him a tight yet gentle hug. "Yes, my son, that is correct. The love you have for your parents reaches all the way to Hillcrest for them to feel. It is like you being there, for they are "seeing" you through their hearts."

"And I'm seeing them through the 'eyes' of my heart." Simon beamed.

Neopoleana smiled with the pride only a mother could know. "You are now mastering the great value and power this bond holds," she commented.

"Thank you so much for answering my question and explaining to me what I have been feeling," Simon obliged with gratitude.

Just then, Razzle interrupted. "Mama, when are we leaving?"

The Mother Rhue chuckled lightly and looked toward Simon. "Why, we are ready now, aren't we?" she asked.

"Yes, I am ready more than ever to move on!" he shouted with confidence.

"Hurry now! All of you board your rides. We have a long journey ahead of us!" Neopoleana commanded as she scooted the Rhues off. "Come to me, Winglet! You and I are walking with Simon," she exclaimed.

The Rhues overheard. They immediately came to a halt with frowns upon their faces. "We want to walk with you too!" Pinka whined.

"That is fine with me. I assumed you enjoyed riding with the creatures," Neopoleana stated.

"Actually, I could use a rest from bouncing around on Trog," Pinka remarked while rubbing her behind.

Winglet flittered to Simon's shoulder and straddled his neck so she could look around during the journey. Chuckatoo and Flutta flew low above the tall trees while the other creatures took their time strolling leisurely behind the group.

Memories

Slowly, the troop made their way through fragrant fields of wild flowers and rose bushes, breathing in the aromatic perfumed air as all eyes captured bold, vivid colors. Soon they walked upon the beautiful red rose bush fence where Neopoleana often stayed.

Simon stared and then shouted for everyone to halt. "I'll be back shortly!" he announced while quickly sliding Winglet from around his neck and handing her to Neopoleana. "I want one last look at Krystallina's monument, and I prefer to go alone."

"We understand and will wait for you right here," the Mother Rhue stated.

Simon quickly ran to the fence and pushed his way through the bushes. Immediately, he began to lavish the breathtaking scene as he crept down the teal-green and fuchsia-pink pathway built by the stone figures. He knelt down to closely examine the intricate artwork displayed in the construction of this magnificent piece of work. *Tealo, Jado, Roza, and Ember are so talented. I guess they are somewhere right now working on a project*, he warmly thought. He then got up and took a seat upon the sturdy stone bench and lightly stroked its surface. *The stone figures are so artistic and amazing. These beautiful works of art are such priceless treasures!* He wondered if he would even see the figures again before leaving Rhueland. A twinge of sadness ran over him.

Simon began to think back and chuckled at how nervous he had been to meet Neopoleana for the first time. Winglet had charmed him, and the other Rhues had left him in complete awe. Never again would he meet such delightful creatures! *Saying good-bye to the Rhues will be one of the hardest things I will ever have to do. I will never see them again, not forever*, he thought as his eyes welled with tears. He then quickly jumped up, wiped away the tears, and followed the pathway.

Once again, Simon entered the captivating yellow rose garden and walked toward Krystallina's monument. This was a solemn moment for him, and he stood quietly, reaching slowly to touch the huge gray stone. "Your kind spirit still shines in Rhueland," he softly spoke. Flickers of crystal light began to dance above the sculpture, yet Simon remained completely at ease. He smiled and whispered, "I feel as though I know you, and I believe you see me. It is like Neopoleana said, 'The light of your spirit lives on.'"

Simon then turned to walk out of the garden, glancing back one last time. "Bye, Krystallina," he spoke and then quickly whirled around to head back down the pathway. He stopped at the beautiful fence of red roses to breathe the sweet fragrance deep into his lungs before exiting to the other side.

Neopoleana smiled, and Winglet immediately flew to him. "Is everybody ready to move on?" the Mother Rhue asked.

"We are! We are!" Razzle shouted.

Simon looked up to see that he and Malo had boarded the bird's back. "Hey, you're starting to talk like Chuckatoo!" he chuckled.

Flutta was close by in a very tall, blue-leafed tree with Blubbles and Gurggles on board. "We're ready too. I'll be flying from tree to tree until we reach an open area," the beautiful butterfly shouted.

Simon looked at the other Rhues. "Do you guys need a ride?" There are plenty of creatures left to board."

"Not us, Simon! I'm sure we can walk another two or three miles without one complaint," Pinka sassily remarked.

"Walking certainly is good for you as long as you don't overdo it," Simon commented.

"Well, I believe Razzle, Malo, Blubbles, and Gurggles are just being lazy," Blinko quietly whispered to Simon, causing him to snicker.

Simon whispered back, "You could be right about that."

Suddenly, the two were caught off guard by the wise Mother Rhue. "Do you have something you wish to share with us?" she firmly asked.

"Uh…uh…no, ma'am," Simon stammered.

"Then we should be on our way," she commanded.

"Our mother doesn't like for us to whisper," Blinko informed him as they prepared to move onward.

Simon agreed. "My mom taught me that it wasn't polite. I should have known better."

Blinko added, "Besides that, we were gossiping. Neopoleana would have had a hissy if she had known that."

"I have a suspicious feeling she did know," Simon analyzed.

An Awesome Surprise

The journey continued through vibrant fields. The Rhues sang joyfully as they marched along, Simon listening intently to their voices in harmony. It reminded him of a choir, and he was certainly going to miss such sweet music.

Soon the group came upon the open area near the bridge built by the stone figures. Trog was ready for a refreshing swim and wasted no time! Without uttering a word, the giant bullfrog leaped past the others, heading toward the stream without stopping! Then he let out one loud bellow and jumped over the bridge as everyone watched in awe. Huge droplets shot high into the air after he plunged in with massive force, causing the others to wonder if any water was left at all for him to swim in.

Flutta and Chuckatoo flew down to the open area to drop off Razzle, Malo, Blubbles, and Gurggles. "They are ready to walk awhile," Flutta commented as the tiny Rhues quickly slid off the creatures' backs and waddled toward Simon. Malo quickly latched on to Simon's right hand while Razzle reached for his left one.

"Is everyone ready to cross the bridge?" Simon asked.

"Yes!" the group shouted together.

Neopoleana held tightly to Winglet as the group marched. Getting closer, Simon noticed what appeared to be a new pathway in the distance beyond the bridge. Teal-green and fuchsia-pink stones glowed with brilliance. "Look over there!" he shouted with excitement. "Isn't that a new road?"

"Why, it is new!" Neopoleana confirmed. "The stone figures have certainly been busy."

"Let's hurry across the bridge!" Simon yelled and then took off running. The Rhues followed with Neopoleana and Winglet trailing in behind.

After stopping on the stone structure to wait for the others, Simon caught a glimpse of the stone figures near the newly constructed road. "Look! There are Tealo, Jado, Ember, and Roza!" he shouted with anticipation.

"They're standing there as if they are waiting for us. Let's go see them now!" Pinka squealed excitedly.

"Calm down now," Neopoleana commanded as Winglet squirmed in her arms. "Of course we are going to see them."

Simon was thrilled at the sight of the stone figures, for he never thought he would see them again. He waved, but of course, they just stood at attention like trained soldiers.

Truffles yelled down to Trog, "Come on! We're going on across the bridge to see the stone figures!"

"Yeah. They have built a new pathway for us to explore!" Tooty added.

"Okay, okay! I'm coming!" Trog shouted as he leaped out of the water and onto the bridge without warning. The Rhues squealed as huge droplets soaked their downy fur coats. Pinka fussed at Trog for drenching her pink curls. Simon and the others laughed, watching her shake the water from her hair.

After the excitement settled, Neopoleana quickly crossed the bridge with Winglet. Simon and the Rhues followed, and Trog leaped behind them. They all waited for the other creatures to cross.

"Only one of you can cross at a time," Simon shouted.

"Well, we certainly know that!" Bunnita blurted as she hopped on across. Fuzzle slinked in behind her, followed by Turckle.

"Where are Flutta and Chuckatoo?" Simon asked.

"There they are!" Slurple yelled, pointing toward the pathway. "My goodness, they're fast!"

"Come on! The stone figures might get tired of waiting for us and leave!" Blubbles expressed while waddling out front.

As the group approached, the figures did a quick turn, marching down the pathway. "I believe they want us to follow them," Simon whispered.

Neopoleana agreed. "That is exactly what they want. Now let's march in an orderly fashion. I will lead with Winglet."

The group was quiet, for the beauty surrounding them was spellbounding. Simon looked down at the newly created pathway to see that all the perfectly oval-shaped stones of teal green and fuchsia pink were in exact sequence of each other. The sides of the pathway were lined with a solid wall of precious red and blue gemstones. Groups of vibrant tulips, pink roses, white carnations, and green plants of every shape were growing and blooming in front of the gemstone fence. This was truly the most beautiful creation of all he had seen!

Simon's eyes finally moved ahead to watch Tealo, Jado, Ember, and Roza march proudly. Suddenly, Neopoleana came to a halt. She and Winglet stared straight ahead in complete awe. Simon walked up to stand beside her. His eyes grew big, his mouth gaped open, and his breath was literally taken away. All the Rhues and creatures gasped at the amazing sight. In fact, no one could speak nor take their eyes off the incredible masterpiece standing in front of them. There, at the end of the pathway, was a statue of Simon, constructed from the coins that once formed Bronzella! Each gold piece was placed with precision to form an exact likeness to him. Even the height of the work of art was correct. Teal green stones were used to put color in Simon's eyes, and a smile was captured upon his face. His favorite cap was made up also of teal-green stones. At the base of the statue, flowers of every color were in full bloom. Ember and Tealo stood at attention on one side, and Roza and Jado stood on the other.

Tears streamed down Simon's eyes, dripping off his cheeks as he marveled at the sight. "Why did they go to all the trouble of building a statue of me?" he softly asked the Mother Rhue.

"This is their way of showing how much they care. The stone figures are expressing their love by paying tribute to you with this magnificent statue," Neopoleana explained with pride. "Since they do not talk, their art work speaks for them," she added.

"We love the statue of you," Pinka said sweetly.

"It is beautiful," Tooty expressed.

Soon all the Rhues and creatures were commenting about the sculpture. Simon smiled and then approached Ember and Tealo. "I want to thank you for loving me so much," he spoke with compassion. "The statue looks just like me. I will never forget how incredible you guys are." Ember and Tealo remained at attention, but Simon knew they understood how much he appreciated what they had done for him.

He then moved to the other side to thank Jado and Roza. "The statue is magnificent! There will be a special place in my heart for you always. I will never forget your beautiful works of art."

Simon then stepped back and glanced toward all four of them. "Thank you from the bottom of my heart! I love you and will miss you!" he cried while turning around to leave.

Neopoleana walked up, getting beside Simon, with Winglet stretching her tiny arms out. He reached for her, and she hugged his neck tightly. Everyone was solemn, sobbing quietly as they walked back down the pathway. Simon turned to get one last glimpse of his friends and the statue.

Neopoleana then put her arm around Simon's shoulder and gently nudged him close. "It's hard to leave friends behind"— she whispered—"but we must move on. You have two wonderful parents who miss you. You belong in their world with them."

Simon cried. "I know, but it still hurts to walk away knowing I'll never see them again. They taught me so much, especially in finding happiness in creative ways. The stone figures find real joy just working, creating beautiful works of art. I have many friends who are like that. I now understand their joy.

A Bad Feeling

Soon the group approached the open area and was ready to continue their journey. "We shall rest a few minutes then be on our way," Neopoleana stated. Winglet quickly flew to her open arms to be rocked gently as the other Rhues plopped down around her.

The creatures (all but Trog) rested close by. That big bullfrog was nowhere in sight! "Trog must have gone ahead," Simon remarked.

"Yes, I'm sure that is what he did," Pinka spoke in an unusually huffy manner. She had her arms folded together tightly, a frown was upon her face, and she jumped up and marched away from the group.

Simon was dumbfounded. "What is Pinka's problem?" he asked.

"She is just in one of her moods, I guess," Blinko analyzed as if they had contended with this behavior before.

Neopoleana was getting ready to go check on her when Simon blurted, "I'll go! There's no need for Winglet to be disturbed."

"Thank you so very much. I appreciate your kindness," the Mother Rhue replied with pride of his good manners.

Simon walked quietly to the area where Pinka was sitting. "What's the matter?" he politely asked.

"Nothing!" Pinka snapped.

"Aw, come on now! Your anger shows all over. You have a pink glow," Simon exclaimed with a chuckle. "I'm sure you are not that upset over Trog going on ahead of us."

"You would never understand!" Pinka yelled.

"How do you know that?"

"Well, I guess I just feel that you wouldn't!"

"Why don't you give me a try? Maybe I'll surprise you," Simon bragged.

"I doubt it." Pinka smirked.

"Okay. If you want to lug all that anger around and let it make you feel bad, there is nothing I can do!" Simon firmly stated then turned to walk away.

Pinka quickly looked back and cried out, "Wait a minute!"

Simon hurried to the little Rhue and grabbed her up in his arms. She sobbed on his shoulder like a baby while he gently patted her back. "It's okay; everything will be all right," he chanted.

Pinka finally calmed down enough to speak. "I have this strange feeling sometimes, and it feels bad. I don't like it, but I can't get rid of it!"

Simon was concerned. "What is this feeling? Describe it," he asked.

"Uh…well, that is hard to do!"

"You must try. I want to help you."

"Uh…uh…I'll try," Pinka stammered. "The bad feeling comes when Neopoleana seems to be giving Winglet all the attention. She holds her all the time. The baby Rhue even gets rocked. I feel left out," she cried with anguish.

Simon hugged her tightly. "Aw, Pinka. I know the Mother Rhue doesn't realize you get *jealous* over Winglet," he stated in a calm manner.

Now Pinka absolutely did not like the sound of this word "jealous" whatsoever. With a grimaced face, she firmly stated, "I am not jealous!"

"Calm down, Pinka!" Simon ordered. "I cannot help you if you're going to be defensive. You are not the only one who has ever felt jealous."

"I'm not?"

"Of course not. I've felt it many times before," Simon assured her.

"You have had this bad feeling?" Pinka squealed.

Simon recanted. "Oh yes. My Mom kept my baby cousin for two days one time when I was younger. I thought she had forgotten I even existed! I really don't like admitting to this… ugh…but at times I felt….uh…hate toward my baby cousin. Isn't that awful?" he cried. "However, I realize now it was from the jealousy."

Pinka gasped. "Oh, Simon, I'm so ashamed for having the same feeling sometimes toward Winglet. She is just a baby and I love her so much. I just feel jealous sometimes. I'm confused!"

"So was I," Simon admitted.

"How did you get unconfused?" Pinka asked with hope.

"Well, my Mom noticed how my behavior had changed. One day she questioned me, and I answered her questions truthfully. It was hard, but I got through it."

"Oh my goodness! You mean that you admitted to your mother you were…uh…jealous over your baby cousin?" Pinka gasped with anxiety.

"I had to get it all out of my system! But guess what?" Simon asked.

"What?"

"It turned out that most of what I was jealous over came from me not understanding!" he exclaimed.

"Huh?" Pinka shrugged.

"My mom explained it to me. A baby requires a lot of attention. They are curious and can get into things that will harm them. When I was a baby, my mom gave me this same kind of attention," Simon informed her.

"So when I was a baby, I received the kind of attention like Winglet is getting now?" Pinka asked.

"That's right. Neopoleana is forever telling you Rhues how much she loves you. She goes in the tallest tree every day and stands for hours with her *golden wings* spread. She does this out of unconditional love for you. She knows you will die if she doesn't provide power and light to Rhueland. Don't let what you think you see overshadow what is real." Simon preached with wisdom he had gained from Neopoleana.

"Do you think the Mother Rhue has noticed my bad behavior?" Pinka asked.

"Oh yes. She was ready to check on you immediately after you walked off in a huff," Simon answered.

Pinka's mouth dropped open as she gasped. She immediately covered it with her hand. "Oh, Simon, I bet my mother already had it figured out about my jealousy."

"I don't doubt that whatsoever," Simon responded.

"Now I'm going to feel funny around her, wondering if she knows my problem," Pinka stated, sounding rather insecure. "What should I say to Neopoleana?"

"Well, you could just give the Mother Rhue a warm hug and tell her you love her and that you know she loves you," Simon suggested. "She will most likely realize that you have worked through your jealousy."

Pinka squealed with excitement. "Oh, thank you, Simon. That is what I will do! You have helped me so much that I feel better already!" She then kissed him on his cheek, causing him to blush with pride.

The two scurried back to the group, and Pinka immediately ran to Neopoleana with stretched-out arms. The Mother Rhue kept one arm around Winglet and latched on to her with the other.

"I love you, Mama! And I know you love all of us," Pinka sweetly whispered.

"It cannot be measured, my child," Neopoleana confirmed as she pulled Pinka close. "Do you feel better now?" she asked, looking toward Simon and winking.

"Yes, I am much better now," Pinka responded while cuddling close to the Mother Rhue's breast as all the wonder and insecurities she had built up inside melted away.

Simon walked over to Fuzzle and laid his head back against his soft body. He closed his eyes and thought of how nice it had sounded to hear Pinka call Neopoleana "Mama" once again. He grinned to himself while thinking, *The Rhues are something else! I just can't help but love them!*

New Places, New Friends

After being refreshed from the cozy nap, everyone was anxious to journey onward. Neopoleana prepared to fly ahead with Winglet as Blubbles, Gurggles, Squiggly, Malo, and Razzle made preparations to ride with Chuckatoo and Flutta. "Simon, you will be traveling down a new road," the Mother Rhue informed him. "The Rhues and I have been down this road many times. It goes through the center of Graywood Forest, which is home to the wild creatures of Rhueland."

Simon gasped. "I thought all the wild creatures lived in Gruhland!"

"Oh no. We have many beautiful, wild, and free creatures existing in Rhueland. Graywood Forest belongs to them. It is their home, but they do not mind if we use the winding road, which goes through the center of the forest, for traveling," Neopoleana explained. "However, we never, under any circumstances, go into their territory," she added.

Simon felt rather anxious. "Why can't we go into the forest?"

"As I stated, Graywood Forest is the wild creatures' habitat. They are happy and contented living there alone. We should always respect this and leave them in peace and harmony, just as they do us," Neopoleana informed him.

Simon smiled. "I understand."

"I shall meet you in the orchid field, beyond the forest," the Mother Rhue said before parting with Winglet. Flutta and Chuckatoo immediately followed behind. Simon and the other Rhues waved until they were out of sight, and the squeals from Blubbles, Gurggles, Squiggly, Malo, and Razzle had faded away.

Simon quickly boarded Bunnita, getting in behind a smiling Pinka. "I hurried to Bunnita so that we would have a soft ride," she giggled in a whisper.

Blinko, Tooty, and Truffles had latched on to Fuzzle and were ready to go, leaving Jetta and Slurple stuck with Turckle's rough ride. However, they didn't complain, because they knew the old turtle would fuss at them.

The group had only traveled a short distance when the open area came to an abrupt end. Simon was in awe of the huge, dense forest directly in front of them. The creatures slowly entered the wide clearing that lead to the winding road to begin their journey through the center of Graywood Forest.

Soon Simon began to notice how the much too quiet forest was becoming thick with plants; and tall trees with huge gray trunks that soared high into the air. He and the Rhues and creatures stretched their necks backward to see enchanting leaves of purple and yellow. Only traces of the coral sky now trickled through, for these thick, tall trees seemed to consume all the space above. The thick, green foliage and plants consumed all the space below, except for the road.

An eerie feeling began to grip Simon's body and mind. He felt as if someone or something was watching him. "This place seems haunted to me!" he yelled out.

"What does that mean?" Pinka asked.

Simon begins to chant in chilling tones. "It means this forest full of vicious, wild creatures could decide to hunt us down and eat us alive!" He then growled, putting his hands in motion as if he were a giant grizzly bear. "Grr…Grr…" The Rhues screamed in terror, causing him to laugh.

Turckle shouted, "Simon! Please! The Rhues have never been frightened while traveling through Graywood Forest! Now look at them! You have them scared half to death!"

The tiny Rhues were trembling fiercely with fright. They could not speak, but loud shouts were displayed with slurps and honks. Blinko's snout flashed on to a brilliant brightness, and Pinka glowed like a candle. Jetta shook so violently that Turckle could feel the vibrations. Truffles's chocolate scent became strong, permeating everyone's nostrils.

"Well, I'm sorry for scaring the Rhues, but I do not like Graywood Forest!"

Turckle spoke with authority. "Let me tell you, Simon. We have been down this road hundreds of times. The creatures have never bothered us, because we know to stay on this wide path. Therefore, they trust us and have no reason to bring us harm. Now calm down and quit upsetting the Rhues. We have a long distance to go to get through Graywood Forest," he scolded.

Simon apologized to the Rhues. "I really am sorry for scaring you. Actually, I was frightened, so I used a scare tactic on you hoping to feel better." He then added, "I was afraid before there was a need to be." He remembered how he had told Malo the exact same thing. "Practice what you preach, Simon," he muttered softly to himself.

Turckle reminded the Rhues of how often they had journeyed down this road before and were never afraid. Soon they had calmed down and were laughing and singing, just like old times. However, these moments of tranquility were very short-lived. Simon suddenly screamed so loud Turckle thought he had gotten hurt. "What is it now?" he asked with despair.

"Look over there behind that thick bunch of plants!" Simon exclaimed while pointing. Everyone turned their heads together to look at the monster-sized gray wolf and enormously huge red fox.

"I knew it! I knew it!" Simon shouted. "Those vicious, wild animals are stalking us! We don't stand a chance!"

The creatures and Rhues now chuckled at Simon's fear. "It's not funny!" he harked in defense. "Now just run! What are you waiting for? Run for your lives and run to save mine!"

"That will be enough," Turckle boldly demanded. The strength of this old turtle's voice caused Simon to become amazingly silent right then. "That is Roxy, the red fox, and Timber, the gray wolf. They are just out scrounging for food and have no interest in us except maybe to stare out of curiosity. As I have repeated several times, they stay in Graywood Forest, living in the wild," Turckle explained. "Now let's travel onward!" he commanded. "Neopoleana and the others will be waiting for us at the lake."

Right then, Simon forgot about Timber and Roxy. 'I didn't know we would be going to a lake!" he squealed.

"What about the far tunnel?" he immediately asked. "I'm supposed to be going home, you know?"

"I guess we forgot to mention it!" Turckle snickered. "We must cross Lake Azure. The far tunnel lies right beyond the other side of it."

"That's cool," Simon stated as he thought of how classy Lake Azure sounded. "Is the lake very big?" he asked.

"Do you remember the other lake you visited when you first arrived in Rhueland?" Turckle asked. Simon nodded yes. "Lake Azure makes that one look like a mud puddle!"

"You must be halfway across before you even begin to see the other side," Fuzzle commented.

Simon's eyes grew big with anticipation of seeing this huge lake. Then he asked, "What is on the other side besides the sealed tunnel?"

"Oh, it's a continuation of Graywood Forest. Lake Azure sits in the middle of the forest," Bunnita explained.

"Well, what are we waiting for? Let's journey onward!" Simon commanded. "I'm anxious to get off this road!"

The creatures pressed forward. Soon the Rhues were lulled in and out of naps. During this quiet time, Simon became so wrapped up in thoughts; they all ran together. He wondered what day and time it was at home and what his parents were doing. He thought about the statue of him the stone figures had built. *I will always be a part of their world,* he thought with pride. Quickly, memories of Gruhland and Rhueland entered into his mind. *These lands in The Third Dimension are just so incredible. It's hard to believe they actually exist.*

Simon's thoughts quickly turned toward Bronzella. *Gosh! I hated, in a way, to see the sphinx fall apart. If it had not been for her, I would have never gotten to see these beautiful lands. I would have never met the adorable Rhues or Neopoleana! I would have never laid eyes upon the wonderful creatures!* he exclaimed in his mind.

Why did the sphinx have to be so selfish? he questioned with anguish. *She actually destroyed herself through the bad attitude she clung to. What a waste of such a beautiful, muscular, and powerful creature!* he thought as one lonely teardrop rolled from his eye.

Simon's thoughts abruptly ended with cheers bellowing out from the Rhues and creatures. He regained his focus, realizing they were headed off this dreadful road. A beautiful green open area was just ahead! "The lake lies just beyond this field. From hereon out, we will be traveling downhill," Turckle explained.

Simon was busy gazing at the huge meadow of clovers and wild flowers when he was jolted by Bunnita's sudden hop into this field of paradise, for she adored the taste of sweet, succulent green clovers. The Rhues were already having the time of their lives frolicking through the fragrant garden. Simon joined the gang for fun and play! Truffles and Slurple took turns with Jetta and Blinko, riding Fuzzle down through the soft, thick bed of clovers. The caterpillar would go very fast then abruptly stop, tossing them onto the soft, green mat. Giggles of delight filled the air!

Turckle munched on plants nearby, listening to the sounds of happiness. *Simon will be missed so much, but I'm glad he was brought to our world, even for this short time,* he thought.

His chain of thoughts was broken when Pinka ran up and asked with excitement, "Will you sing and dance with us, Turckle? Tooty is going to play special music on her snout!" The old reptile swallowed his last mouthful of tasty, young clovers and then followed her back to join the group.

They sang and danced together right there in the field until it wore them out. "Well, I think we overdid it," Simon laughed as he collapsed to the ground. The Rhues fell asleep one by one beside him, snuggling close for a short nap. Turckle, Bunnita, and Fuzzle stood close by to catnap.

Simon's mind drifted into the most terrible dream he had experienced. He had just exited the far tunnel, but instead of Karen and Jim greeting him, Bronzella was there in waiting! She grabbed him up, snarling and laughing right in his face. "We're going back to Gruhland, and you are going to do all my dirty work for the rest of your life," the sphinx taunted, shining her sharp razor teeth. "This time you will stay forever, for I'm going to keep you locked up!" She smirked with vicious tones before scooping him into her huge mouth, clenching him between her deadly razor teeth. She quickly darted away, running as fast as she could go with Simon screaming at the top of his lungs.

Thank goodness he was awakened by Flutta's call. "Wake up! Simon, wake up!"

Slowly he opened his eyes to see the beautiful, colorful butterfly staring down at him.

"You were screaming in your sleep," she told.

Simon responded in frightful tones while sweating and shaking in terror. "I had a nightmare about Bronzella. She had me clutched between her teeth, heading back to Gruhland!"

"Thank goodness it was only a...uh...*nightmare*, as you called it. Shouldn't it be called a *daymare?*" Flutta asked with a snicker.

Simon immediately frowned. "Haha! How cute! Just never mind about that. I don't feel like explaining about a figure of speech. Can't you see that I'm totally distraught? This is not the time to be joking!" he scolded.

"Well, excuse me! I'm sorry, but actually I was serious," Flutta rebutted. "Anyway, it was only a dream! Forget about it," she encouraged.

"It's just that it seemed so real!" Simon exclaimed, shaking his head in disbelief.

"Why were you sleeping here anyway? You know we've been waiting for you at the lake," Flutta scolded. "Neopoleana was starting to worry and sent me to check you."

"We stopped to play in the field and then got tired," Simon explained. "The Rhues must have been exhausted to have slept through my screaming!" He laughed while nudging them awake.

"I'll fly back down to the lake and let Neopoleana know you are safe and on your way," Flutta stated as she took off.

Simon finished waking the group. Soon the sleepyhead Rhues were boarded upon the creatures' backs and ready to go. The slow ride down the rather steep hill was quiet, for no one was yet fully awake. "I wasn't ready to get up!" Pinka sassily fussed.

"Neither was I!" Jetta agreed.

"It was really a very short nap," Bunnita pointed out.

"Oh, but Lake Azure will soon be in sight. That will wake us up!" Turckle promised.

"I can't wait to see it!" Simon exclaimed as the group continued to journey downward. In a few short minutes, open, grassy land was in sight.

"The lake is over there beyond this long flatland area," Fuzzle spoke with excitement while pointing.

"Hurry, go fast!" Blinko commanded. "I want to see Mama."

The creatures moved at a fast pace, but as usual, Turckle was left behind. "We'll be the last ones there!" Pinka griped in frustration.

"Now don't start your whining! We'll get there soon enough!" Turckle scolded.

"Look!" Simon suddenly screamed out. "There's the lake! There's Lake Azure!"

The creatures and Rhues looked to see Neopoleana gazing their way. "There's Mama!" Blinko yelled out with a blink of his snout. "Let me down!" he shouted to Bunnita.

"I want down too!" Tooty screamed at Fuzzle.

Soon all the Rhues, except for Pinka and Simon, had slid down the creatures' sides and took off running toward the Mother

Rhue. Tooty was tooting her snout loudly as Slurple slurped and Blinko flashed his snout. Truffles's scent was stronger than ever, and Razzle glowed like a luminous raspberry! Malo bounced along as Jetta ran ahead of them in her usual fast, waddling pace. "Mama! Mama!" she shouted with delight.

Neopoleana walked farther out to greet them. Winglet was in her arms, squirming almost beyond control to get down, so she turned the baby Rhue loose. Immediately, she flew toward Jetta, who grabbed her in her arms. Whoops! She was too big for Jetta to hold, and both tumbled to the ground. Neopoleana laughed at the sight while running to help them up.

Soon the other Rhues were with their mother, scampering for hugs. Flutta and Chuckatoo rested quietly by the lake's shoreline waiting to complete the journey while everyone else was on the lookout for Turckle and Pinka. Suddenly, Blinko shouted out, "Here they come!"

The old turtle slowly made his way out of the grassland where the others were patiently waiting. Pinka quickly jumped from his back and into Neopoleana's arms, squealing with pure delight. She reached around her neck hugging her tight. "I love you, Mama!" she said with excitement and planted a kiss on her cheek.

"I love you too, Pinka," the Mother Rhue warmly responded.

Jetta was tugging at Neopoleana's long downy coat. "What is it, Jetta?"

"I also love you!" she exclaimed.

"Well, I certainly know that, just as you know I love all my little Rhues," Neopoleana confirmed as she looked down into the innocent eyes of each one.

Suddenly, everyone's attention was captured by Simon's exciting shouts. "This is beautiful and marvelous!" he cried while looking around. Lake Azure was calm and peaceful. The huge ocean of crystal water was surrounded by the green beauty of the forest on one side. On the other side, teal-green and fuchsia-pink mountains soared beyond the coral sky. Nothing but sparkling, clear water could be seen straight ahead. It appeared to have no end!

Simon squealed, "What awesome mountains! They are so tall I can't even see their peaks."

"The mountains peek far beyond the coral sky. The Rivers of Strength lie on the other side of those massive boulders," Neopoleana explained.

"Do they get their color from the rivers?" Simon asked.

"Yes, they do. These huge mountains protect us from the excess hot molten by carrying it away from our lands," the Mother Rhue informed him.

Simon gasped as a thought ran through his mind. *I wonder if this is where our volcanoes back in my world come from.*

He quickly diminished this thought and looked out across the lake. In the distance, two white figures appeared to be moving in their direction. The objects were traveling slowly side by side. This reminded Simon of two huge ocean liners. "Look over there!" he bellowed. "What are those things?"

"They are swans! They are swans!" Chuckatoo shouted loudly from high up a nearby tree.

"The lake is their home! The lake is their home!" Blubbles added, repeating himself.

"You are beginning to sound like Chuckatoo," Simon exclaimed.

"I am? I am?" Blubbles asked with a giggle.

"Yes, you are!" Simon yelled. I guess when you rode with him, you picked up his way of talking without realizing it."

"Well, I'm glad you made me aware of it! Well, I'm glad"— Blubbles stopped in the middle of his repeat sentence—"I see what you mean," he stated. Simon laughed along with him over the issue then walked closer to Lake Azure's border with all the creatures and Rhues strolling down to join him.

"The swans are Fredrix and Grace," Neopoleana informed Simon. "You can ride with them across the lake to reach the far tunnel, if you'd like."

Simon became totally excited. "Wow! I would love it! I could pretend I'm on a cruise ship headed to a remote island!" The Rhues and creatures laughed at his sense of humor.

"The swans' names—Fredrix and Grace—they sound rather ritzy, if you know what I mean," Simon remarked to Neopoleana. "Are they *high fu-luting*?"

As wise as she was, the Mother Rhue looked dumbfounded to this question. "Simon! I have no idea what you are talking about! I don't like the sound of this phrase 'high fu-luting.' What does it mean?"

Now Simon was perplexed. He had heard his mom use this word a couple of times but never really knew its full meaning. After pondering a minute, he spoke. "Well, I'll try to explain it the best I can. You use this word when you think someone believes they are...uh...upper class...uh...better than you...I guess that's how to put it," he stammered then sighed, being glad he had gotten through that explanation.

Neopoleana also sighed. "Well, Simon, all I can say is that Fredrix and Grace are very nice swans. Yes, they are very prim and proper, but that is just their style. I'm sure our style is a bit odd to them also," she informed him. "You know, I believe 'graceful' and 'elegant' are much better words to use to describe these swans," she added. Simon nodded in agreement.

As Fredrix and Grace glided closer in, Simon realized just what Neopoleana was talking about. These huge swans were truly graceful and elegant! They were also very classy. Both were white as pure snow, but Fredrix had black markings around his neck resembling a fancy bow tie. Grace was wearing a necklace of fuchsia-pink and teal-green stones made by the stone figures, which complimented her enchanting green eyes. Fredrix had contrasting pale-blue eyes.

As the swans reached the shore, the Rhues and creatures cheered. Neopoleana greeted the sophisticated pair and then introduced Simon.

"It is utterly delightful to meet you," Fredrix spoke in his strong style.

"And it is nice to meet you, sir," Simon cordially responded.

"How do you like Lake Azure? Do you not find it simply gorgeous?" Grace questioned with class.

"Oh, it is beautiful, madam," Simon replied as the swans smiled with pride. "I'm going across the lake to the far tunnel. Neopoleana is unsealing it so that I may journey home," he informed them.

"That sounds very interesting," Fredrix commented as Simon looked them over. They reminded him of a rich millionaire couple from Bellaire. He most certainly liked their style!

Simon was a bit hesitant but asked the swans anyway, "Uh… may I ride with you across the lake?"

"We shall be leaving shortly to cruise back over to the other side. It shall be our pleasure to give you a ride," Grace answered with sheer elegance.

"Do you think some of the Rhues could also ride?"

"I do not believe that shall be a problem," Fredrix answered.

Simon thanked them, and the Rhues immediately clapped then began arguing over who would get to ride which swan. Of course, Neopoleana was standing close by to help solve the hopeless case. "Why are you arguing?" she calmly asked.

"I want to ride with Grace!" Pinka whined.

"I do too," Jetta added.

"I want to ride with Fredrix!" Squiggly cried.

"We do too!" Gurggles and Tooty exclaimed.

All the other Rhues then chimed in. The Mother Rhue could not understand which Rhue wanted what due to all the chatter. "Silence right this minute!" she scolded in a firm voice. The Rhues obeyed without question. "It's a wonder either Fredrix or Grace would want any of you to ride with them! Just listening to you arguing is enough to give anyone a headache!" she exclaimed.

"We understand how the Rhues may show differences of opinions in a loud manner, but they must behave while crossing the lake," Fredrix made clear.

"I believe you owe Fredrix and Grace an apology," Neopoleana stated as the Rhues downed their heads.

They slowly looked up, then each took their turn apologizing. "I'm sorry, Mr. and Mrs. Swans," Pinka spoke with compassion.

"I'm sorry too," Truffles followed. Soon all the apologies have been made, Fredrix and Grace accepting them with honor.

"Now I have something to say to the Rhues," Neopoleana boldly spoke, causing big eyes and bewildered looks among the group. "Have you forgotten that you have ridden the swans before?"

The Rhues' mouths dropped open, and they looked at each other sheepishly. "Oh me, there's plenty of room for all of us!" Razzle blushed.

"Yeah, I can't believe we forgot that!" Gurggles yelled out.

"See? You were so excited that you were not clearly thinking. You were arguing for no logical reason at all," the Mother Rhue pointed out. Simon couldn't help but snicker, causing the creatures to join in. Even Neopoleana and Fredrix and Grace chuckled softly.

"We were being silly, weren't we, Mama?" Blinko asked.

"Yes, but we are all silly at times," the wise Mother Rhue proclaimed as Blinko hugged her.

"Well, is everyone ready to go?" Flutta asked loudly.

"Yes! Yes!" the Rhues shouted together as they ran to board the swans.

"Hold it! Halt right there!" Fredrix commanded. "Surely you haven't forgotten that we must first extend our steps."

Pinka stammered. "Uh...uh...We haven't forgotten that."

"Just like me! Just like me!" Chuckatoo screeched.

"That's right, Chuckatoo. The swans can extend their wings down into steps the same as you," Malo acknowledged.

Everyone stood back and gazed in awe as Fredrix and Grace extended their strong white wings downward, creating a set of long staircases. The Rhues quickly scurried up, half boarding upon Fredrix and half upon Grace.

Neopoleana noticed Simon looking around in wonder. "What is it?" she asked.

"Where is Winglet?"

Neopoleana smiled and looked toward Fuzzle. Simon's eyes followed. "Well, isn't that cute!" he squealed to see Winglet buried inside the caterpillar's soft coat. All that was showing were her closed eyelids and short snout, which was bobbing up and down as she snoozed. The Mother Rhue quietly walked over and dug the baby Rhue out then laid her gently across her shoulder. "We'll meet you on the other side of Lake Azure," she whispered. "Are you ready, Chuckatoo?"

"I'm ready! I'm ready!" the hyper bird responded while shaking his Indian headdress feathers.

"What about you?" she softly asked Flutta.

"Shoot! I've been warmed up for several minutes already," she replied.

"Well, let's fly on over!" the Mother Rhue commanded as she took to the coral sky. The group watched as Chuckatoo and Flutta joined her, noticing how majestic the three looked, soaring high against the background of teal-green and fuchsia-pink mountains.

Simon then hurried along to catch his ride with Fredrix. Just as he was about to climb the "wing steps," he suddenly stopped in wonder of the creatures. "Hey! How are you getting to the far tunnel, or can you even get there?" he asked with concern.

Bunnita chuckled. "Of course, we can get there, Simon! We always swim the distance."

"What!"

"You heard Bunnita right. We swim across Lake Azure," Fuzzle confirmed.

Simon then roamed his eyes at Turckle with a look of great concern. "What kind of expression is that upon your face? Why are you giving me such a worried stare?" the old turtle questioned.

Simon became tongue-tied. "Uh...uh...well...uh...I'm concerned," he stammered.

"Why?" Turckle asked in a gruff manner.

Simon recanted. "Uh...well, don't you remember what happened back in the orchid field when you found Winglet missing? You took off running and gave out of air in no time. You passed out! How could you possibly make it even halfway across Lake Azure?" he shouted, becoming anxious.

Turckle grimaced. "That only happened because I was overwhelmed with fear. I was already breathing hard before I started running!"

"Uh...well, you are not as young as you used to be. Your body has slowed down. You could get out there and tire out...uh... then drown!" Simon anxiously evaluated.

"So you think I'm too old to swim the distance of this huge lake, don't you?" Turckle shouted defensively.

"I'm just concerned, that is all. You lack the stamina a young turtle has," Simon rebuked.

Now Turckle was really hot! His preaching began. "Let me tell you something! I walk, exercise, and eat plenty of good food every single day. Why, I'm as fit as any young turtle around, even more so than the lazy ones. I may be a bit slow, but I certainly measure up!"

"Oh, I didn't realize you had been taking such good care of yourself," Simon responded, sounding surprised.

"You may also like to know that I can stretch out my legs and float on the water if I choose. I most certainly will not drown," Turckle emphasized.

"Wow! I didn't know you could float," Simon exclaimed.

"You assumed too much." Turckle smirked. "Age is just a number, having no limits. It does not mean that when I reach a certain number in age, I'm supposed to stop living as I choose. In other words, as long as I can walk, swim, or anything else I choose to do, then I'll keep doing them. That is what keeps me young."

"Calm down, Turckle! I understand what you are saying. I'm sorry for criticizing you," Simon apologized.

"Aw, I guess it's okay. You really didn't know any better," Turckle responded. "Just remember to always stay in good health so you can enjoy life at any age."

Simon smiled. "You can count on that, Turckle. My mom and dad tell me the same thing. I promise to listen to them and you.

Shouts from the Rhues suddenly broke their conversation. "Hurry up! We're ready to go!"

"Okay, I'm coming!" Simon exclaimed as he turned to scurry up the "wing steps."

"Bye, Turckle! I'll see you on the other side of the lake."

Simon plopped down close to Razzle and Malo atop Fredrix's huge, flat back. Squiggly, Blubbles, and Tooty sat directly across from them. Jetta had found a cozy spot near the swan's long neck. The other Rhues were seated atop Grace and were shouting back and forth to each other until Grace called them down. "Sh! Sh! Now don't be so loud, and please stay seated during the trip. Is that understood?" she firmly asked.

All the Rhues replied with "Yes, ma'am."

Fredrix and Grace wheeled in their "wing steps" in sequence. Slowly, they pulled away from the shore, traveling side by side.

"We'll swim close by the swans," Fuzzle suggested as he slinked into the crystal blue water. Bunnita and Turckle followed.

Simon stretched out to be more comfortable. "Man, what a smooth ride. It's just like taking a cruise!" he stated with contentment. He looked up at the enchanting coral sky and then glanced toward the gigantic teal-green and fuchsia-pink mountains. The sounds were faint, but he could hear hot molten churning inside these tall, massive boulders. A pink-and-green haze mingled together near the mountains, creating a magical beauty that would take your breath away.

Soon Simon decides to turn over and then crawls near the edge of Fredrix's back. He stared down into the deep, crystal water. Suddenly he screams out, "There are giant fish in this lake!"

"Of course. They are our main source of food," Fredrix explained.

Simon was totally fascinated with the huge, fast-swimming fish. Actually, they weren't much bigger than goldfish compared to the size of the swans. "Wow, these fish have the shiniest gold color I've ever seen!" he exclaimed and then chuckled loudly as their giant suction-cup mouths opened and closed.

The Rhues watched in anticipation as Simon began to play with the golden fish, which reminded him of giant bars of gold. Cautiously, he stuck his hand down in the water near where a couple was swimming. Quickly, he pulled his hand up when they came near. Over and over, he did this as the Rhues watched with big eyes. Suddenly, a suction-cup mouth sucked his hand in! Simon screamed in terror, setting off a chain reaction of frightful screams from the Rhues! He wasn't in pain, but he didn't like this strange, constrictive feeling around his hand. He screamed at the top of his lungs. "It's going to suck my hand completely off!" Thank goodness this scared the golden fish, making it turn loose.

"Simon, were you taunting the fish?" Fredrix firmly asked.

"I just wanted to play with them," he whined while examining his hand. The Rhues giggled as they thought of how funny the incident had been.

"It's not funny! That fish could have sucked my hand off!" Simon protested.

"Well, you cannot be playing with them like that. The fish become upset!" Fredrix scolded.

"Yes, sir!"

Right at that moment, something jumped out of the water flying low above the swans. Simon and the Rhues ducked down screaming and placing their hands quickly over their heads. Simon peeped between his fingers to see one of the golden fish soaring. Suddenly, another jumped high from the water and began flying around. "My goodness! These are flying fish!" he muttered to himself with anxiousness. He and the Rhues watched in awe as the golden fish flew up, down, and in circles. At one point, they dove close to their heads with their suction-cup mouths opening and closing in fast motion. This brought distressful thoughts to the group, for it reminded them of Sqhawk! They certainly did not want to contend with a flying fish snatching one of them up and taking them under water!

Finally, the two golden fish dove back down through the water. Simon and the Rhues remained still for a minute or so until they heard Fredrix speak. "They won't be back. Only a few of them fly once or twice daily."

"Whew! I'm glad that's over!" Simon stressed.

"I am too," Jetta agreed. "I thought those fish were going to eat us alive!"

Fredrix and Grace chuckled. "I believe the golden fish flew at this time in show of their agitation," Grace contended.

"Well, I certainly will not be playing with them anymore!" Simon clearly stated.

"Just relax and enjoy the rest of your cruise. We're already halfway across Lake Azure," Fredrix informed him.

Simon and the Rhues calmed down and then lay back. Being serene once again, Tooty began playing a nice, slow tune on her saxophone snout. Blubbles lay on his back, blowing bubbles out and over the crystal blue water as Simon counted each one that passed above in his direction. The Rhues watched with contentment.

Soon the peaceful music and watching and counting bubbles had lulled them all to sleep. Fredrix and Grace just smiled at one another as they continued to cruise along.

Beyond Lake Azure

Simon and the Rhues napped for the rest of the journey. As Fredrix and Grace approached the lake's shore, they could see Neopoleana looking out over the water. Winglet was in her arms, pointing toward them. Bunnita, Turckle, and Fuzzle were sprawled out in a small open area, drying off. Chuckatoo was resting in a nearby tall tree while Flutta dozed beneath it.

Fredrix and Grace cruised slowly up to the shoreline and stopped. Neopoleana walked out to greet them with Winglet squirming in her arms. "Go to Simon!" the Mother Rhue prodded. Immediately, she flew near him yelling, "Wat up, wat up!" Her baby talk awakened the entire gang.

It took the group a while to realize where they were. "Gosh, we missed half the trip!" Simon complained as he wiped sleep out of his eyes.

"But you got some good rest," Grace stated.

The Rhues were stretching and yawning as Winglet flittered around them. "Stop being a pest!" Pinka scolded.

Simon chuckled while turning his eyes toward Fredrix and Grace. "Thanks for the ride," he remarked while watching their beautiful wings flow down and become steps.

"You are quite welcome," they remarked.

"I don't guess I'll be seeing you again," Simon commented with a twinge of sadness.

"We will never forget you," Grace responded.

"It was a pleasure to have gotten to meet you," Fredrix added.

"May I give you a hug?" Simon blushed.

"Why, we would be honored," Grace replied elegantly.

Simon quickly hopped down the "wing steps" and ran to face the graceful swans. They bent their heads low for warm hugs.

"We hope you get home safe and sound, Simon," Grace spoke.

"Oh, I'll be just fine," he remarked with confidence while scurrying off to help the Rhues climb down the steps.

"Come on, Winglet!" Simon commanded. The baby Rhue giggled as she flew down into his arms. All the other Rhues quickly waddled down the steps and ran to Neopoleana's side.

"We're going to fish for food now," Fredrix stated as he and Grace reeled in their steps. Slowly, they floated away, moving into deeper water. Simon and the Rhues shouted "bye" until the gracious pair was out of sight.

"I'm glad I got to meet them," Simon told Neopoleana as he handed Winglet to her.

She smiled and said, "Me too, Simon."

As the group turned to walk toward the trees, the splashy sound and cold feel of gigantic water droplets caused them to chill in their tracks. "Hey! Wait for me!" the deep voice shouted.

Simon would recognize that baritone sound anytime and anywhere. Immediately, he whirled around and gasped with happiness. "Trog, you old bullfrog. You came!"

"Of course, I did!"

"Where have you been?" Simon asked as the Rhues jumped and played around him.

Trog bellowed, "Well, I walked off to find a quiet place to myself so that I could rest peacefully. I guess it worked, because I fell asleep and slept a very long time. When I awoke, everyone had already left. I hurried to Lake Azure, jumped in, and swam fast to get here!"

"I'm certainly glad you caught up with us," Neopoleana commented.

"We are too," Pinka agreed, speaking for the Rhues.

"We are heading to the far tunnel now," Simon informed Trog.

"That's what I had figured."

"Which way do we go, Neopoleana?" Simon asked.

"Well, there is a narrow path that way inside Graywood Forest," she answered while pointing toward a collage of trees.

Simon snapped, "Graywood Forest!" I didn't think we would have to go in there again!"

"Calm down," Neopoleana whispered. "Did the wild creatures bother you when you traveled the road leading to Lake Azure?" she asked.

Simon stammered. "Uh…well…no, but there could always be a first time," he determined, causing the creatures and Rhues to snicker at his unfounded fear.

"Simon, have you not realized by now that the creatures of Graywood Forest will not harm you as long as you stay on the right path?" Neopoleana asked.

"How do you know which path is right?" he returned.

The Mother Rhue smiled, moved close to Simon, and looked down into his eyes. "As long as you can see light, then you are assured of being on the right path. If the path you take leads to darkness, then you know to turn back," she explained with wisdom.

These words sent a chill down Simon's spine, but he understood. "The deep woods of Graywood Forest are dark and scary. This is the wild creatures' territory. It is always dark and frightful. Am I right, Neopoleana?" he asked.

"You are correct, Simon," she replied with pride. "If you get off on the wrong path, you will know it by the feeling you get—there will be no mistake."

Simon swallowed hard. "Oh, you don't have to worry about me. I'll stay on the right path!" he promised.

Everyone chuckled, and then Bunnita yelled out, "Let's get going!"

"I agree to that," Fuzzle blurted.

"You want a ride?" Trog asked Simon.

"No thanks. I'll walk with Neopoleana and Winglet," he replied, showing his anxiety.

"May Truffles and I ride?" Pinka sweetly asked the bullfrog.

"Of course, you can. Hop on up!"

All the Rhues boarded atop the creatures and were soon heading down the narrow road into Graywood Forest. Even Flutta and Chuckatoo had decided to walk with Neopoleana this time.

"This path is short. We are very close to the far tunnel," the Mother Rhue informed Simon.

He felt his stomach knot up from both anticipation and fear. "Well, I don't guess it will be much longer before I'll be heading home."

Neopoleana gave him a warm smile. "Oh, your mom and dad will be completely overjoyed to see their 'little boy' again," she commented.

"I'll be happy to see them. I've really missed my parents a lot," Simon responded as he glanced toward the Rhues. Great pains of sadness showed upon their faces, for so much love had grown between him and the Rhues.

Squiggly spoke out, "The statue of you is nice, but it will never replace the real you."

"It cannot move, nor can it talk!" Pinka sassily pointed out.

"It can't play with us, and it can't make us laugh!" Razzle sadly added.

Blinko sobbed. "We will enjoy looking at the statue and thinking of you, but it will never have feelings like you."

Simon slightly downed his head, for he had no idea what to say to the Rhues. Neopoleana stepped in. "Okay now, you're getting all worked up, though you knew the time was coming when Simon would be returning home."

"Yes, ma'am," Slurple acknowledged. "But we still wish he could stay here with us forever!"

When he heard the word "wish," Simon remembered the stones he had kept. He quietly slid his hand down inside his pocket to make sure he had not lost them. *Yeah, they're still there*, he thought with gratitude while feeling each tiny, oval stone.

The Rhues finally calmed down and slid off the creatures' backs to walk with Simon, wanting to be close to their friend. Quickly, they grouped around him and then took turns, two at a time, holding his hands while moving onward.

The rest of the journey was quiet except for a few rustling sounds down in the brush. Simon wondered if Timber and Roxy were slinking around, watching their movements. These thoughts quickly vanished when another huge field of orchids seemed to have appeared right before his eyes. "Oh man! I had no idea there was another nectar field left in Rhueland!" he exclaimed through drools of hungry joy.

"Oh yes, my child. Nectar fields are plentiful here. There is at least a dozen more that you have not seen," Neopoleana exclaimed.

Simon's eyes had grown big. "Wow!" he shouted.

"I'm hungry!" Pinka whined in.

"We are all hungry!" Malo announced.

"Can we eat?" Jetta asked the Mother Rhue.

"That was my intention," she replied, causing the Rhues to dance around in delight.

"Now listen to me!" Neopoleana commanded. All the creatures, Simon, and the Rhues immediately became attentive to her words. "I am going to feed Winglet then go to the tallest tree to spread power and light to all of Rhueland. The far tunnel, as you Rhues and creatures already know, is right beyond this field. Simon will need to rest before beginning his long journey home. After all of you eat, I suggest that everyone take a nap. However, under no circumstance whatsoever are you to leave this orchid field. You must stay put until I return. Is that understood?" she firmly asked.

"Yes, ma'am!" the group responded together.

Neopoleana smiled and said, "That's good. Now, there is one more thing."

"What is that?" Simon asked.

"Please do not overeat. If you get too full, you will become sluggish and want to sleep far too long. Then you will be droopy for the rest of our journey to the far tunnel," she explained.

Malo remembered back to when he had hogged so much nectar down he floated away. "Don't worry, Mama! We'll just have a snack of nectar!" he assured her.

"Okay then, you may go eat now," the Mother Rhue instructed in a tone that reminded Simon of one of his teachers back at Hillcrest.

The Rhues jumped up and down and clapped as they scurried along with Simon toward the huge paradise of colorful orchids. Flutta and Chuckatoo flew very low above the field and then lit close to the giant blue flowers. Bunnita and Trog hopped and leaped near them, stopping at a nice spot to munch on orchid leaves. Turckle and Fuzzle slinked in between two rows of yellow orchids. Fuzzle enjoyed a few tender flower heads while Turckle devoured the plant's bottom leaves. Simon helped feed Winglet as Neopoleana ate so she could soon fly to The Red-and-Blue Forest.

"I shall return in a couple of hours," the Mother Rhue announced before taking off with the baby Rhue. The group was so busy feeding their faces, they did not really pay much attention when she took off.

After Squiggly ate his fill of nectar, he retrieved his usual snoutful of the luscious liquid for Simon. He gobbled up the sweet confection and then boasted of his restrain. "I could use more, but Neopoleana doesn't want us to be sluggish for the journey." He then yelled, "Okay, Rhues, I think all of you have eaten enough. It's time to take a short nap!"

Truffles and Tooty snuggled up against Trog. It wasn't all that cozy, but they wanted to be near the big bullfrog, so they didn't really mind. Gurggles and Slurple bundled up inside Bunnita's fur while Blinko, Malo, Razzle, and Blubbles found comfort in nestling under Flutta's and Chuckatoo's wings. Jetta and Pinka curled up next to Simon, almost hidden inside Fuzzle's soft coat. Turckle had already fallen asleep in his own private, quiet spot.

On the Wrong Path

All the Rhues, except for Jetta and Pinka, had no problem falling fast asleep. "Simon, I can't get to sleep," Pinka whined.

"Why not?"

"Well, because I'm not sleepy!" She chuckled.

"I'm not sleepy either!" Jetta whined.

Simon stretched and yawned. "Man, I'm tired! Can't you two just rest quietly?" He begged.

"I've already done that!" Pinka fussed.

"Me too!" Jetta agreed.

"Okay! Okay! Let's not wake the others, for Pete's sake!" Simon exclaimed.

"Who is Pete?" Pinka whispered.

Simon became more agitated. "Oh, never mind. I'm getting up now. We'll walk quietly around the orchid field. Maybe this will help you get tired enough to sleep," he snapped.

The two Rhues bolted up. "I'm sure that will help," Jetta agreed.

"That's a really good idea!" Pinka bragged.

The group proceeded to tiptoe out of the rows of orchids. "Now don't make any noise! I'm certainly not in the mood to deal with more cranky Rhues!" Simon whispered. "We'll walk around the outside of the field, but that is as far as we go. Is that clear?" he firmly ordered. Jetta and Pinka nodded yes as to understanding his instructions.

The three began their walk around the huge field. "Gosh, this is boring," Simon mumbled within only a short time.

"We can walk by ourselves if you want to go lie down," Pinka stated.

"Are you kidding me? You two would probably wander off somewhere, and then I would be in trouble!" Simon exclaimed with a snicker. Jetta and Pinka grimaced at his assuming remark.

Suddenly, Pinka yelled lowly as she pointed, "Hey, look over there at that path!"

"I wonder what is there," Jetta remarked rather hauntingly.

Simon became very curious himself as he stared up the narrow, darkened road. However, he didn't let on. "Don't even think about it! You know what the Mother Rhue said!" he exclaimed.

"Yeah, we need to stay here," Pinka agreed. Jetta nodded in agreement with them.

"Come on now, get going!" Simon commanded while scooting the two along. They had walked only a short distance when he began complaining again. "Aren't you two sleepy yet? This is just so boring!"

Pinka fussed. "It is making me dizzy! I feel like I'm walking around in circles!"

Simon snickered. "That's what we are doing. This field is one big circle, you silly girl!" he teased. Pinka rolled her eyes at him but didn't say anything.

Soon Jetta whined, "I'm still not sleepy."

"Me either!" Pinka shouted. "You know, Simon, I believe it would be all right for us to walk a short distance up that path," she smoothly added.

"Now what makes you think this?"

"I figure as long as we don't lose sight of the orchid field, then we would be safe. What harm could that bring?" she pointed out.

Simon looked somewhat puzzled but felt that what Pinka said really made sense. "You're right! It wouldn't be like we were wandering a long way off. In fact, as long as we can still see the orchid field, it would be like not leaving at all," he evaluated, trying to justify his reasoning.

Jetta was elated. "Yes. Walking up that path won't be so boring!"

Quickly, they turned around and headed toward the darkened path. "Remember when the orchid field is no longer in our sight, we turn around and head back," Simon firmly instructed.

"We sure will," Pinka agreed.

"Of course," Jetta added.

Simon looked up through the long, narrow path. His eyes then skimmed the dense trees of Graywood Forest, which surrounded the entire area. It was quiet; almost too serene. Right then, something deep inside him started gnawing away. He just passed this feeling off as being anxious. "Okay, you guys. Are you ready to go?" he asked.

"Yes!" they replied with big smiles.

Pinka grabbed his right hand and Jetta latched on to his left one. Slowly, they moved down the darkened path. Simon glanced back every once in a while to make sure the orchid field was still within their view. "Wild creatures will not bother us as long as we stay on this path, right Simon?" Pinka asked with much apprehension.

Her question sent a chill down his spine, but he kept it to himself. "They don't bother anyone on the other roads and paths," he replied.

Neopoleana's words began to haunt Simon, for the path was getting darker and darker. *As long as you can see light, then you are assured of being on the right path. If the path you take leads to darkness, then you know to turn back.* Her message spun around in his head.

Jetta was becoming anxious. "It sure is dark and quiet up this way, isn't it?" she asked.

"Yeah, there is probably nothing up here," Simon answered, sounding a bit unsure as he glanced behind. The orchid field was barely visible, which actually gave him a sense of relief. Soon they would have to turn around and head back.

However, Jetta suddenly screamed out. "Hey, what is that?" she asked while pointing to a huge cave at the very end of the path.

"Could that be the far tunnel?" Simon asked with hope.

Pinka chuckled. "No, the tunnel is on the other side of the field. Besides, if this was the one, it would be sealed. Remember, Simon?" she asked, jarring his memory.

"You're right. I guess I was just having wishful thinking," Simon remarked as he stared at the giant black hole in the entrance to a mysterious cave.

"I don't hear anything in that old cave," Jetta pointed out. "Can we take a peek just inside the entrance?"

Simon looked back and realized the cave would be out of sight of the orchid field. However, curiosity was killing him. *It's just a few steps away*, he thought.

"Okay, we'll take a quick peep then leave!" he replied. "Is that understood?"

"Oh yes," Jetta and Pinka agreed.

Slowly the three made their way toward the cave's haunting entrance. They became somewhat nervous, but their curiosity outweighed the fear. With caution, Simon peeped inside the darkened hole first. The Rhues immediately followed. Of course, there was no light inside the cave, so they would see nothing anyway.

"Hey! Hey! Is anyone in there?" Pinka shouted, her voice echoing deep inside the cold chamber.

Jetta scolded her. "What are you doing? There could be a wild creature hiding in the darkness! He could eat us alive!"

"Then why did you want to look, if you are so afraid?" Pinka sassily asked.

"I'm not afraid. I'm just careful. That is all!" Jetta proclaimed.

"That is enough, you two!" Simon exclaimed. "We need to get back to the orchid field. Now come on, let's get going!" he ordered while scooting them along.

As they walked away, Pinka glanced back. "Hey. I saw something peeping at us!" she screamed.

Simon and Jetta turned to look but saw nothing except darkness. "There is nothing at the entrance. It must have been your imagination," Simon determined.

"I know I saw something!" she insisted.

"Then that gives us more reason to leave this place!" Simon exclaimed as he pulled her along.

They took several more steps, Pinka straining hard to look back. She shouted out, "There it is again! There's a creature or something inside that cave, and it is peeping out at us!"

"Well, we need to keep moving on. If there is something inside that cave, it will be wild, and it will shred us to pieces!" Jetta determined with anxiousness.

"Pinka, are you really sure that you saw something?" Simon asked out of wonder.

"Yes, sir!" she pronounced loudly.

"Well, I don't believe whatever you saw is wild, or it wouldn't be so shy about showing itself," Simon remarked with wit.

"You're right. I believe it is a nice creature, like us," Pinka boasted.

"Well, it could be a wild creature just trying to fool us into coming back. Then it will grab us up and swallow us whole!" Jetta screamed as her eyes grew big. Her statement created a few pangs of fear in Simon and Pinka, but they realized she was just guessing.

"A wild creature would not have hidden from us when we were at the cave's entrance," Simon analyzed.

"Simon's right. I know it is a nice creature. It could be lost, cold, and hungry," Pinka stated with compassion.

"We can't be sure of anything," Jetta argued.

Just then, Simon got a glimpse of what Pinka had seen. He shouted with anticipation, "I saw it! I saw it! It was a rather small creature, seeming to be frightened!"

"I knew it," Pinka bragged.

Simon gave instructions. "We'll walk back very slowly. That way, maybe it will not run from us."

"I'm scared! I don't want to go back!" Jetta cried.

Pinka quickly smirked. "I knew you were scared!"

"Hush up, Pinka!" Simon scolded.

"Jetta, you can wait here," he suggested.

"No!" she blasted. "That is even scarier. Let's just go back to the orchid field!"

At that point, Simon reached down to pick the shaking Rhue up in his arms. He apologized in a comforting manner. "I'm sorry. I didn't realize you were so frightened. We don't have to check on that creature if it scares you."

"Come on, Pinka!" he commanded. She stomped off in a huff, glowing like a pink lightbulb.

"Pinka's mad because she wanted to see the creature, isn't she, Simon?" Jetta whispered.

"Yes, but she will get over it. Pinka is just concerned that the creature is lost and hungry. She's probably wondering if the poor thing might starve to death or something," he explained, laying on the pity act very heavily. Maybe Simon picked this up from Bronzella; who knows?

These words stabbed at Jetta's heart. She thought, *Maybe I'm being too scared. After all, that creature hasn't even tried to get us. What if Simon and Pinka are right? It would be my fault if that creature starves to death, or if a wild creature gets it!*

Soon Jetta's fears and thoughts became overwhelming. She screamed out, "Simon, I want to go back and check on that poor creature!"

Pinka heard the remark and turned around with a smile upon her face that went from ear to ear. She ran back to Simon, clapping and cheering. "Are we going to check on the creature?" she asked excitedly.

"Yeah, we'll go back," Simon replied while putting Jetta down. "We'll go slowly. We must be careful, you know," he advised.

"Oh yes, we will be really cautious. If the creature acts mean, we'll run!" Pinka assured him.

"Okay, let's go!" Simon commanded.

They walked fast, heading back down the path, slowing as they neared the cave. "Let's wait right here to see if the creature peeps out again," Simon ordered.

"It could have already run off," Jetta speculated.

"We'll soon find out!" Simon exclaimed lowly. "Now be quiet, and get down behind this bush."

The three waited patiently for what seemed like hours for the mysterious creature to show its face Just as Simon was about to give up, there it was peeping again! "There's the creature!" Jetta shouted.

"Sh! Sh! We must keep very quiet," Simon scolded. "Let's wait to see if it will come out," he whispered.

They sat quietly, hoping the creature would soon reveal itself. Soon it slowly began to make its way out into the open. Simon, Pinka, and Jetta became excited with mixed emotions. They did not move a muscle as the creature came out into full view. Soon there it was, standing just yards from them. Their eyes grew big and their mouths dropped open as they stared at the sight just outside the entranceway of the cave. "Gosh. It looks just like a giant teddy bear!" Simon gasped.

"A what?" Pinka asked with wonder.

"A teddy bear," Simon replied. "Kids play with them back home where I come from. In fact, when I was really little, I had one that looked almost like the one we now see."

"Oh!" Pinka squealed. "I just know he is nice. Look at how cute he is."

"Hold on, Pinka!" Simon exclaimed. "The teddy bears I played with were toys. They were not live creatures. They could not walk, feel, or anything!"

Pinka was still viewing the three-feet-tall bear that was covered from head to toe in plum-colored fur. He walked on his two hind feet rather stiffly but with pride. "Well, I still know he is nice. You can tell by looking at him. He is adorable." She sweetly smiled.

"What do you think, Simon? Do you believe the teddy bear is friendly?" Jetta questioned.

"I'm not sure yet, but I don't believe he is wild."

"Well, he may look nice, but we can't go by that," Jetta clearly stated.

"I'm certainly not basing my opinion just on that," Pinka sassily remarked. "Look at his mannerisms. He isn't acting vicious. You can tell he is a good teddy bear."

The three chuckled as the bear tilted his head back, sniffing his nose high into the air. He then planted all four feet to the ground and began tumbling. Simon and the Rhues laughed almost out loud as they listened to his grunts of pleasure.

"You know what? This bear is just a young creature like us," Pinka whispered with anxiousness.

"I wonder if he has a mother." Jetta asked.

"I'm sure he does—unless something happened to her," Simon answered. Jetta and Pinka sighed.

Right at that moment, another bear poked his head out of the cave. Pinka squealed, "Oh my! There are two of them!"

"Not so loud! We don't want to scare them away!" Simon scolded.

"That one looks like a girl," Jetta commented as they observed the bear who was wearing a soft-looking amber-colored fur coat. They also noticed that she stood the same height as her sibling.

"I bet they are brother and sister," Simon commented.

"What do you mean?" Jetta asked.

"It means they have the same mother."

"Like all of us Rhues. We have the same mother, Neopoleana," Pinka whispered in excitement.

"Pinka and I are brother and sister!" Jetta exclaimed.

Simon covered his mouth, stifling the noise from his giggle. "No! No! Both of you are girls, so you are sisters," he explained. "Also the boys would be brothers to each other. Only a boy and a girl can be brother and sister. Do you understand?" he asked.

Pinka and Jetta looked at one another with dumbfounded expressions, but they still nodded that they understood.

"Do you think the bears will let us play with them?" Pinka asked.

"I don't know. Let's walk out very slowly and stand in one spot. Maybe they will not be frightened away," Simon suggested.

They stood up and then cautiously made their way out from behind the bush. Immediately, the bear's attention was captured. The three did not move a muscle as the cubs stared at them with deep reservation. Simon made a quick decision to speak. His tone was gentle.

"Hello there! My name is Simon, and this is Pinka and Jetta. We want to be your friends."

However, the young bears became frightened of these strange intruders. They quickly scampered back to the cave's entrance. Surprisingly, they did not hide but peeped out at them with caution. "May we come into your territory?" Simon softly asked without taking one step.

The two bears looked at each other and then glanced back at the unwelcome guests. "What for?" the amber-colored one asked.

Pinka smiled. "We want to play with you," she replied.

"What are your names?" Simon asked. The bears were very reluctant to answer. "Oh, come on. I told you our names. Why can't you tell us yours?" he begged.

"Well, I guess it wouldn't hurt to do that," the bear answered.

"I'm Carey and this is Beary," she announced.

"It is nice to meet you," Simon stated as Pinka and Jetta smiled and nodded.

"May we come closer?" Simon asked.

"You seem nice enough. Come on, but go slow—real slow," Beary ordered.

The three walked very slowly and cautiously toward the cave until they were within five feet of the bears. "That's far enough!" Beary shouted. They halted dead in their tracks. Simon then looked into Beary's small, round black eyes and realized the cub was still very wary of them. Carey's deep-set brown eyes showed the same expression. After all, these were complete strangers standing in front of them.

"We are young like you," Simon informed them.

The bears weren't impressed. "What are you doing here?" Beary asked.

"Jetta and Pinka couldn't sleep, so we took a walk around the field of orchids. We spotted the path that leads to your cave and wondered what was up here," Simon explained.

"Well, I guess that sounds logical," Carey replied.

Pinka showed compassion. "We thought maybe you were lost and hungry."

Beary and Carey chuckled. "No, this is our home."

"Do you have a mother?" Jetta asked.

"Of course. She is out gathering honey in Graywood Forest," Carey replied.

That means these cubs are wild creatures, Simon thought to himself. Immediately, he found a good excuse to leave. "We can't stay long. The Rhues' mother, Neopoleana, will soon be returning to the orchid field. She will worry sick over us."

"Oh, but I want to play with Beary and Carey!" Pinka whined in.

"I do too!" Jetta cried.

Simon didn't want to appear antisocial. He stammered. "Uh… well…maybe for just a few minutes, but only if the bears want to."

He then looked toward the fuzzy creatures. Beary and Carey had calmed down, determining that Simon and the Rhues could be trusted. "We never ever have anyone to play with. Sure, we'll give it a try," Beary announced with anticipation.

"What about your mother?" Simon asked with much concern.

"Oh, it will be quite some time before she returns. It takes her forever to fill the honey pots," Beary assured him.

Jetta and Pinka's eyes grew big as they filled with wonderment. "A honey pot?" Pinka questioned.

"Yes, we have many of them. Our mother stores our food in them," Carey explained.

"Let's play awhile, then we will show you the honey pots," she volunteered.

"Oh, that sounds so cool!" Pinka exclaimed, having picked up Simon's way of talking.

"We get to see the honey pots! We get to see the honey pots!" the Rhues sang as they clapped and jumped around. Beary and Carey laughed at the sight of them.

Soon Simon joined in the fun of frolic and play, forgetting all about the wild mama bear who was due back. First, the bears played tag with Simon and the Rhues. Then Pinka chased Beary but would run and hide from him when he chased her back. Jetta chased after Carey but never could catch her. Even though Jetta was fast, she had met her match with this feisty teddy bear. The Rhues had Beary and Carey singing as they skipped around together in a circle. Finally, they plopped to the ground, tumbled through the leaves, and did somersaults.

"This is the most fun we have ever had in our entire lives!" Carey exclaimed.

"It sure has made me hungry," Beary growled. "I guess you will see the honey pots now."

"Follow me," Carey ordered as she began walking toward the right side of the cave on the very edge of Graywood Forest.

Simon and the Rhues couldn't believe their eyes! There were at least a dozen large, brown clay pots lined up against the cave's outer wall. Each had a clay lid covering the luscious golden liquid inside. "Are all these pots filled with honey?" Simon asked.

Beary's mouth was drooling. "Yes, and our mother took two to Graywood Forest. She will bring them back, and they will be pouring over with the stuff!" he shouted.

"Can we look at the honey in one?" Pinka asked.

"Sure you can, because I'm getting ready to devour some of the sweet treat right now!" Beary replied as he quickly removed the clay lid from a pot.

Jetta and Pinka leaned over to look inside. "It looks like thick nectar," Jetta proclaimed.

"Have some," Beary invited.

Before Simon had time to warn her, Jetta had jumped up on the rim of the pot and plunged her snout completely down into the thick, gooey honey. "Jetta!" he screamed anxiously. "Your snout will get stuck! The honey is too thick!"

It was too late! Jetta was holding on to the rim of the pot with both hands and both feet as she strained and pulled, stretching her tiny snout to the limit. She made loud grunting sounds as she worked to break loose from the thick glue-like honey. Sweat beads popped out on her forehead and rolled down into her eyes. "Help me! Help me!" she screamed in muffled tones since her mouth was grazing the sticky goo.

"Don't try to talk, Jetta! The honey will get down your throat and strangle you!" Simon warned. "Just don't worry. I'll get you loose!" he assured her as Beary, Carey, and Pinka watched in horror.

"Gosh, I was fixing to stick my snout in that other pot of honey!" Pinka cried with anticipation.

"Jetta could be stuck there forever!" Carey howled.

"Stop talking like that. You will scare Jetta into hysteria and make matters worse," Simon scolded.

"I'm sorry. I wasn't thinking about how that sounded," Carey apologized.

"Is there anything I can do to help?" Beary asked.

"I'm going to try to pull her out. Get behind me and hold on to my waist, and then pull on me as I pull on Jetta," Simon instructed. The bear cub quickly did as Simon had asked. They pulled and tugged, straining and grunting. Jetta did her own share of groaning and then let out a muffled scream.

"I know it hurts, but we must get you out," Simon firmly stated yet feeling compassion for her. Again, he tugged hard on the little Rhue as Beary pulled on him with all his might. Jetta's snout stretched out so tight everyone thought it was going to snap. Carey and Pinka stood frozen with cringed faces, their hands covering their gaping mouths.

Just as Simon started to tug once again, a low, growling voice could be heard from deep within the cave. "What was that?" he screamed, knowing in his mind what it was but hoping he was wrong.

"It is our mother! She's coming in from the back entrance of the cave!" Carey answered with much anticipation.

"Oh no!" Simon shouted with panic. "Will she realize that we are your friends?"

"I don't know! She is very protective of Beary and me. She may become very upset and not even listen to us!" Carey cried.

Pinka immediately latched on to Simon's leg, screaming and crying like a baby. "She's going to eat us alive!"

Simon quickly snapped her loose from his leg, bent down, and looked into her eyes. "I know you're very frightened, but right now, we must help Jetta. We don't have much time!" he firmly spoke, giving her a brief hug.

He then immediately tugged on Jetta one last time, using strength mustered up from his fear. Suddenly, the agonizing Rhue's snout popped loose and snapped back, hitting her in the face. "Ouch!" she yelled while rubbing her sore, throbbing snout.

"Sh! Sh!" Simon hissed while helping her down from the rim of the honey pot. "The wild mother bear's growls are growing louder. She is getting very close. We have got to get out of here now!" he commanded while scooting her and Pinka around to the front of the cave.

"Now run back down the path and don't stop until you have reached the orchid field," Simon ordered.

"You're coming too, aren't you, Simon?" Pinka asked with hysteria.

He quickly explained. "I must keep the mother bear occupied until you are a safe distance away. She can outrun any of us. You wouldn't stand a chance. Plus there is no telling what she might do if she sees all of us strangers with her cubs!" He then cried, "Now hurry! Run! Go! I'll be there soon, I promise!"

Pinka and Jetta quickly darted away, running as fast as they could in their waddling manners. Their hearts were pounding with fear, and tears streamed from their eyes.

Since they dared not look back, the Rhues had no idea that Beary and Carey were running right in behind them! Simon couldn't yell for the bears to come back because the mother bear was just too close at emerging from the cave.

Though almost frozen in fear, Simon realized he must keep a clear head. That was the only way he would survive. Suddenly, the grunts and growls were at the entrance! He hunkered down and peeped around the corner to see the most humongous black bear with fiery red eyes he would ever see in his entire life! Her giant stature and the wild tones of her growls were the complete opposite of her teddy bear children's gentle nature. Now completely frozen in fear, Simon felt doomed, for he had lost his clear head!

The old grizzly spoke, startling him to no end. "Beary! Carey! Where are you? Now stop playing games with me! I know you're hiding!" she shouted ferociously.

Simon had managed to crawl back and hide behind one of the large clay honey pots. He looked around at Graywood Forest surrounding the cave and determined the deep woods would be his only escape route.

The wild mother bear was now getting very anxious over her children not responding to her calls. She stood up on her hind feet and growled so loud it seemed to shake even the leaves on the nearby trees. As the huge, outraged creature journeyed around to the side of the cave, Simon knew he must make a run for it. *My legs feel like rubber. I sure hope they will carry me into Graywood Forest!* he thought.

Fast, without a second thought, Simon made his dash toward the thick woods of more wild creatures. With her keen eyesight, the mother bear spotted him immediately. Her growls were the most ferocious Simon would ever hear as she tailed close behind! The mad creature swiped her sharp claws toward his torso! As he felt the rush of air created by the force of the dangerous claw weapons, he jumped inside a deep thicket.

Immediately, from deep inside the twisted vines, he cried out to the mother bear, "Beary and Carey are safe!"

The raged bear growled intensely as she raked her claws through the thick, low shrub. "Where are my babies?" she asked.

Simon stammered. "Uh…uh…" He then realized Pinka and Jetta already had time to reach the orchid field. "They ran down the path!" he cried out.

"You mean child! You frightened my babies away from their home! I'm going to shred you to pieces!" the angry bear growled at the top of her lungs. Simon covered his ears, cringing with fear.

"You had better be telling me the truth of this, and my babies had better not be harmed! If I do not locate them, I'll be back to get you!"

A chilling wave traveled down Simon's spine and his stomach knotted up. He listened in silence to the rustling sounds as the giant, wild bear turned to run down the path. *Man, I hope Neopoleana is back*, he thought. Suddenly the what-ifs set in. *What if the mother bear can't find Beary and Carey? What if they went off somewhere else? What if another wild creature got them?*

Simon worked himself up into a total frazzle. *Oh no! I can't go back out there! I can't take the risk! I'll have to find a different route of escape!* he anxiously thought. He cautiously peered out of the thicket, wondering if he should stay put or make a dash toward the tall trees.

The angry mother bear was running fast down the path, calling her cubs by name. "Beary! Carey! Beary! Carey! Where are you?" she shouted in desperation.

Pinka and Jetta heard her desperate cries just as they reached the field. "Mama! Mama!" they cried out.

Neopoleana had returned from the tall tree and was close by. She immediately emerged from the orchid field and scooped the frightened Rhues up into her arms. She saw Beary and Carey as they stopped short, halting at the end of the path. "Oh my goodness! What are those bear cubs doing here?" she frantically asked.

Jetta and Pinka turned to look. Their eyes grew big with surprise of seeing them. "Oh. Mama, that is Beary and Carey! We made friends with them at the cave," Pinka jabbered.

"We didn't know they followed us here!" Jetta exclaimed. "The mother bear was coming out of the cave! Simon stayed so we could get away," she cried through tears of guilt.

"Oh my goodness!" Neopoleana gasped while setting Pinka and Jetta down then gasped again when she looked to see the mother bear approaching in the distance. There was no sign of Simon.

As the bear cubs stood and stared in disarray, Neopoleana added to their confusion when she spoke. "Your mother is coming for you. She will be angry!"

"We just followed Pinka and Jetta because we wanted to play some more," Carey tried to explain.

"I sure hope our mother will not be too angry," Beary cried.

"Well, you should not have run off and given her cause to worry!" Neopoleana scolded, glaring also at Pinka and Jetta, causing their faces to turn red with embarrassment.

All the Rhues and creatures quickly gathered around Neopoleana at the edge of the field to listen and observe. The wild mother bear's growls were getting very loud. "Beary! Carey! You know better than to just run off like that!" she shouted as she neared the cubs.

"We're sorry. We were just excited and didn't think right," Beary weakly explained.

"You had me worried half out of my mind," their mother scolded yet hugged them at the same time.

Suddenly, silence prevailed when Neopoleana spoke loudly, calling the mother bear by name. "Berthina, where is the boy? Where is Simon?" she firmly asked.

Berthina snickered. "Aw, he is okay, I guess. My growls frightened him to no end. He ran and then jumped into a thicket on the edge of Graywood Forest," she responded.

The Rhues gasped with fear. "Simon will be eaten alive!" Tooty squalled as the other Rhues and creatures joined in with sobs of anguish.

Of course, Neopoleana also felt a rush of panic run through her body. As usual, she let it pass, replacing her fears with hope. "Listen to my words," she shouted. The Rhues and creatures became silent right then. The Mother Rhue proclaimed, "Simon is extra smart. He has a good chance of escaping from Graywood Forest without being harmed." She then hugged each Rhue.

Berthina had not left with her cubs and had listened to the conversation. She could see the love Neopoleana had for the Rhues, creatures, and Simon, but she could not feel compassion. Berthina was wild and knew only certain basic instincts, one of which is protecting her young. Very casually, she scooted Beary and Carey back down the path toward the cave as the Rhues watched in confusion. "Mama, how come Berthina doesn't want us to play with her cubs?" Pinka asked.

Neopoleana explained with wisdom. "I know it is hard for you to understand, but she is a wild creature, knowing only how to care for and protect her young. She is actually helping her cubs to develop their wild instincts."

"Beary and Carey sure don't seen wild," Blinko spoke out.

"Oh, but as the bear cubs get older, their wild instincts will grow with them. That is the way they were meant to be. Right now, Beary and Carey are curious because they are learning.

They are exploring a whole new world," the Mother Rhue enlightened them.

"But if they stayed with us long enough, Beary and Carey wouldn't have to turn wild," Blubbles pointed out.

Neopoleana possessed great insight. "Well, it would change them somewhat, but on the inside, the two would always yearn to be wild and free. Their instinct for survival in the wild would haunt them always."

"So the bear cubs would never really be happy living like we do. Is that right?" Gurggles asked.

"That is correct," the Mother Rhue confirmed. "It would not be in the bears' best interest to try and change their nature."

"Mama, are you worried over Simon very much?" Squiggly asked.

"Of course, I'm very concerned," Neopoleana answered.

"We are very concerned also," Truffles repeated her words. "Shouldn't we search for him?"

"Graywood Forest is deep and very dangerous because of the wild creatures," Neopoleana spoke as Winglet tugged on her leg.

She reached down and picked her up. The baby Rhue immediately snuggled her head against her mother's neck.

"I want Timon," she cried.

The Mother Rhue patted the baby's back gently to help soothe the bad feelings away.

"Can't you and Flutta fly over Graywood Forest to see if you can spot Simon below?" Slurple asked.

"I'm sorry, but the forest is just too dense. We would never find him. Besides, Simon knows the risks of being there. I'm sure he is in hiding, waiting for just the right opportunity to make his escape," Neopoleana responded.

"Well, I think we creatures are huge enough to scare off any wild creatures. Why can't we go into Graywood Forest and search for Simon?" Fuzzle asked in anticipation.

"Look, the forest is very widespread. I can't take the chance of anyone getting lost," Neopoleana explained.

"Simon is probably lost!" Pinka cried out.

"That is a possibility, but I'm sure Simon is smart enough to find his way out," Neopoleana responded.

"Maybe Simon just climbed back out of the thicket. He could be hiding at Berthina's cave right now," Razzle determined.

"That is another possibility," the Mother Rhue remarked. "However, we cannot bother the mother bear or her cubs again. Berthina is already agitated enough."

The creatures downed their heads, and the Rhues began crying from fear of the worst. Neopoleana comforted them the best she could, but it was hard because her heart was also filled with concern. They sat quietly, huddled together, wondering if Simon would ever get out of the woods of the wild Graywood Forest.

Lost and Alone

Simon had decided to take the chance of climbing out of the thicket. He had slowly made his way through thick foliage, vines, and brush and was now among the huge trees of the forest. Thick piles of dead leaves crunched beneath his feet as he wandered along. *"Man, I thought for sure going this way would lead me quickly out of here,"* he thought while leaning his hand against one of the trees just to find it sticking tight to the trunk. *What in the world?* he cringed while straining to set his hand free.

While examining the tree closely, Simon found that the sticky goo was oozing from within it and then flowing down the trunk. He realized quickly what this thick liquid was. "This is a honey tree!" he squealed with excitement as he checked out other trees. Each one was overflowing with the sweet, sugary treat. With a smile of delight, he licked his hand clean of the concoction and then let more of the luscious honey trickle over his fingers, lapping up each scrumptious bite. "Boy, that was good!" he moaned with pleasure of having a full belly.

While Simon was resting a minute, reality set back in. *I guess it's time for me to start searching for a way out of here*, he thought as fear once again began to build up inside him. *I'll try going this way*, he decided while making his way out from the stand of trees. He passed several dead tree stumps and then cautiously entered thick weeds, tripping and falling over the mass of twisted vines. At that moment, the dreaded thought he had been denying crept in. He cried out in anguish, "I'm lost! I am really lost! What am I going to do? I want to see my mom and dad again! I don't want to be stuck in these woods forever!"

Suddenly, to make matters worse, Simon heard a nearby rustling sound. Quickly, he crawled under the thick brush. Then everything was quiet again—too quiet. Simon dared not scream for help, for the wild creatures would surely find him. He lay completely still for what seemed to be hours but actually were several minutes. *I can't lie here forever!* he thought with despair.

Noticing that things were still quiet, Simon determined it had probably just been his imagination of hearing sounds. Slowly, he crawled from beneath the brush, making his way to another group of huge trees. He ran fast from tree to tree, pausing a minute or so behind each one before peering out to see if the coast was clear. Through the deep, dark woods, he ran in this manner until becoming completely out of breath. Looking ahead to see no end in sight, Simon wondered if he was just traveling around in circles. He cried silently, but with desperation. "Mom and Dad, I'm so afraid! I wish you were here to hug me tight and make me feel safe! Mama! Daddy! I want to come home!"

Suddenly, right at that very moment and out of nowhere it seemed, Timber, the wild wolf, leaped right in front of his face! Simon was so terrified the entire bottom half of his mouth shook violently, and his eyes became in a fixed gaze upon this treacherous-looking gray wolf. Saliva drooled from the hungry mouth of this wild beast, and his teeth glistened like the sharp edge of a sword. His fiery red eyes were the most taunting of all the wild creatures in *Graywood Forest*, appearing to look right through Simon with chilling meanness.

Without warning, the terrorizing wolf spoke. "Are you lost, boy?" he asked in arrogant, heated breath.

Simon had already felt the color drain from his face. Now he thought he would pass out. In fact, he was wishing for it. Just then, Roxy, the red fox, walked up. Simon glanced into her pale-green eyes. He could see that she was wild but didn't appear to be as vicious as Timber.

"I asked, 'Are you lost, boy?'" Timber repeated as he raked his sharp claw slowly down the side of Simon's face, leaving a light, tender scratch. Simon could not move, nor could he speak.

"Oh, stop messing with him!" Roxy suddenly blurted out. Timber just looked at her with a sneaky half-smile.

By this time, severe anxiety had consumed Simon. His heart was racing away, causing sweat beads to roll off his forehead. Timber moved very close to his face. With a look of sheer arrogance, the wild wolf let out a snarling growl as thick, sticky saliva dripped from his mouth. Simon could not move his eyes but felt the warm, slimy drool coat his forearm. All that he could see was Timber's razor-sharp teeth and smell his stinking, hot breath. At that precise moment, he passed out completely.

"Now see what you did?" Roxy screamed.

Timber just snickered loudly. "Well, I had to have some fun. I want to make sure the boy never enters our territory again," he replied.

The sly fox became agitated. "Timber, you know very well we had been watching the boy. He did not intentionally enter our domain. He became lost after running from Berthina. Now look at him! He could be dead," she exclaimed, heavily scolding the mean gray wolf. Timber just laughed.

"There is one thing I can't figure out."

"What is that, Roxy?" Timber asked.

"I don't know if it was your vicious growl or your bad breath that caused the boy to fall out like he did," she quipped with a chuckle.

Timber snarled and snorted. "That is very funny and cute, Roxy, haha! You're so hilarious!"

Roxy rolled with laughter at having got the best of him. After regaining her composure, she walked over to check on Simon, nudging him with her large paw. He was limp as a noodle.

"Come on, Roxy! Let's move on!" Timber demanded.

"I think the boy just passed out. Maybe we should wait awhile for him to come to."

Timber growled in a firm manner. "I don't have time to mess around! I'm getting gnawing hunger pangs, and I want to hunt now!" he exclaimed. "What's up with you anyhow, Roxy? Are you getting soft?"

The sly fox smirked at Timber's insulting question. "I most certainly am not becoming soft! The boy was lost and did not realize how close he was to being out of Graywood Forest. It wouldn't hurt us to stay here a few minutes!" she firmly responded.

The impatient wolf snapped, "Well! I am not waiting!"

"Well! If you can't wait, the least we could do is drag the boy out to the path!" Roxy loudly suggested.

Timber sighed heavily. "Good grief! I will never hear the end of it if I don't abide by your wishes! Okay! Okay! We'll drag him out there. Then, will you be happy and get off my back?" he exclaimed with criticism.

With a look of disgust, Roxy nodded her head yes.

"Now, where do we start?" Timber asked.

"You get on one side, and I'll get on the other. I guess we can latch on to his shirt and drag him," Roxy assumed.

"It might work, unless our sharp teeth shred the material to pieces," Timber informed her.

"Well, let's try it anyway!" Roxy exclaimed as she gripped Simon's shirt into her mouth at the shoulder. Timber quickly latched on to the other side. Slowly they began to tug, dragging Simon through the prickly brush of the woods. The thick leaves acted as a carpet, protecting him from getting scratched and bruised.

Roxy halted right before they reached the path. "What are you stopping for?" Timber asked, still sounding put out.

"I want to check the boy to see if he's coming around yet," Roxy replied then gently stroked Simon's face with her huge paw. She got no response and sighed, "He's still out cold."

The coldhearted wolf just snickered. "I must have scared him out of his wits. He will never want to return to Graywood Forest," he bragged.

"Come on! Let's get the boy up to the path," Roxy ordered as she grasped Simon's tattered shirt.

After making their way through the last group of tall, dense trees and thickets, Timber looked all around before he and Roxy dragged Simon onto the path. "We need to take him toward the end, near the orchid field," Roxy remarked.

Timber fussed. "This is good enough! I've already done more than I should! If any other wolves were to find out about this, I would be the laughing stock of the entire pack!"

Roxy rolled her eyes. "The creatures of Rhueland can't spot the boy this far back! You know they are probably searching for him. The boy needs help!" she exclaimed.

Timber shook his head back and forth in disbelief. "Roxy, for the life of me, I just can't understand you!" he shouted. Why should you even care?"

"I've already told you my reasons. Now stop wasting valuable time. After we move the boy in sight of where the creatures from Rhueland can easily see him, then you will not have to lift another finger!"

Timber snarled at her last remark. "Well, good, because if I don't soon go hunting, I'm going to starve to death!" he yelled then snickered as he raked his eyes over Simon. "In fact"—he growled—"I'm so hungry maybe I could just nibble on—"

"Don't even go there!" Roxy firmly cut in. "Come on! Let's get this job done," she ordered.

Slowly, the two dragged Simon down the path until the field of orchids was in sight. Roxy could see all the creatures and Rhues huddled around Neopoleana. Without any warning to Timber, she suddenly shouted, "Hey! Hey! Over here! The boy is over here!" All eyes glanced toward the path to see Simon's limp body.

"You fool!" Timber shouted as he leaped into the thicket beside the path. Roxy followed, and soon, the two were well hidden in the deep woods of Graywood Forest.

Without hesitation, the Mother Rhue took the short flight to where Simon lay. She reached down, gently picked him up, and cradled him in her arms.

The creatures and Rhues soon arrived at the sight. "Oh, Mama. Is Simon…uh…uh…*dead*?" Pinka cried.

"No, my sweet child. I believe he has been terrified into a deep sleep."

"Will he now sleep forever?" Blubbles asked with sadness.

Neopoleana smiled with wisdom. "Oh, I believe Simon will bounce back as good as new! He not only loves us, but he loves his mom and dad and wants to see them again. All this gives him a strong will," she explained.

"Look at Simon's shirt, Mama! It is ripped almost to pieces!" Razzle exclaimed. "Did Timber and Roxy do that?"

"Yes, but they did it while dragging him back to us."

"They could have eaten Simon alive. Why didn't they, Mama?" Tooty asked, sounding a bit confused.

"I'm not really sure, but Timber and Roxy did know that we have never disturbed their privacy. I believe they realized Simon was lost," Neopoleana evaluated. "Now listen! I'm going to help Simon so that he can get well faster," she announced.

"Like you did with Winglet?" Slurple asked as he glanced toward the smiling baby Rhue.

"That is correct," the Mother Rhue answered. "Now, Winglet, I want you to behave while I'm nursing Simon back to health. Go to Fuzzle and stay with him," she ordered.

"O Tay, Ma-ma." Winglet obeyed in baby talk as she flew to the cuddly caterpillar.

The Rhues and creatures gathered around Neopoleana to watch this awesome event. As she spread out her powerful *golden wings*, they quickly covered their eyes, shielding them from the brilliant light. The Mother Rhue then sat upon the ground, laying Simon across her lap. Slowly, she laid the elegant wings over him and then folded them gently around him, covering and encasing his entire body with pure power and light. The group removed their hands from their eyes and sat quietly while Tooty played a soothing tune on her clarinet snout. The beautiful melody was calming, lulling Winglet to sleep. Neopoleana was now being a caring mother to Simon, trying to nurture him back to good health. Unconditional love poured from the magical *golden wings*, flowing through his weak body.

Several hours passed. The Rhues and creatures had dozed off into a restful sleep, and Winglet was still napping deep inside Fuzzle's soft coat. Neopoleana was finally resting comfortably. With all of Rhueland being so quiet, you could have heard a pin drop. Suddenly, Simon flung the *golden wings* away from his body and then abruptly jumped off her lap while screaming at the top of his lungs! Of course, this startled everyone to no end. "Gosh, I thought I was in a *coffin!*" he shouted, shaking with fear. "I am really here, aren't I?" he asked with anticipation.

"Calm down, Simon!" the Mother Rhue softly ordered. "Of course, you are here. You were out for quite a while."

"Man, was I having a severe nightmare!" he exclaimed. "I dreamed the wild wolf tore me to shreds, but I was at home, not here! My mom and dad were looking down at me as I lay in a coffin!" he relayed in a most terrorizing manner.

"Simon! Calm down right now, or you will pass out again," Neopoleana strongly advised.

"What is a coffin?" Truffles chimed in.

"Well, it's what they put you in when you're going to be gone forever!" Simon explained as the Rhues listened with big eyes.

"It was just a dream, and dreams seem real," Neopoleana reminded him. "Don't dwell on it. You are fine now."

"You're right, Neopoleana. I am okay! Thank you for putting me underneath your wings. I love you!" he cried with a warm smile while hugging her tight.

"I love you too, Simon."

He then glanced calmly toward the Rhues and creatures to quiet them. "Now, come here you guys! I want your hugs too!" he stated while reaching his arms out. They ran to him, and each took their turn giving hugs as Winglet nestled in Neopoleana's arms. Razzle was last in line to get his hug, but it was just as warm as the first that Simon had given out.

Good-Byes Can Be Hard

"It is time to go," Neopoleana spoke softly to Simon. He smiled and nodded as Winglet flew to his arms. The creatures and Rhues prepared for this final journey, for the far tunnel was right beyond the orchid field.

As they began their walk, Blinko pointed out Simon's tattered shirt to him. "Gosh! What in the world did Timber and Roxy do to me?" he asked with anxiousness. Neopoleana explained how the wild wolf and sly fox dragged him onto the path and how Roxy shouted for her to come for him.

Simon sighed. "Yeah, Timber was teasing me bad! I took him seriously. Then, when he opened his big mouth and came toward my face, I figured I was a complete goner!" he exclaimed.

"We're glad you weren't a goner," Pinka sassily stated.

Soon this conversation faded out, and the group walked quietly. Simon looked up at the enchanting coral sky and then moved his eyes to focus on the majestic blue and pink mountains. Karen and Jim entered his thoughts. *I bet Mom and Dad think I'm never coming home. They may have given up on me by now. Boy, will they be happy and surprised!* His thoughts then rambled to other things. *Doug probably never thinks of me anymore. I'll never get caught up on my school work. All my friends will be asking questions.*

Simon then looked over at Neopoleana, who smiled and winked as if to know he was wrapped up in some deep thinking. *Man, I'm certainly going to miss the Mother Rhue*, he conceived as his eyes roamed from her to the creatures—Fuzzle, Trog, Flutta, Turckle, and Bunnita. He remembered back to the great fun they had together and all they had taught him. He watched the Rhues and smiled in delight of how sweet and innocent they were. Pinka was being prissy with the way she tousled her curls as she sashayed along in her waddling walk. Blubbles and Gurggles were skipping together as they made tiny gurgling and bubbling noises. Simon laughed to himself while watching Squiggly roll his snout up and down like a yo-yo. Jetta captured his heart as she danced around to a tune Tooty was playing on her saxophone snout. Razzle was walking in step with Blinko as they glowed and blinked in sequence. Slurple walked quietly beside Simon but was slurping with each step. Truffles walked behind Malo, pushing him along the path as the sweet scent of chocolate filled the air.

Suddenly, Simon's thoughts became rather confusing. *If Bronzella had never brought me to this land in The Third Dimension, then I wouldn't have to worry about saying good-bye to my friends—*

good-bye forever! I would have never known them, and I would not love them!" he cried deep inside himself. Suddenly, his thoughts shifted. *What am I thinking? I'm glad I met the Rhues and creatures. I'm thankful I was given the opportunity to love them! It's…uh… uh…I don't want to leave them. I will be sad forever. They will be sad forever!* Now Simon began to have racing thoughts. *I have to return home, or I'll be sad for Mom and Dad, and they will be sad for me forever! This is hard! I can't think straight! I'm totally confused! Why is this so difficult?*

Soon Simon was so overwhelmed he stopped in his tracks and screamed out. "I can't deal with this. It is too much. Help me, please, Neopoleana. Help me," he wailed with passion.

Simon's sudden outburst startled Winglet, and she flew to the Mother Rhue's arms just before he dropped to the ground, screaming and crying in anguish. The creatures and Rhues stood back in silence, not knowing what to think or do. Neopoleana quickly put Winglet down inside Fuzzle's soft, secure coat and hurried to Simon's side. She gently lifted him to a sitting position and looked deep into his eyes. "Oh, Simon, my dear, sweet child. You are grieving for us already. It is okay," she consoled. "Let it all out. Let the pain of grief flow out of you. Your tears shall carry it away. It is very healing, my precious child," the Mother Rhue spoke with compassion.

Soon all the Rhues and creatures were crying along with Simon. Neopoleana rocked him gently in her loving arms as he cried until he felt there were no more tears left in his eyes. "Why does sadness have to hurt so badly?" he asked in a sobbing manner while looking into her deep, caring eyes.

Wisdom poured from Neopoleana. "Sadness is a feeling like happiness is a feeling. With grief or sadness, you experience tears. With happiness, you feel joy and laughter. Both feelings help us in totally different ways, but at the time, we do not realize they are helping. All we feel at the moment is happiness or sadness." Simon looked a bit puzzled, but he was beginning to understand.

Neopoleana continued. "Let me put it this way. Laughter helps to release all the good anxiety we have built up inside us. Bad anxiety or awful feelings are released through our tears. So both are very healing to our minds and bodies."

Simon smiled, for now he understood almost completely what the wise Mother Rhue had told him. Winglet let out a cute giggle as she flew back into his arms. The Rhues and creatures gave him hugs, for they were feeling much better also. Happy to be together for a while longer, they walked on to their destination, playing and laughing all the way there.

⊙〰〰〰〰☉

"Well, we are finally here," Neopoleana pronounced as they entered a rocky area.

Simon was surprised at the short time it took to get there. "We are? I don't see the tunnel. Where is it?" he questioned. Everyone chuckled as Neopoleana pointed toward the huge, smooth and round gray boulder at the very edge of Graywood Forest. "That's the tunnel?" Simon uttered in astonishment.

"Yes, that is the tunnel, my dear boy. It only appears to be a solid rock because it is sealed," the Mother Rhue explained.

"Oh, I forgot! Of course it would look differently than an open tunnel," Simon chuckled as he walked over to pat the thick boulder with his hand. He then glanced back at Neopoleana. "This is it, isn't it? I'm really going home, aren't I?" he asked, having a mixed bag of feelings once again.

"Yes, my son," Neopoleana replied while walking near and placing her arm around his shoulder. Simon looked up into her eyes and smiled. She then spoke with love, "You will soon be returning to your parents and to the world you belong in. Your mom and dad love you dearly and will be so happy to have their little boy back. However, before you leave, I have a surprise."

"You do?" Simon asked in anticipation.

"Yes, I do, and this surprise is truly just for you," the Mother Rhue answered. "Come on out everyone!" she immediately yelled.

Simon could barely contain his composure when he saw what was happening right before his eyes. All the wonderful creatures he had met in Gruhland were coming out of hiding! There was La'Zar, the gigantic, scaly lizard, and Icky, the huge, slimy snail with the rock shell on his back. Frieda, the spider who could spin strong, silk ropes, stood nearby. Cutter and Crawly, the giant worms, slinked out from behind a boulder. Rattles the snake slithered out of a large hole, shaking his huge rattle to no end. Simon could hear and see smoke churning around Grundel's nostrils as the massive dragon emerged from behind a thick tree trunk. Brat followed, giving him a nod. Simon returned the gesture to the oversized rat.

"I can't believe you guys are here!" Simon squealed. "How did you do it?" he asked while making himself around the group for hugs.

La'Zar looked at Neopoleana. "Ask her," he blurted.

Simon ran to the Mother Rhue. He already had it figured out. "You enlarged the tunnel that connects Rhueland to Gruhland, didn't you?" he asked in excitement.

Neopoleana smiled with delight. "Yes, Simon. I realized how much you cared for these creatures, so I just had to make it possible for you to see them one last time. They love you too, Simon," she softly spoke with brightened eyes.

"Are you going to leave the tunnel enlarged?" Simon asked.

"For now, I am. All the creatures from both Gruhland and Rhueland will be free to visit one another," she replied with a warm smile.

Just then, a screeching noise from the coral sky caught everyone's attention. All heads looked above to see that old hawk, Sqhawk circling the area.

"Come on down!" Simon shouted as the Rhues joined in with excitement.

Soon Sqhawk descended from the open sky. The group stepped back to give her landing room. To everyone's surprise, the gigantic bird landed in the area with precision.

Simon immediately ran to her. "Thank you so much for coming to see me off!" he cried out.

"Oh, I wouldn't have missed seeing you again for anything!" Sqhawk spoke as she lowered her head for a hug.

"Not even for a big, juicy rat!" Brat chimed in, creating laughter among the group.

Sqhawk rolled her eyes but didn't really mind the joke. She then looked at Simon. "After what I put you through, yet you were kind enough to forgive and trust me, it just made me a better old bird. I just couldn't let you leave without thanking you one last time!" she exclaimed.

Simon squeezed Sqhawk's neck a little tighter. "I'm going to miss you, you know?"

"Me too," the old bird replied with tears swelling in her eyes. "Uh...I love you, Simon."

"I love you too, Sqhawk."

"Oh my goodness, I cannot believe my eyes!" Simon suddenly shouted while breaking his grip around Squawk's neck.

Everyone turned to look toward the open area in the direction of the orchid field. There, marching proudly toward the far tunnel, were the stone figures, Tealo, Jado, Ember, and Roza. And behind them were the graceful swans, Fredrix and Grace.

Simon ran out to greet them, squealing with joy. The creatures and Rhues shouted and clapped with excitement as Pinka, Blinko, and Malo trailed in behind Simon. The stone figures gave their usual salute and then continued to march forward. They kept their distance from the crowd, stopping and standing silently at attention near the far tunnel.

"Everyone has come!" Simon elated as he and Malo climbed upon Fredrix's back. Pinka and Blinko quickly climbed up to ride with Grace.

As they made their way to the tunnel, Simon spotted Berthina and her cubs, Beary and Carey, peeping out from the thicket at the edge of Graywood Forest. Timber and Roxy were nearby, peering his way. He just smiled and kept their warm presence a secret so their privacy would not be invaded.

Soon the entire group had gathered in a huddle. Neopoleana clapped her hands a couple of times and then called for everyone to get quiet. Silence came quickly with her command. "Simon, we have a farewell song for you," she announced. He swallowed hard, for he knew this was it! This was good-bye forever! Tremendous emotion began to consume his body, but he tried to keep it hidden.

"As we sing, each Rhue and creature will give you their last farewell hug," the Mother Rhue spoke.

Simon choked back all tears of sadness. "Oh, that is so nice of you to have memorized a song just for me!" he exclaimed in a trembling voice then took a seat upon a nearby rock.

The elegant Mother Rhue took center stage in front of Simon. Tooty took her place directly behind her, preparing to play the music for the song on her *pan flute* snout. The other Rhues grouped together in front of the creatures, standing behind Tooty, to sing the chorus.

Simon listened in awe as Neopoleana's sweet, angelic voice filled the air with beautiful, powerful notes. When the Rhues and creatures joined in the chorus, their voices were like a choir of angels. Never before had he heard such majestic music, and the words to the song went straight to his heart.

As they sang, each Rhue and creature took their turn going up to Simon for a final farewell hug. It was truly an emotional, magnificent moment! Neopoleana's song went like this:

We Touch with Our Hearts

Your world, my world
Are so far apart
But I'll be beside you
For we touch with our hearts
So close your eyes and see with your dreams
Feel me close by you
For your heart touches mine

I'll feel all your joys,
Your heartaches and pain
And hear your laughter
And know when you cry
So close your eyes and see with your dreams
Feel me close by you
For your heart touches mine

You're deep in my heart
And that keeps you near
Your presence I'll feel
When you reach with your heart
So close your eyes and see with your dreams
Feel me close by you
For your heart touches mine

After the group finished singing, everyone remained quiet as Neopoleana walked gracefully toward Simon. She extended her hand and he placed his hand in hers while sliding gently off the rock. His eyes remained fixed, looking into the Mother Rhue's enchanting eyes. "Come, Simon," she spoke softly. "You are going home now. You have loved ones in your world waiting for your return."

Simon smiled into her deep, caring eyes. "Thank you for the beautiful song, Neopoleana. I understood the message, and it will make leaving somewhat easier."

The Mother Rhue smiled back and then slowly led Simon to the sealed tunnel as the Rhues and creatures followed. Winglet flew to his arms to be held one last time. He stroked her soft face as she looked at him, bubbling with love that shined out of her huge, innocent blue eyes. "I will wuve you fo-evr," she spoke in baby talk.

"I wish I could see you grow up, but I must return home. You're going to be so magnificent with your magical *silver* fully developed wings," Simon spoke, choking up inside.

"Now, fly back to Fuzzle so the Mother Rhue can open the tunnel," he prodded Winglet as she clung tightly to him. She hesitated a moment then quickly flew into Fuzzle's coat, burrowing herself deep inside to sob. Simon's heart was bursting with emotion. "I will love you forever, Winglet!" he shouted

Simon's eyes went to each Rhue and creature. He took one last look at the stone figures and then glanced toward Graywood Forest to see Berthina and her cubs. He sucked in the sight of Timber and Roxy.

His eyes then went to Neopoleana, and he nodded. The Mother Rhue turned to directly face the sealed tunnel. She spread her *golden wings* up and out, looking very glorious and dignified. In a short time, bright beams of golden light began pouring from the powerful wings, penetrating into the thick, gray boulder. For a brief moment, the popping and crackling sounds brought the Zappers that patrolled the orchid fields to Simon's mind.

For what seemed to be an hour or so, hot and flickering, finely ground rock speckled from the massive boulder. Everyone watched in amazement as a tiny peephole began to slowly appear in the center of the huge rock. With big eyes, they watched this tiny opening grow into a large entrance, exposing a breathtaking view of pure, clear, and dazzling crystal.

Finally, the crackling and popping ceased. Neopoleana stepped back as she folded in her wings. Brilliance abounded with speed from the tunnel, traveling out and over the group of Rhues and creatures. Oooohs and ahhhs prevailed for several minutes, and then Simon quietly slinked forward to peer inside the newly created entrance. Never before had he seen such beautiful walls of solid, uncut crystal. *Wow! I wonder if this is solid diamond rock?* he exclaimed in thought. This conception quickly diminished when he turned to see all the faces of the Rhues and creatures. The love beaming from their eyes outshined the value of any crystal, for it was priceless.

"Simon, it is now time to leave," Neopoleana softly spoke. She then smiled as a lone tear gently trickled down her cheek. "In a short time, you shall be back in your world with your mom and dad," she elated with joy, being completely unselfish.

Simon smiled and then took his place in the brightness of the tunnel's entrance. While looking around at his friends, tears began to flow from his eyes. The light reflected each one, capturing the sparkle hidden in each drop. Slowly, he sucked in a long, deep breath and prepared to give his farewell remarks. "I love you—never forget that!" he cried. "And remember, I will never forget you!"

Pinka was sobbing. "You will always be close to our hearts. Nothing can ever take that away."

Simon was hypnotized as he watched colorful tears flow from her eyes like they did when Winglet was sick. Soon all the Rhues were crying the beautiful tears of color.

Neopoleana's voice broke the trance. "Turn around now, Simon, and begin your journey back home." Her heart was breaking, but she could not let it stop her from doing the right thing, even though this was the most difficult task she had ever faced.

Simon slowly turned around, but he could not put one foot in front of the other. "Go ahead," Neopoleana gently encouraged. "Remember, we shall always be just a heart-breadth away. No distance can ever break our connection, for it is of love, and it is sealed in our hearts."

Those incredible words just spoken by the wise Mother Rhue helped. Simon moved his feet, taking one small step, but then he glanced back and cried out, "It's hard to leave, Neopoleana!"

The Mother Rhue's instinct of pure love and devotion told her to run to Simon, but she knew this would be wrong. Instead, with wisdom from the heart, she spoke to him with compassion. "I know it's hard to leave friends behind who are near and dear to your heart, but you must focus on your mom and dad. Think of the love and joy they will feel when they see you. They will hold their 'little boy' once again in their arms. Your mom and dad are waiting for you, Simon. Above all, you need them in your life. Now, turn back around and go to your parents. I'll be right here until you reach your world," she instructed.

"I love you, Neopoleana!" Simon cried one last time.

She smiled and winked as he turned around and quickly took another step. The Rhues and creatures began to sing the chorus to "We Touch with Our Hearts." Simon listened deeply to the words, "So close your eyes and see with your dreams, feel me close by you, for your heart touches mine."

Soon he was walking onward, realizing how near the creatures and Rhues would always be to him through his heart. As the beautiful, heartfelt singing and the music from Tooty's pan flute snout faded, he paused and then turned around. All he could see was dazzling walls of diamond.

Simon then dried the last of his tears and said to himself, "You're right, Neopoleana. It's time for me to return home to my mom and dad. Man, are they going to be surprised to see me. I can hardly wait to see them!"

As he turned to continue his journey home, Simon slid his hand down inside his pocket. "Yeah, the stone pebbles are still there," he thought with a smile. He then began to whistle and to skip at a steady pace, knowing he was on the right road, and it truly would lead him back home!

Sweet Memories

Karen's Hope, Jim's "Reality"

FOR DAYS, KAREN'S thoughts of Simon had been muddled with confusion. Her sleepless nights had returned, and when she did sleep, it was filled with either very good dreams or haunting nightmares of her son. Jim noticed the change in her, for his wife had become unusually quiet during the days. At night, she would awaken him with terrorizing screams, crying out in her sleep for Simon.

This morning, during breakfast, Jim questioned her. "Karen, I really thought you were getting a grip on life again, but it never lasts. You seem to be more down now than ever. Maybe...uh... you should see a doctor," he cautiously suggested.

"I'm okay, Jim. I don't want to see a doctor!" she firmly replied.

"Well, I'm very concerned. You just can't keep letting these horrible feelings consume your very being. A good doctor could help," Jim assured her.

Karen snapped. "Feeling like what, Jim? You don't know what I'm feeling. A doctor—of course, we know you mean a shrink— sure wouldn't know!"

"Calm down now, Karen. I didn't mean to get you so uptight."

She took a long, deep breath and sat down at the kitchen table. "Jim, I know you still think I'm crazy or something, but the strange feelings I had before have returned. They are real, and they mean something," she spoke with compassion, hoping he would finally understand.

Jim sighed. "Karen, I don't think you are crazy. I just believe severe anxiety is causing your problems," he gingerly expressed his opinion.

Of course, Karen's expression immediately changed. "Jim, I'm sorry, but I absolutely do not agree with you!" she exclaimed. "How can you even think they're just anxiety attacks after what we both experienced at the wishing well? I'm telling you, something is going on with our son, but I don't believe it is something bad. Things have changed for the better for Simon. This is what I strongly feel."

Here we go again, Jim thought as he rolled his eyes upward for a moment. "Of course, I had strange feelings back at the wishing well. Our son is gone. We feel and see crazy things, but the reality of it all is that these strange feelings are from anxiety and distraught!" he blasted. "Can't you just face the truth, Karen?"

She stared at Jim with a blank look, determined not to show any emotion as he continued speaking his mind with questions of authority. "Don't you realize these feelings are different because they do involve Simon, our own flesh and blood? Don't you see that you are living in this hope of yours—a hope based on some make-believe legend?"

Jim then got up from the kitchen chair and placed his arm gently across Karen's shoulders, drawing near to her face. "Please make an appointment with a good psychiatrist today, for your own sake and for mine—for our sake," he whispered as if begging but now feeling in complete control of the situation.

Karen rolled her eyes back and shook her head in frustration. Quickly, she pulled away from Jim and hustled from her chair. *If only he could understand*, she thought while walking near the double sinks and peering out the small window. She sighed deeply from feeling defeated and then whirled around to give what he wanted to hear. "Okay, Jim! I'll call a shrink today. Anything to make you happy!" she smirked.

"Oh, come on, Karen," he whined like a whipped pup while walking near and scooping her up in his arms. "You act as though I'm punishing you or something. I love you and just want you to have a better perspective of reality."

"Whatever!" Karen snapped, squirming and breaking loose from Jim's tight embrace. She immediately turned her back on him.

Jim didn't like her gesture and quickly walked around to face her to speak boldly. "Look, Karen! I care for you and Simon more than anything in this world, but we can't live forever on the hope of some make-believe legend coming true! Our son has been gone over two weeks now! You need to face the possibility he could be…uh…well, you know," he lingered the sentence, realizing he had said far too much.

"*Dead!* Say the word!" Karen screamed in anguish. "You believe our son could be dead!" she cried out while running into the living room and plopping down on the sofa. Her fast movements startled Bingo, causing the dog to jump and whine.

Jim followed behind her. "Karen, I'm sorry, but this is the sort of thing I'm talking about. You can't face any real possibilities!" he spoke out, holding firm.

"That's because that is all they are for now. They are just possibilities! What is so crazy with me holding on to hope and believing in something that goes beyond what we have *learned* to be real? That is my possibilities! Why can't they be accepted for what they are?" Karen preached, leaving Jim speechless.

She had actually gotten to him, but after a few minutes of sighing in weak thought, Jim meekly muttered, "I do have hope and belief, but I also realize that hope can run out. That is when reality sets in."

"Well, it hasn't run out for me! In fact, my hope is stronger than ever before. I feel Simon's presence, and I know deep inside my heart that he is still trying to get home. Not you, nor any psychiatrist, can take that away from me!" Karen firmly responded while wiping her tear-soaked face with the back of her hand. "Can you not understand that?"

Once again, Jim was feeling compassion for his wife. "I have been trying. I really have. You think I have given up on Simon, but I haven't, Karen," he replied.

"Well, you act as though you have!"

"It's just that I'm not as emotional as you," Jim responded.

Karen became critical. "Yeah, you keep everything inside. You always have! I know deep down in my heart that what occurred at the wishing well meant something to you! You are just shrugging it off as coincidental circumstances!"

This sharp criticism hit Jim hard, but he didn't show emotion. Instead, he turned away, hoping she wouldn't notice his sheepish face. "I've got to get to work," he spoke, quickly changing the subject.

"See! You can't even talk about it!" Karen exclaimed as she followed in behind his every step.

Jim suddenly turned around and firmly spoke, "That is because there is nothing to talk about!"

"Yeah, right!" Karen snickered.

Without warning, Jim grabbed her up and planted a kiss on her lips. "You are so stubborn! You know that, don't you?" he jokingly asked with a chuckle.

Karen couldn't help but smile. "Well, what about you?" she laughed while goosing his stomach.

Jim laughed and grabbed his stomach area to slow down the tickling sensations. "I guess you're right. We're both pretty stubborn."

"Now let me get out of here," Jim stated before giving Karen a peck on the cheek. Quickly, he headed to the front door then turned to slyly slide in a reminder, "Now don't forget your appointment, Karen!"

"Okay, Doctor Sphinx!" she teased.

Before Karen knew it, Bingo had squeezed through the half-opened door and run down the steps, wagging his tail and yelping. Jim patted him on the head and then scooted the hyper dog back to the front porch. "See you this evening!" he yelled as he hurried to his car.

Bingo barked as Karen watched until Jim's car was out of sight. "Come on, Bingo! I've got to look a doctor up in the phone book!" she fussed while shutting the front door.

As he drove to work, Jim began to think about how Karen seemed to read his mind. *She knows I saw something more at the wishing well, but I can't tell her the truth. If she knew I saw Simon's reflection, she would read far too much into it.*

"I would never hear the end of it!" Jim exclaimed out loud. *She's too wrapped up in deep emotions. Sure, I have strange feelings, but I know they are caused by stress and anxiety. I must stay focused on reality,* he determined then reached for the knob and turned on the radio. The soft, relaxing classical music was soothing to his mind and faded the thoughts away, for the time being.

A Dream of Hope

Karen plopped the phone book down on the kitchen table, pulled out the chair, sat down, and opened it up to the yellow pages. She then looked up "psychiatrists." "My heavens!" she shouted. "Is the entire world insane? Look at all the psychiatrists listed here! There are three pages full!"

Before beginning the task of deciding which "unknown good doctor" to choose, Karen got up to pour herself a cup of steaming hot, black coffee. She sat back down, sighed, and then slowly went down each page with her index finger. "Now, how am I supposed to decide on which one to call?" she asked out loud.

Bingo perked up his ears then whined and yawned before resting his head against her feet.

"I'm doing this for Jim only because he doesn't understand my feelings," she muttered then closed her eyes and placed her index finger upon the page. *Which name I point to, that's the one I'll call,* she thought while sliding her finger down the page.

After stopping half-way down the page, Karen opened her eyes to read the name Dr. R. B. Dollar. She busted out in laughter. "Well, I'm sure the name suits him with what he'll charge per hour just to tell me what my thoughts and feelings mean!" she exclaimed.

Karen picked up the cordless phone receiver she had laying on the table and then took a deep breath. "There's no use in putting this off," she whispered while dialing the number.

Suddenly, she heard the voice at the other end. "Dr. R. B. Dollar's office. How may I help you?"

"Hello, I'm Karen Sphinx. I would like to make an appointment to see Dr. Dollar," she nervously spoke into the receiver.

Before the receptionist could even speak, Karen rattled, "My husband seems to think I need help. My son is missing, and I've been anxious. Gosh, what does he expect! I'm Simon's mother!"

Finally, Karen got quiet when she heard the voice on the other end speaking very loudly. "Mrs. Sphinx, Mrs. Sphinx!"

"Uh…uh…oh, I'm sorry for going on and on like that," Karen apologized. "Now what were you saying?," she asked while thinking, *I bet she already thinks I'm a nutcase* after *hearing me mutter like that!*

"If you would like an appointment with Dr. Dollar, I have a cancellation for 10:00 a.m. tomorrow morning. If you do not want that one, there isn't another available for two weeks," the receptionist spoke in a professional manner. "Would you like the 10:00 a.m. appointment?"

"Well, that's kind of fast, but I'll take it," Karen replied.

"I need to ask you some questions, if you do not mind. It will save so much time to get this out of the way before your arrival," the receptionist pointed out.

"That will be fine," Karen obliged.

She went through about fifty questions (some seeming very silly to Karen) with the receptionist and then called for Bingo. "Come on, Bingo!" she ordered while whistling for the tired dog. "Let's go upstairs!"

Karen made her and Jim's bed up and then proceeded to dust and vacuum. As she finished up the work, she realized what a good mood she was in. *Gosh, I sure am feeling better*, she thought before leaving the freshly cleaned room.

As Karen approached Simon's room, she paused and stared at the closed door. One of her strange feelings came over her, but this time it was different, being rather soothing and calming. For some odd reason, she felt the need to spruce up her son's room. As she slowly opened the door, Bingo pushed his way through and immediately jumped upon Simon's bed, sniffing it thoroughly.

Karen didn't question her "new" feeling too much. She just went to work with the dusting and vacuuming then scooted Bingo off the bed and changed the linen. After making sure everything (including Simon's rock collection), was neat and in place, she breathed deeply and smiled.

"Come on, Bingo!" she called. The frisky mutt whined, holding back.

Karen grinned. "Okay, boy, you can sleep on Simon's bed. He would like that." Bingo ran and jumped in the middle of the soft, crisp and fresh linen as Karen walked away, leaving the door open.

She hopped down the stairs and crashed on the sofa. *Gosh, I'm tired. I can't believe all the work I've done. I'll just stretch out here and rest awhile*, she thought. She fluffed the sofa pillow and laid her head back on it, stretching out completely. As she looked up toward the ceiling, her thoughts went to Simon. *Why did I have the urge to clean your room, Simon? What's going on with you? I feel something, but it doesn't feel bad*, she whispered as if he were there.

Soon Karen had talked herself to sleep, drifting fast into a dream—an extraordinarily realistic vision. She was at the wishing well looking down inside at Simon's reflection and listening to his screams. "Mama! Mama, I can't get out! Help me, Mama!"

"Climb the sides of the well!" Karen shouted in desperation.

"I'm scared! I might fall!" Simon cried.

"Don't be afraid! I'll be right here to help guide you," she promised.

Simon took a deep breath then stretched his arms out, pressing his hands tightly against the well's inner round concrete wall. He lifted his left leg up and put his foot against the wall. He then pulled his right leg up and put that foot against the other side of the wall. Simon then took another deep breath before beginning the strenuous climb up the wall, sliding one hand then the other, sliding one foot then the other.

Karen was right there to lend her support. "Come on, son, you're doing great! It won't be long until you reach me!" she cheered.

Sweat beads popped loose from her son's forehead and began to trickle down into his eyes, causing an almost unbearable stinging sensation. He batted his eyes rapidly, but this caused the pain to worsen. Soon his eyes were completely blinded by the sweat brine. He panicked. "Mama, I can't see, and my eyes are hurting bad!" he screamed in torment.

"I know, baby. The sweat from your brows is dripping into your eyes. I know this is painful, but you mustn't turn loose!" Karen begged.

He shouted with fear, "But I can't see! I'm so afraid!"

Karen gave assurance. "That is okay. You don't need to see. Just feel your hands and feet against the concrete wall and work your way up. Concentrate hard on this instead of your burning eyes," she pleaded.

"I'll try, Mama!" Simon cried as he slowly inched up the wall.

"Come on, sweetheart! You're almost here!" Karen prodded as she extended her hand down inside the well, stretching as far as possible without risking falling in.

She could hear Simon's grunts and groans as he struggled with all his might to make it to his mother. "That's it, Simon. Just a little farther, and I can reach you!"

Simon inched upward, pausing within reaching distance of his mom. Slowly, he removed his right hand from the wall as Karen stretched her arm downward with all her might, preparing to grab hold of his hand, her heart pounding and racing with excitement.

Just as their fingertips were about to touch, Karen suddenly woke up. She was breathing hard, and the sweat from her own brows was burning her eyes. Quickly, she ran to the bathroom and splashed cool water on her face. "Gosh, what a dream. It seemed so real!" she said to herself while staring in the mirror above the sink. "I almost touched you, Simon. I now know that you are nearing the end of your journey home. I feel you so strongly," she whispered then smiled at her image before walking away.

A Nice Surprise for Jim

Karen was in good spirits the rest of the afternoon. She even called her friend Patricia Shatterly to chat and to check on Doug.

"You sound better than I've heard you in a long time," Patricia commented.

"I am doing better," Karen replied but decided again not to discuss her deep, innermost feelings.

"Enough about me. What about you and Doug?" she asked, taking the focus off her.

"I'm doing fine since Doug has gotten better emotionally. His grades are back to where they should be," Patricia answered. "I know he thinks of Simon every day, so do I, but life goes on, doesn't it?" she subtly asked.

Karen agreed. "Yes, it does. I will never give up hope on Simon, but I must go on with my life also. I have an appointment with a psychiatrist tomorrow," she blurted, surprising Patricia.

"Oh, that is wonderful—I mean it's good that you are getting help to deal with your emotions," Patricia explained.

"Well, actually, it's Jim's idea, but I figure it won't hurt me to spill my guts to a professional counselor," Karen spoke with tones of resentment.

"You sound somewhat reluctant. You could try to have a good attitude about it, you know?" Patricia advised.

"Oh, don't worry. My attitude is just fine," Karen boasted rather arrogantly. "I'm sure that Dr. Dollar will know me inside and out after I spend an hour or so with him. He will know what my every thought means. Imagine—a complete stranger will talk to me a short while, asking me all kinds of personal questions, and then he will proceed to analyze my answers. From this, Dr. Dollar will glean out what I feel and why I feel it!" she cockily emphasized.

Patricia chuckled. "Karen, you are so dramatic! Psychiatrists are highly trained to recognize problems. I'm sure Dr. Dollar can help you."

"Whatever!" Karen blurted.

"Well, let me know how your first visit with him goes," Patricia spoke with concern.

Karen snapped, "My first visit? So you're already counting!"

"You know what I mean. He may or may not need to see you again. I don't know," Patricia spoke out.

"Well, I'll call you tomorrow and let you know how it went, okay?" Karen responded. "Right now, I'm going to fix Jim a special dinner," she spoke with excitement.

"Ooh la la, that does sound nice. Now don't forget to call me!" Patricia reminded her before hanging up.

Karen scurried to the kitchen and pulled open the top drawer of the china hutch. She reached in, pulled out her favorite blue apron, shaking it to its original shape. She then tied the apron around her waist and went to work.

First, she would make the luscious chocolate mousse that Jim always raved over. Then, while it was chilling, she would change into something gorgeous but not too elegant. For a different look, she would even put her hair up.

After getting dressed into the perfect long black skirt and red satin blouse, Karen finished preparing the food, spaghetti and meatballs, salad, and French bread. She went all out, covering the table with their antique white lace tablecloth. For a final touch, she lit two long red tapered candles and placed them in the center of the table.

Jim will be surprised! He will love this! Karen bubbled with excitement.

The smell of the scrumptious meatballs caused Bingo to awaken and drool at the mouth. Soon he was down the stairs, heading straight to the kitchen. "Now look, Bingo! I can't have you yelping and jumping around during dinner!" Karen scolded. "I made a couple of extra meatballs for you. Now calm down and eat them!"

Bingo devoured the tasty beef plus a bowl of dog food. He then finished off with a large bowl of water. "Well, that should hold you!" Karen exclaimed. "Now go lie down in the living room," she commanded while pointing her finger. Bingo immediately obeyed, running to the sofa and jumping up to his favorite spot.

Within minutes, Karen heard Jim's car pull up in the driveway. Quickly, she untied the blue apron and yanked it off then hid behind the kitchen door.

"Hello, I'm home!" Jim greeted as he came through the front door. Of course, Bingo immediately jumped down from the sofa and ran to get his usual pat on the head.

"Where's Karen?" he questioned. The frisky dog yelped a couple of times and then whined.

"Karen, where are you?"

Delectable aromas led Jim to the kitchen. "Boo!" Karen playfully joked as she jumped out from behind the door, startling him.

"Hey! Scare somebody to death, would you?" he chuckled while stopping in his tracks to stare. All he could say was, "Wow, look at you!"

"So you like it?" Karen asked with a cute, blushing smile.

"Do I like it?" Jim repeated. "You look ravishing!" he exclaimed while hugging her tight. "Speaking of ravishing"—he whispered in her ear—"what do I smell cooking?"

"I fixed all your favorites—spaghetti and meatballs, French garlic bread, and for dessert, chocolate mousse," Karen spoke, emphasizing the word "chocolate." Just the sound of this luscious treat caused Jim's taste buds to dance, making his mouth water.

During their candlelight dinner, Jim couldn't help but wonder about Karen's good mood. *She must have made a doctor's appointment and is feeling better already, knowing she is going to be helped*, he analyzed. *I want to ask her about it, but I'd better wait. Maybe I can get her to bring it up.*

Jim began his prodding. "Well, it looks like you had a good, productive day, sweetheart."

Karen smiled. "Oh, it was nice. How was yours?"

Jim gave a quick grin. "It was okay. Business was slow, so I caught up some paperwork. Did anyone call today?" he quickly asked.

Karen looked at him oddly for asking that question and then responded in a put-out manner. "No, but I called Patricia.

"Well, how are she and Doug?" Jim asked.

"They are fine," she answered, deliberately being short.

"Did you call anyone else today?" Jim asked, digging deeper.

Karen screeched loud, "Oh, for crying out loud! Why don't you just come out and ask me if I called a psychiatrist today?"

"Uh…I was pretty obvious, wasn't I? I'm sorry," Jim apologized in an embarrassing manner.

A feeling of relief came over him immediately as he thought, *Yeah, I was right. Karen feels better just knowing she will be getting the help she needs.* He smiled back at her, and they finished their dinner without any talk of strange feelings or legends.

Silent Conversation

After dinner, Jim and Karen snuggled up on the sofa while Bingo rested on the floor in front of them. Jim had eaten so much, he fell asleep during the movie they were watching. Even this did not bother Karen. She actually felt herself getting sleepy for the first time in days.

"Jim! Jim! You need to get up and get ready for bed," she quietly yelled, nudging him with her hand as Bingo yelped.

"Uh...uh...oh, I'm sorry. I dozed off, didn't I?"

"That's what too much good food will do," Karen chuckled. Jim smiled and then sluggishly got up with her. She guided him toward the stairwell and up the stairs. He was too groggy to even notice Simon's open bedroom door. Karen made sure he had his pajamas on and was in bed before she took off to the bathroom. *Bam!* He was asleep as soon as his head hit the pillow.

Jim can shower in the morning, Karen thought as she ran herself a hot bath. She reached for her favorite bath oil and added a few squirts to the running water, breathing in the wonderful scent of jasmine. She then slid down through the tub of hot bubbles. *Oh, this feels so soothing*, she thought as bubbles pooled around her neck.

Karen enjoyed the warmth of the water while reminiscing of good times. Pictures passed through her mind as her thoughts went to Simon's first birthday party at the age of two. He tried so hard to blow out the two green candles on the cake. She could still see the tiny bubbles gurgling from his mouth, and she smiled.

Next, she thought of Simon's Christmas at the age of six. That's when he got his first bicycle (from Santa, of course). Jim had insisted to not leave the training wheels on. *Simon will learn to ride much faster without the crutch those wheels provide!* she remembered him saying. She then laughed. *Gosh! How I fretted over Simon getting broken bones! I didn't want Jim to turn loose of the bike, but he did anyway!*

She then drifted into thoughts of Simon after he learned to read. *His imagination was always wild! From the minute he learned to read, Simon seemed to be drawn to books about dimensions in time and of other worlds.*

Soon a picture of the book Karen had found in Simon's room after his disappearance came into her head. The title appeared in big, capital letters: THE LEGEND OF THE SPHINX. "That was a true legend," she whispered. "Simon, after thousands of years, it was you who ended up with the 'evil eye' of the sphinx. It was you who happened to have the last name of Sphinx, and it was you who was obsessed with other worlds and wished every day at the well to see one!" Karen spoke as if her son could hear her.

"Simon, I feel you so near, yet you're still far away. I only hope you can feel my presence as strongly as I do yours. There was closure to the legend after I crushed the 'sphinx eye.' Your Dad and I saw how the crystal powder made the water rush and bubble when I sprinkled it over the well water. After the water settled, a peaceful feeling came over me. I had no doubt the sphinx had been destroyed. It was at this point I knew beyond anything I had ever believed that you were going to return home," Karen softly whispered with assuring tones.

"Of course, I've had doubtful times, but they have never outweighed my hope and faith. This entire ordeal just seems so far out, but many odd and unexplained happenings occur throughout this world every day, even to the point of being unrealistic," she analyzed.

"You will be home. I know it. I know it deep down inside my heart!" she firmly stated with a smile then sat up and reached for the soft, fluffy bath towel beside the tub. She dried off, put on a cozy cotton gown, and then went straight to bed.

After having had a "silent conversation" with Simon, Karen was now the most relaxed she had been since his strange disappearance, and it would not take her long to fall into a deep, peaceful sleep. Even Bingo's yelp didn't disturb her when the mooch decided to sleep in their room.

Several hours passed with Karen sleeping soundly. She had no idea just how close to home her son was getting.

Reassurance from Neopoleana—
Getting Closer to Home

SIMON TROD ONWARD through the beautiful, glistening diamond tunnel. The sparkling crystal was now beginning to resemble hard, thick ice. This made him feel very cold, and he shivered. For a long while, he had been excited over his homecoming, but now Simon had begun to notice the eeriness of the silence. Plus, the tunnel seemed to have no end.

He stopped about every thirty minutes to rest, his thoughts always mixed with images of his mom and dad and the Rhues and creatures of Rhueland and Gruhland. Even Bronzella taunted his brain from time to time.

After walking and running another hour or so, anxiousness set in. Simon's stomach knotted up as thoughts of doom entered his mind and became overwhelming. "I wonder when I'll reach the end?" he asked himself. "I feel as though I have been in here for days. I'm tired and hungry and thirsty! I could perish soon!"

One what-if question after another flooded Simon's mind. "What if this tunnel has no end? What if I get sealed up in here forever? What if it this cave crumbles down, crushing me to mush?" All these what-ifs soon worked Simon into a panic. As fear gripped his every fiber, he took off running and screaming. "Help! help! I want out of here!" His voice echoed loud and deep within the tunnel, causing him to feel even more closed in.

Finally, Simon was so out of breath from running he had to stop. It took several minutes of panting for him to start breathing normal again. Feeling helpless, he curled up into a ball on the cold, solidly packed black dirt floor. "I'm feeling so afraid for some reason. I should have already reached the end of my journey home," he cried.

After several minutes of sobbing, Simon thought about the Mother Rhue. "Neopoleana wouldn't send me through this tunnel if it wasn't the way home. She loves me and would never lie to me. She is much too wise to make such a mistake." He remembered what the wise Mother Rhue told him, "Think of your mom and dad and how much they love you. Feel with your heart". He could see and hear her speak these words almost as if she were standing over him.

"But I'm scared, Neopoleana," Simon cried as he closed his eyes and hoped she would really be there when he opened them. Something marvelous and wonderful occurred right at that very moment! As he slowly opened his eyes, he could really see Neopoleana! The Rhues and creatures were even grouped together, looking down at him. They began singing the chorus to "We Touch with Our Hearts." He listened intently as the beautiful words rang out, "So close your eyes and see with your dreams. Feel me close by you, for your heart touches mine."

After receiving comfort from these words, Simon began to sing it out loud. He got up with determination to continue his journey home. "Mama, I'll be there soon! I hope you can hear me," he whispered with renewed excitement.

The images of his friends had faded, but Simon was now ready to travel onward. "Thank you, Neopoleana," he exclaimed while moving ahead, singing over and over the chorus to this most heartfelt song. With renewed strength of the heart and mind, Simon walked fast, for he knew he was getting closer and closer to the end of his journey and nearer to home.

He didn't know, but something glorious and spectacular was also taking place within his mom's heart as he sang and whispered to her.

The Wait

The Promise

KAREN SUDDENLY AWAKENED from her deep sleep, feeling her son's presence as never before. She sat up in bed and closed her eyes, enjoying the feeling of the moment. *Simon, you are so near. I must go to the wishing well, for I feel that you will be home soon, and this is where you will return.* She became ecstatic and hopped out of bed with a smile upon her face. For the first time in weeks, Karen had absolutely no fears.

"Jim! Jim! You must get up!" she called while shaking him.

"What on earth is wrong?" he sleepily exclaimed.

"Oh, honey, there is nothing wrong—nothing at all! Everything is so right!" she elated with pure joy.

Jim rubbed his foggy eyes. "What do you mean?"

Karen shouted with anticipation, "Simon is getting closer to home. We must go to the wishing well and wait for his return!"

Jim went ballistic. "What! It's 2:00 a.m. Are you crazy?" he spoke with disgust. "Never mind—I already know! You're having one of your strange feelings again!"

Karen snapped, "Oh, please, Jim! Don't ridicule me now! We've got to get going. This is more than an urge!"

Jim shook his head in disbelief as he sighed and thought, *I'm so thankful Karen is seeing a psychiatrist tomorrow.*

"Jim, if you will go with me, I promise you—this will absolutely be the last time I ever ask," Karen pleaded. Before he could say one word, she added, "I know that I made this promise once before, but this time it's different. I know in my heart our son is coming home tonight!"

Her pleading continued, "Please, Jim, come with me! If Simon doesn't return, I promise to tell the shrin—uh…psychiatrist—tomorrow about my strange feelings, even about this last trip to the wishing well!"

"Calm down, Karen!" Jim firmly ordered. "You're too emotional, and it's really making me nervous! Look at yourself! You're in frenzy!"

Karen took a long, deep breath, held it a moment, then slowly let it out. "I'm sorry, Jim, but I'm just excited, that's all," she calmly spoke while fumbling around, trying to get dressed. "Well, are you going with me?" she asked in a matter-of-fact manner after realizing he had not moved from the edge of the bed.

"For gosh's sakes, Karen, this is insane!" Jim scolded as he got up and slid into his tattered brown bedroom shoes.

"Jim, we don't have time to argue. If you are going to the wishing well with me, you must get dressed, okay?" she ordered in a pleading manner.

He sighed heavily. "All right, Karen. I can't have you messing around out there alone. But remember, this is the last time for good!"

Karen smiled and nodded at him. "Thank you, sweetheart. Now hurry and get dressed. We're wasting valuable time!" she prodded.

Bingo had moved off their bed to sleep in Simon's room, but Jim and Karen's loud voices had awakened him. The dog ran into their bedroom wagging his tail. "You want to go with us, boy?" Karen asked. Bingo yelped a couple of times as if answering yes then ran to her for a quick pat on the head. "Simon's coming home tonight, you know," she spoke with tones of excitement. Bingo barked twice and then jumped around and around. "Okay, okay!" Karen fussed while bending down for a couple of wet tongue laps just to calm him down.

"You can go with us, but you can't be barking loud in the park," Jim ordered as he glanced toward Bingo. Again, the dog yelped a couple of times.

"Oh, he will be fine," Karen spoke out.

Jim had dressed and was ready to go in less than ten minutes. Karen was surprised when he shouted, "Let's go and get this over with!"

As they walked out the back door, Karen overheard Jim's mutters. *This is just so crazy! I can't believe I'm going through this again! We should be sleeping!*

"Jim, please!" she scolded with frustration. "I told you this will be the last time I go to the wishing well. Why can't you stop complaining so much?" Before he could answer, Karen added, "You act as though you have no hope left of Simon returning home. That bothers me!"

"Karen, we have been over this a hundred or more times. I do have hope, but I'm trying hard to be realistic. I'm telling you your emotions are out of whack!"

"Whatever!" Karen snapped as they walked to the car. She opened the door, got in, and slammed it hard.

Jim ordered Bingo to hop into the car. The pooch leaped onto the backseat and began pouncing from one side to the other, whining and yelping loud. "Settle down, boy!" Jim demanded while cranking up the car, causing the dog to howl in a distressed manner as if saddened by his tone. However, he quickly obeyed, stretching out across the seat and becoming quiet.

Before he pulled out of the driveway, Karen tried to reason with Jim, speaking much calmer. "I do understand how crazy you must think my feelings are. However, I truly meant what I said.

If Simon doesn't return home tonight, these excursions to the wishing well will cease. I will not pursue this any further."

Jim swallowed the lump in his throat as he glanced toward Karen with a look of compassion. She was so full of love and hope for her son. Why did he have to be so hard on her about facing reality? He smiled into her eyes and then reached out to pull her close and hold her tight before taking off to the wishing well.

The Confessions

The night was cool, crisp, and a bit foggy, creating an eerie setting in the park. Jim and Karen began the tranquil walk, hearing nothing but buzzing music presented by the crickets and tree frogs. They gazed into the distance, noticing how the sparse lighting throughout the park cast a haunting image of the well.

Suddenly, Bingo stopped and lay down, unwilling to budge. His whines of insecurity were making Karen very nervous. "What's wrong, Bingo? You've never been afraid of the dark," she uttered.

"I guess the high-pitched tones of the chirping crickets are hurting his eardrums," Jim analyzed. Karen bent down to give the mooch reassurance with a hug and pat on the head. He wagged his tail with excitement but the whining continued when the petting stopped.

The two then moved on toward the wishing well, trying to ignore Bingo's pitiful cries as he lagged behind. Soon they were there, and Karen immediately had an urge to peep down inside the well. Bingo yelped as she stepped upon the bottom railing and slowly leaned over to peer down through the water.

"What are you doing?" Jim shouted. "Do you think Simon is going to come up through the well or something?"

"He could, you know," Karen sharply replied as she stared down at the dark, calm water.

"You need to sit down so Bingo will calm down!" Jim demanded. "We don't want him barking. The cops might show up," he lectured.

Karen noticed how Bingo was still fidgeting around. "Come on, boy!" she softly called while stepping off the railing. She then sat down and called again, "Come over here!" Bingo quickly ran to get his fur frisked a minute or so and then lay down at her feet. She gently stroked his head, hoping the dog would remain settled.

After several minutes of total silence, Jim popped a question. "What brought this on? I mean, what possessed you this time, Karen?"

She sighed heavily. "Jim, you know that it's hard for me to explain these types of deep feelings."

"Just try, please," he pleaded. "I'm trying to gain some understanding of where you're coming from."

Karen took a deep breath. With a look of serenity upon her face, she thought for a minute as if she were searching for the correct explanation. "Okay, I'll try to explain 'where I'm coming from' she quipped. "You know I carried Simon for nine months inside of me."

Jim chuckled and then interrupted. "Of course I know that!"

"Well, a special bond was formed between us just from having had Simon that close before he was even born.

Again, Jim interrupted. "I know all that!"

"Just let me finish, okay?" Karen scolded. Jim swallowed and didn't speak again.

At that moment, Karen began to confess her innermost feelings. "The bond I have with Simon seems to go extra deep. I've always had this 'sixth sense'—a feeling of knowing when he was happy, sad, sick, or hurt. Remember that time when I suddenly felt so ill at work that I had to come home? I wasn't in the house more than thirty minutes before the school called. Simon was sick and I had to go pick him up."

Jim listened attentively as Karen continued. "Do you remember the time my knee throbbed the entire day and then Simon came home from playing basketball with a hurt knee? I can feel our son's emotions. That is why and how I know he is alive. That is how I know he is on his way home. I can feel it inside my heart!" she elated.

Jim stared into Karen's compassionate eyes as she finished speaking. "All the strange feelings I've been experiencing are actually coming from Simon's emotions. We have a special connection through our hearts. This is how we touch."

"That's deep, Karen," Jim responded. "I know you're Simon's mother, and I can see why you would sense things when they involve him, but this is kind of far-out!" he spoke with reservation.

Karen smiled while giving some good points. "Well, if you can see that I sense things going on with Simon, why can't you see how it's possible for this connection to go deeper? There is no set rule on a stopping point, is there?" she questioned with confidence.

Jim had a funny look come upon his face. Karen had gotten to him with these questions. "Well, you do have a point," he muttered, trying to appear casual.

"I have a good and valid point!" Karen confirmed. "I'm telling you, I can feel Simon's presence. We touch with our hearts!"

As a smile came across his face, Jim reached out and wrapped his arms around Karen. He now truly understood "where she was coming from." His wife possessed such a complete, ultimate, and unselfish love for her son. Her faith, hope, and belief were strong, real, and true. They let her travel beyond what anyone could actually see in the reality of this world, for they were her "eyes" coming from the heart and letting her "see."

"Karen, I love you, and I do understand these deep feelings you have," he softly whispered into her ear.

With surprise, Karen pulled back, breaking his embrace. She then looked straight into Jim's eyes. "Are you trying to tell me something?" she asked with anticipation.

Jim downed his head. Karen put her hand under his chin and pushed gently upward, holding firm. "Please don't hold anything back!" she begged. "I just spilled my guts to you. Now is the time for you to do the same."

Jim took her hand into his and then reached for her other hand. As he held them tightly and stared deep into her eyes, he began to confess. "Karen, when I was at this wishing well that day you and Patricia saw me, I did experience something."

He then paused and looked away, causing Karen to become anxious. "Oh, please, Jim! Let it out! What was this experience?" she pleaded while nudging his shoulder.

Jim hesitated a moment longer then quickly turned and stared straight into his wife's eyes. "I saw Simon's reflection in the wishing well," he blurted out.

Karen squealed with both excitement and relief that Jim had finally shared this special happening with her. "Oh, Jim, I just knew in my heart that you had experienced something marvelous. Thank you from the bottom of my heart for confessing this to me!" she cried.

"I'm sorry for keeping it inside me so long, but I was afraid. I figured it was just my nerves, and with the way you were having strange feelings, well, I didn't want you reading too much into it," Jim explained.

"That's okay! I'm glad you told me now. You do understand my feelings!" she elated and then laid her head gently on his lap. Jim began to stroke her face and hair gently as they quietly sat in waiting. Soon they drifted off into a light snooze as Bingo lay stretched beneath their feet, sleeping soundly.

Getting Anxious

The two slept a couple of hours before Jim woke up. He looked at his watch and then nudged Karen. "Wake up! Wake up!" he called. "It's 5:00 a.m. It will be getting daylight soon."

"I can't believe we dozed off like that," Karen sleepily spoke while rubbing her burning eyes. "Where's Bingo?" she asked.

Jim looked around while quietly calling to him. "Bingo! Where are you, boy?" The mooch ran out from behind a small group of nearby bushes. "You're getting hungry, aren't you?" he asked as Bingo yelped and wagged his tail.

"Karen, we can't stay here much longer," Jim exclaimed, causing her to sigh.

For the first time, she felt horrible pangs down in her heart, and for the first time, she was feeling the agony of losing a bit of hope. "Just a little while longer, please, Jim?" she begged with anxiousness.

Jim took a deep breath. "Okay, we'll stay another hour, but if Simon hasn't returned by then, we must leave."

"He'll be here, Jim. I just know it!" Karen beamed as her eyes roamed the dusky darkness of the park in anticipation.

The Surprise

Simon was still walking onward at a steady pace, singing his song. He was starting to feel hunger pangs when he noticed how the inside of the tunnel was starting to look different. The solid, glistening diamond walls were coming to an end, for just ahead, they were nothing more than gray rock and packed red clay. The floor of the tunnel was getting damp and cool. He became totally excited. "Oh my gosh! I must be nearing the end!" he shouted.

Just before stepping inside the walls of dull, gray rock, Simon turned to take one last look at the dazzling diamond fortress he would be leaving behind. His breath was taken away for a moment, his eyes grew big as saucers, and his mouth dropped open at what he saw. There, lying within five feet of his reach, was the biggest, most magnificent uncut diamond he would ever see! It was flawless! "Why didn't I see that awhile ago?" he asked himself while slowly creeping toward the beautiful creation. "Oh man, wow!" he exclaimed while kneeling down for a closer view.

For a few moments, Simon just stared at the gleaming jewel with big eyes and then reached down to gently pick it up. With the beauty clutched in both hands, he peered down through the sparkling tunnel. "Thank you, Neopoleana," he whispered with a soft smile. He then slowly opened his hand to examine the rare crystal. "I think Mama will love this. She can have all kinds of stuff made just from this one huge diamond!" he shouted out loud with excitement. He took one last look and then forced the magnificent jewel inside his pocket, straining and grunting to push it down. He gently slid his hand down inside the other pocket. "Yeah, the stone pebbles are still there!" He beamed.

Simon patted the bulging pocket before turning around to take off again, going very fast. He had gone only a short distance before seeing that the tunnel's floor was beginning to puddle with red, muddy water. The walls were becoming mostly packed dirt. His heart began to beat just a little faster with joyous anxiousness. He picked up speed as he shouted, "I'm getting close to home, Mom and Dad! I'm almost there!"

Doubt Closes In

The hour went by fast, and Karen had become overwhelmed with anxiousness. Her heart begged her not to give up, but her body was tired. She began to wonder if all she had felt and experienced was just her imagination. This doubt made her feel lost, cold, and confused.

"We must go home now, Karen. It's 6:00 a.m. We both need rest, and Bingo is hungry and thirsty," Jim spoke, knowing she would not want to leave.

She cried in vain. "Oh, Jim, where is Simon? Why didn't he come back home?"

Karen's emotions caused him to experience heartfelt compassion. "I don't know. I don't have all the answers. Gosh, I hate to see you hurting like this," he responded.

Karen became desperate. "Simon! Simon! Where are you? Please hear me! I know you are not dead! Please, Simon! Let me see you!"

Feeling lost and hurt himself, Jim's eyes filled with tears. "Come on, Karen," he softly spoke while clutching her by the arm.

He wailed with "I know this is emotional anguish, Karen! My heart is also ripped out, but it's now time to turn loose. Come on. Let me take you home," he cried as he nudged her along.

Karen pulled back harder, this time breaking away and running fast to the wishing well, screaming for her son. Jim followed, begging her to stop.

"I don't want to go! I want to wait for Simon! It's just taking longer than I anticipated," she cried in desperation.

Jim was completely knotted up on the inside. Seeing Karen like this was almost more than he could bear. He approached his wife slowly and cautiously. "I'm so sorry, sweetheart. You did all you could," he cried. Bingo even sensed the pain and hurt, showing it with sorrowful howls.

"I still feel him close, Jim. Tell me this hasn't been my imagination! Tell me I haven't had all these feelings in vain!"

"I wish that I could take all your pain away," Jim cried with more compassion than he had ever known. He removed his jacket and gently placed it around her shoulders then put his arm around her. "Now come on. You need some rest," he whispered.

Karen was so emotionally drained she could barely focus. She just sighed heavily and then became quiet. Slowly, with Jim holding on to her, she walked away from the well. Not once did she glance back as they left the park.

Bingo's "Sixth Sense"

As his mom and dad exited the park, Simon could see flickers of light as he neared the end of the tunnel. "Oh man! I'm at the end of my journey home," he squealed while running the rest of the distance through murky, muddy water. With slimy mud covering him from head to toe, he stopped abruptly at the entrance and stood quietly. With caution, he began to peer outside the entranceway. "I sure hope I'm close to familiar surroundings," he whispered in anticipation. His eyes went to the lighted areas around the park. The early morning was still foggy, giving the area a misty look. The moon was full but barely visible through the thick blanket of clouds.

Slowly, Simon stepped outside the tunnel onto solid, grassy sod. Immediately, he stooped low to brush his hand through the cool, damp grass. He tasted the dew, lapping the liquid from his fingers. It really felt soothing inside his hot, dry mouth. Simon then rose up and looked around, not realizing where he was, since the fog distorted his surroundings. Taking a deep breath, he moved forward a couple steps. "Mama," he called softly and cautiously. Nothing but silence prevailed.

Simon took a few more steps and then turned to look back. Suddenly, the tunnel's entranceway shrank very fast away right before his eyes, leaving only a grassy hill in its place. He stared a minute or so in wonderment. *Neopoleana has sealed the tunnel back up.* Slowly, he walked back to the hill and patted it gently. "My friends are safe. Now I've got to figure out where I am and get home," he whispered.

Simon began to walk using the lights in the park as a guide. Just as he shouted once again for help, Jim shut the car door and cranked up. He and Karen could not hear Simon's cries as he screamed, "Mama! Daddy!"

Bingo suddenly began to bark then scratched at the car windows, for his keen sense of hearing picked up his best friend's desperate cries and his keen sense of smell picked up his scent.

"Calm down, Bingo!" Jim demanded.

The anxious dog whined the loudest they had ever heard. He paced back and forth across the backseat as Jim pulled away from the curb. Louder and louder, Bingo barked. Harder and harder, he scratched at the side windows, leaving claw marks on the glass.

Jim yelled, "Bingo! Lie down and be quiet!" The smart dog would not listen this time, for he knew Simon was out there.

As Jim drove onto the road, Bingo barked even more frantically, getting louder and louder, even growling in desperation. "Stop the car!" Karen suddenly cried out.

"What's the matter?" Jim asked with a tone of frustration as he drove on.

"Stop the car, Jim!" she screamed. He slammed on the brakes. Karen jumped out of the car with Bingo leaping out behind her taking off running toward the wishing well barking nonstop.

"Come on, Jim!" Karen demanded, as she ran in behind Bingo.

Simon was in the area just beyond the wishing well, but the fog camouflaged his view. However, in a short time, he began to hear the faint barks. Right then, he knew beyond any shadow of a doubt that it was his dog! "Bingo! Bingo! Bingo!" he screamed while running toward the sound of the barks.

Karen faintly heard her son's screams. "Simon! Simon! Is that you?" she cried with exciting anticipation while running as fast as she could go.

"Mama! Mama, it's me! I'm over here! I'm home now!" he cried with pure joy.

"Simon, we're at the wishing well!" his Mom breathlessly shouted as she approached the area. She stopped and gasped for air as she looked beyond the area. Her heart melted when she got a glimpse of Simon just as Bingo reached him. Just then, Jim ran up behind her, and both took off running toward their son. They were shouting his name and feeling so much joy that they felt as if they were flying!

"Simon! Oh, Simon! Is it really you?" Karen cried out.

Bingo already had him down on the ground, lapping his face with his drooling, wet tongue. The happy, excited mooch was pouncing all over his best friend! Simon was laughing and hugging Bingo as they rolled around together on the damp sod.

Karen shouted again as she and Jim got closer. "Simon, it is you, isn't it?"

"It's him," Jim confirmed. "Our son is home," he cried.

Simon broke loose from Bingo and ran to his mom and dad's open arms as Bingo trailed behind with barks of delightful happiness. Jim and Karen kneeled down to catch him as he flew into their warm embrace.

"Mom! Dad! It's real! I'm really back at Hillcrest!" Simon cried as his parents hugged him tightly for several minutes. Tears of joy flowed from their eyes as they kissed his muddy face.

"Yes, son. It is real. You are home," Jim spoke as he squeezed him tight.

"Oh, Simon, we love you and have missed you every minute!" Karen exclaimed.

"But you are home now, and we are so happy and grateful," Jim spoke with excitement.

"Come on, Simon! We need to get you to the house so you can get cleaned up. I know you are hungry," Karen stated as her motherly instincts took over. "I'm sure you have much to tell us," she added.

"Oh, Mama, I do! The sphinx came out of the wishing well and took me to a land in The Third Dimension. I met the Rhues and Gruhs. They were my friends, but the sphinx, Bronzella, was not. She was selfish and wanted everything for herself."

Jim chimed in. "Calm down now, Simon. We know you have had quite an experience. You will have plenty of time to tell us all about it after you have rested."

Karen hugged her son again and then reached for his hand. With sparkling, joyful eyes, she looked at him. "Come on, Simon. Let's go home." He smiled while latching onto her hand as Jim grabbed hold of his other hand. Bingo yelped and wagged his tail in delight.

In order to avoid the wishing well, Jim was leading his family out of the park a different way. However, Simon kept glancing back, for he could not keep his eyes off the opening, which had led him to new worlds. He didn't let on, but inside, he was feeling drawn to this well once again. "Dad, I want to go the way we always do," he begged.

"Simon, you have been through so much, and it all started with that wishing well!" Karen cried out.

"I know, Mom. But I met some very special creatures in Gruhland and Rhueland. They are my friends. I want my journey to end the same way it started—at the wishing well," Simon explained.

Jim and Karen looked at one another and smiled, because they knew their son had connected with his new friends in a very beautiful and magical way. They also knew everything was going to be just fine. "Okay, we'll go out the same way we always do— past the wishing well," Jim agreed.

Simon hugged his dad's neck. "Thank you. I love you!" he cried.

Bingo yelped a couple of times as the reunited family slowly walked toward the enchanting well. Strange feelings came over Karen again, but this time she wasn't afraid. In fact, she felt a wonderful presence of love and friendship. Jim felt it also, for she could see it in his eyes.

The sun was starting to peep through the clouds and the fog was lifting, creating a mystic light above and all around the wishing well. It now appeared to stand out from all its surroundings. The crickets and tree frogs had ceased their musical overtures. Even Bingo was now unusually serene.

As they neared the area, Simon stopped. "I want just one more look down inside the well," he quietly spoke. Karen understood, nodding in agreement. Quickly, he darted away!

Jim followed, but Karen rushed forward and grabbed his arm, pulling him back. "Let Simon go alone," she whispered.

Jim gave her a half-smile. "You're right. He needs this time to bring closure to his journey," he responded.

He and Karen watched quietly as Simon approached the well and stepped upon the bottom railing. Slowly, he bent his head over the clear, calm water and gazed downward for several minutes, becoming almost hypnotized. Suddenly, the entire inside of the well became very bright, causing his eyes to squint. Warm golden rays of light began to travel straight up from the water. The low sunrise shined through the perfectly straight beams, making them appear luminous. Sparkles of gold dust floated gently inside each ray. Jim and Karen stood motionless, watching in awe at this miraculous sight. Their eyes followed the length of the shining rays as they reached toward the dusky sky. Bingo did not move, nor did he bark during this breathtaking event. Peaceful silence prevailed all through the park.

Soon the faint sound of music could be heard traveling upward from deep inside the well. *They know I'm home,* Simon thought as he stood very still. He could hear the beautiful voice of Neopoleana come alive as she sang "We Touch with Our Hearts." Tears streamed down his face as the magnificent "choir voices" of the Rhues and creatures joined in the chorus. Jim and Karen were overwhelmed with heartfelt emotion as beautiful notes joyfully rang out into the night. Never before had they heard such love pour from a song.

As the music ended, the golden light beams slowly traveled back down inside the well. Within a minute, they had faded completely away. Simon leaned his head over the water to see Neopoleana's reflection very slowly appear beneath the water. She was holding Winglet in her arms, which made his face light up. With a smile of joy, he yelled down, "Thank you, Neopoleana, for teaching me to see and to feel with my heart. All of you will always be near. I love you!" The Mother Rhue gave a smile and a wink, and Winglet waved her tiny hand. Simon returned the jesters and then waved until the reflection faded slowly away.

After staring down through the water a few minutes longer, Simon turned around and looked at his parents. "I'm ready to go home now," he spoke while running toward them. Jim brushed his fingers through his son's hair and then patted him on the back. Karen watched, smiling warmly.

Bingo suddenly yelped loudly, causing everyone to laugh. As Simon got busy frisking and playing with the pooch, Jim walked over to Karen and put his arm around her shoulder. He whispered, "Thank you, sweetheart."

Karen smiled but looked somewhat bewildered. "For what?" she asked.

"For showing me how to feel and see with my heart," he replied with love. Karen chuckled as she snuggled close against his chest.

Simon looked up from petting Bingo and smiled at the two. When he went back to playing with the dog, he noticed his bulging pockets and remembered the huge diamond and the stone pebbles. "Mom! Dad!" he exclaimed in excitement while quickly jumping up from his kneeling position. "I almost forgot! I brought something back from Rhueland for both of you!"

"Oh, now this is really getting exciting!" Jim elated with anxiousness as he looked at a smiling Karen.

"Hold out your hand, Dad," Simon instructed as he slid his hand inside his pocket, going all the way to the bottom. He ran his fingers all around until he felt the pebbles and then pushed each one into his hand while Jim and Karen waited patiently for their big surprise. He brought out the handful of stones, keeping them hidden in a tight fist. "Stick out your hand, Dad," he ordered.

He placed his hand over Jim's then let the teal-green and fuchsia-pink stones fall. My goodness, they sure seemed much tinier in his Dad's big hand!

Karen was looking on. "Oh, how precious!" she squealed.

"The stone figures make them all day long," Simon informed his parents.

"Each one is a perfect oval," Jim remarked, realizing what an awesome, magical place their son had been.

With excitement, Simon cut in. "Now hold out your hand, Mom! And close your eyes! You close your eyes also, Dad!" he demanded.

"Okay, we can do that," Jim agreed.

"Don't peek now!" Simon ordered as he wiggled his hand down inside the other pocket. He could barely grab hold of the monster-sized diamond to inch it upward. He grunted and strained and pulled and tugged the huge rock on up. Finally, the brilliant diamond popped out. "Now don't open your eyes until I say so!" he exclaimed with anticipation.

"Okay, we won't!" they answered.

Simon gently placed the magnificent beauty in his mom's small extended hand. "Now you can open your eyes!" he shouted with pure elation.

Jim and Karen opened their eyes and immediately gasped! They were completely spellbound at the incredible sight of the huge, perfect, uncut diamond.

"Do you like it, Mama?"

Karen did not, nor could not, answer right away. "Mama, are you all right?" Simon asked.

With glowing, wide eyes, she turned toward her son. "Oh, it is absolutely radiant!" she answered breathlessly.

Wow, what a land our son must have seen! Jim thought as he viewed the radiant jewel. He then quietly watched as Karen hugged Simon for the gift. As he looked into her eyes, Jim saw something even more precious than the deep sparkles the diamond was reflecting. It was the unconditional love she possessed for Simon. He knew the outstanding, uncut rock would be worth millions, but Karen's love was far more beautiful, and it outshined this huge crystal. A lone tear trickled down his cheek as he thought of how she had clung to her hope while Simon was missing. *I always looked at myself as being strong and brave, but it took the greatest of strength and courage for Karen not to give up. She stuck to the feelings deep inside her heart and never wavered, even when I preached to her on "reality."*

"Jim! Jim!" Karen was calling, awakening him from his deep thoughts.

"What were you thinking?" she questioned.

"Oh, I was just thinking of how much I love my family."

Karen chuckled. "Well, come on, Mr. Reality. Simon gets to sleep in his bed today, and I have an appointment to cancel," she announced with a playful wink.

Jim couldn't help but laugh. "You sure do, honey!" he exclaimed.

"Oh boy, I can hardly wait to get home!" Simon chimed in. Bingo yelped a couple of times as his best friend got between his parents and held their hands. Together they walked out of the park with Bingo running ahead of them.

"Simon, I'm going to run you a nice, hot bath when we get home," Karen spoke.

"I want to soak for at least an hour!" he giggled.

"After your bath, I'll fix you some steaming hot soup."

Simon cringed. "Anything but mushroom!" He then busted out laughing.

Karen and Jim laughed along with him as they got into the car to head home. As he cranked up, Jim glanced back at the wishing well in the distance, which looked lonesome and eerie to him now. Karen and Simon couldn't fight the urge to also look back.

The wishing well was now ready once again to hold all the hopes, wishes, and dreams of those who cast them there. As far as legends go, the well may hold many more, but Karen brought closure to *The Legend of the Sphinx* through her own hope and belief. Today, she will rest peacefully with no strange feelings to haunt her.